THE $\mathcal{H}$OLLOW $\mathcal{K}$INGDOM

CLARE B. DUNKLE

THE HOLLOW KINGDOM

Henry Holt and Company
New York

Special thanks to my editor, Reka Simonsen,
for her keen interest in developing good fantasy for children
and for all her hard work on this book.

Henry Holt and Company, LLC
Publishers since 1866
115 West 18th Street
New York, New York 10011
www.henryholt.com

Library of Congress Cataloging-in-Publication Data
Dunkle, Clare B.
The hollow kingdom / Clare B. Dunkle.
p. cm.
Summary: In nineteenth-century England, a powerful sorcerer and
King of the Goblins chooses Kate, the elder of two orphan girls recently
arrived at their ancestral home, Hallow Hill, to be his bride and queen.
[1. Goblins—Fiction. 2. Magic—Fiction. 3. Sisters—Fiction.
4. Orphans—Fiction. 5. Coventry (England)—History—19th
century—Fiction. 6. Great Britain—History—19th century—
Fiction.] I. Title.
PZ7.D92115Hol 2003   [Fic]—dc21   2002038899

ISBN 0-8050-7390-6
First Edition—2003
Book designed by Amy Manzo Toth
Printed in the United States of America on acid-free paper. ∞

1 3 5 7 9 10 8 6 4 2

*This book is respectfully dedicated to
Lloyd Alexander, who gave the world Eilonwy
and brought Gwydion back to life.*

THE *Hollow* *Kingdom*

Prologue

She had never screamed before, not when she overturned the row-boat and almost drowned, not when the ivy broke and she crashed into the shrubbery below, not even when Lightfoot bucked her off and she felt her leg break underneath her with an agonizing crunch. She hadn't even known that she could. Screaming was Lizzy's job, and Lizzy was terribly good at it. But now she screamed, long and loud, with all her breath.

"My dear," came a mild voice from beneath the black hood. "Do you mind? You're hurting my ears, and I'm surprised at you. You've always been so brave."

She hushed up then, her pride roused, and instead put all her efforts into breaking free, thrashing and writhing in the grip of the black-cloaked figure. It did no good. He carried her steadily and unhurriedly through the deep evening gloom of the woods, and she could see as she twisted about that those others, those bizarre things, were still all around them, following.

The strange crowd broke from the forest and stopped a few feet from the steep bluffs of the Hill. "This is what you've been looking for," remarked the hooded one. "Our front door. You wanted to walk right in, as I recall, and here's your chance."

He set her on her feet, his arm still around her waist. She imme-diately tried to slide to the ground, her feet scrabbling on the loose dirt. Doubled over, kicking and clawing, she felt him drag her forward. "There, you've walked in, more or less." She straightened up to find herself in a broad, dimly lit corridor of polished black stone. "You're inside now. You don't see anywhere to run, do you?" She shook her head. "So you'll stop this scrambling around. You shouldn't have come looking for us, my dear, if you didn't want to find us."

The tall figure released her and unfastened his cloak, stepping back a pace to study her gravely. She stared at him openmouthed, unable to look away. His eyes were beautiful, large and black, like the eyes of Christ on her father's Greek icon. His face was broad, with high cheekbones, and his smooth skin shimmered in the lamp-light with a strange silvery gray color. He had no hair on his head, no beard, not even eyebrows. His mouth was a little too wide, and his ears were long and narrow and rose to sharp points. She was tall for a girl, but he was half a head taller than she, and his broad shoulders and thick arms explained how he had been able to carry her away so effortlessly.

He saw a very young woman of sturdy, athletic build, her lean, pretty face very pale, black hair straggling about it rather wildly. Her green eyes glared desperately at him. No tears were on her cheeks yet, but the trembling lower lip indicated that they weren't perhaps too far from falling. He gazed at her for a long moment and then gave her a smile.

"You see what a lucky girl you are," he said in a low voice. "I'm very handsome for a goblin. And you were going to catch a goblin, weren't you? With your bare hands." He reached out and laid one of her trembling hands on his muscular silvery gray forearm. "You've caught a goblin, my dear, all for your very own." The hand ended in what looked like well-kept dog claws, and she tried to pull away. He chuckled quietly, and she glanced up to discover that the teeth in that gray face were the color of dark, tarnished silver.

"Where's your spirit of adventure gone?" he said encouragingly. "You wanted a goblin, remember? And you wanted to walk right in here, too, didn't you? Is there anything else you'd like to do?"

"I want to go home," she whispered, and the first tear escaped. He watched it thoughtfully. She was doing pretty well, all things considered.

"I'll take you home," he promised. "Come with me now." Comforted, she let him keep the hand he held and lead her down the polished corridor. They came to a broad, high iron door, which swung open as they approached and then clanged shut behind them. She stopped and looked around in startled wonder.

"Here you are, my dear," he said quietly. "My kingdom. And your home. It's been a long wait, but it's over at last."

"No!" she gasped, her eyes searching that inhuman face for some other meaning. The monster smiled at her warmly.

"Indeed," he assured her. "You haven't seen me, but I've watched you since you were a baby. I've watched over you, too. I tightened your teeth back up when you knocked them loose tumbling out of the snow sled you'd tied to the pony's tail. I fixed your knee after you fell from the ivy when you were eight, and I healed your leg the night you broke it getting thrown from the horse." His smile broadened. "I was glad the doctor didn't know about that, though. Eight weeks' rest was something we all needed at that point." She stared at him in bewilderment.

"It was good for you to grow up outside." His voice was kind. "You certainly enjoyed it. But you were always intended for here, and now you're finally old enough. Barely, but old enough." He chuckled. "I'd have left you outside for another year or two, but you showed such a lively interest in us. You just couldn't wait to meet goblins. So you're home now. In all the years you live here, this door won't ever open for you again. You're underground with me until you die."

"No!" she cried, jerking away from him and flinging herself at the door. "I want out! I want to go home!" She pounded on the iron with fists and forearms. She kicked the door and threw herself against it. The goblin watched all this with a fond forbearance, but when she tried to claw the door open, he intervened.

"Now, now," he said gently, capturing her wrists and surveying her bruised hands. "Let's not break off all those pretty nails, my dear. We'll need at least three for the ceremony." And arm around her waist, he led the sobbing, stumbling girl away.

Seventy years passed over the land, and they passed underneath it, too. Anguish and grief faded to a dull throb, and finally only the mysteries themselves remained, forgotten by all but a concerned few.

PART I

Starlight

Chapter
One

"It's so nice to see new faces at Hallow Hill, isn't it, Prim?"

Gracious and white haired, Celia Whitaker beamed across the dinner table at her great-nieces, and Kate and Emily Winslow smiled shyly back. The girls were grateful to find a smile at the end of their journey. It had been a hard two months. Their father had died suddenly. By scrupulously legal tradition, his house and lands near Coventry now belonged to his nephew, the next male relative, and this man had refused to become their guardian. The Hallow Hill estate belonged to Kate from her late mother, but she had never visited it. It had been rented to another branch of the family for generations. Now Kate and her younger sister were coming home to land and relatives they had never seen. Hugh Roberts, a bachelor cousin of their mother's, had become their legal guardian, and the two great-aunts, Celia and Prim, had agreed to raise the sisters.

Excited and exhausted, Kate and Emily tried to eat their meal. They had arrived only minutes before. Days of bouncing along in a carriage, nervous and bored, had carried them from their father's tame green meadows to this remote country. Last night they had stayed in a little village on the shore of Hollow Lake. The innkeeper had pointed across the great oval lake to the forested hills beyond. A high, bald promontory faced them on the other side, and cliffs and bluffs tumbled haphazardly down to the smooth surface of the water.

"That's Hallow Hill land, miss," he had said to Kate. "The tall rocks there, that's the Hill itself. But it'll take you all morning to get around the lake and the forest. No roads go through the woods by the Hill. They'd not dare to put a road there." My land, thought Kate in surprise. She hadn't expected it to be so wild.

"And what a beauty you are, my dear," Aunt Celia said to Kate. "You favor your mother, doesn't she, Prim? She was slender and small boned, too, such a graceful woman. She had the pick of the men in her day."

Kate tried to smile at these kind remarks, but she found them rather embarrassing. She didn't think of herself as a beauty, although she knew her mother had been one. In fact, Kate was uncommonly pretty. Her long blond hair formed small curls around her face, and she had a dignity and poise unusual for her age. Perhaps this was because she had spent so much time with her father. That lonely gentleman had lavished hours each day on her education. He saw a strength in her gentle nature that he openly admired, and this strength had carried the quiet Kate bravely through the last two months without him.

Rawboned and large handed, Primrose Roberts didn't smile as often as her sister Celia, but this didn't mean she was ill-tempered. She studied the blushing Kate, noting her fair skin and large, dark blue eyes.

"Now, you know Kate's mother was dark, Celia, with that black hair. I think you're like your mother in your build, though; such a little thing she was." Kate sighed. She hated being so short. No one but her father seemed to take her seriously.

"I think you must favor your father, dear." Aunt Celia had turned to Emily. The younger sister frowned by way of answer. Thin and dark, Emily certainly possessed her sister's strength of will, but she didn't always use it quite as sensibly. Her narrow face was very expressive, and her conduct often unexpected. Lively, intelligent, and quite immature, she usually burst out with exactly the comment that summed up the situation beautifully and therefore could never in politeness be said. It is true that she had her father's plain brown hair and brown eyes. It is also true that it is annoying to live with a real beauty if you yourself are not one. Emily thought that she would have loved being a beauty and breaking men's hearts. Kate just didn't appreciate what she had.

"*Hallow* means 'holy,' doesn't it?" asked Emily. "Why is this place called Hallow Hill? Is there a church nearby?"

"Oh, Hugh can tell you about that," Aunt Celia said. "Hugh's quite a scholar, you know. He's writing a book of family history, all about Hallow Hill."

Their legal guardian was a large, corpulent bachelor with a round face and ink stains on his hands. Emily kept staring at him because he wore a curled white wig. No one but lawyers and grand-fathers wore wigs anymore. Except for the barest pleasantries, he had been silent since their arrival. He had brought a book to the table and was reading it as he ate, his spectacles resting low on his nose. Now he raised his pale eyes from the pages and glanced dismissively at Emily.

"I don't suppose someone of your age and gender is going to sit through a linguistic analysis," he remarked. Kate saw her little sister's face darken and spoke quickly to prevent a catastrophe.

"We'd love to hear about Hallow Hill's name," she protested with a bright smile. "Place-name etymology is so fascinating. The words come out of Old English, don't they, so the name can't date back to the Roman times, but it could certainly predate the Norman Conquest."

Hugh Roberts fixed Kate with a critical stare. She noticed an ink stain on his nose and hoped her sister wouldn't mention it.

"So we've read a book or two," he commented dryly. "Yes, the word *hallow* is Old English, but we don't know that *hallow*, or *holy*, is what was intended at all. Perhaps *hollow* is what was meant. Some early documents call the bald peak behind this house Hollow Hill, and there certainly are caves throughout the area. And 'Hollow Lake' may just be a short way of saying the 'lake by Hollow Hill.'

"However, we aren't even positive that is the original Hallow Hill. Near the Lodge house is a smaller hill with a flat, circular crown, and around this crown is a double circle of ancient oak trees. The site was obviously an important druidic center. There are those who say that is the real Hallow Hill, but probably to the early inhabitants this whole region was sacred. It has never been mined, the forests haven't been logged, and the locals retain to this day a tremendous superstitious lore about the area. Calling something *hallow* for hundreds of years has a way of making people treat it as holy whether it really is or not." He picked up his book again. "It's a fascinating human phenomenon, the tenacious preservation of ignorance," he remarked caustically and ignored the conversation around him for the remainder of the meal.

In another half hour, Emily and Kate found themselves back out in the sunshine, facing another carriage ride. Their guardian lived in this large estate house, the Hall, but the girls were not to live here with him. They were to go on to the smaller house, the Lodge, where their greataunts lived.

The Hall faced a large, open green that was not in the least interesting. It contained rigidly geometric pebbled walks, square garden beds, and bench seats set primly by the straight, treelined borders. But the ground to the sides and back of the house began rising at once into small, tumbled hills, and through the windows of the dining room the girls had seen tantalizing views of a shady terrace, mosscovered rock walls, and paths disappearing into the dim forest that reached down and enclosed the Hall on three sides. Kate and

Emily were wild with delight at the thought of those secret paths winding through primeval woodland. They could hardly bear to climb into the carriage for the sedate jog over to the Lodge.

The ride proved more satisfying than they had expected. The gravel track passed the front of the Hall and rapidly left the depressing tidiness of the green behind. It skirted the very edge of the forest and rose and fell with the unevenness of the landscape, providing a view on the one side of windblown meadows full of wildflowers and on the other of those gloomy, green-dappled forest depths that they already longed to explore. The track passed through a grassy orchard as it climbed a steady slope, and the Lodge house stood before them, shaded by large, well-trimmed trees.

Kate and Emily stared up at the big white house. Emily was surprised by its size; hearing that she was to live in the "small Lodge house," she had expected to see a two-room hut. The Lodge had three stories, the top one peeking out through small dormer windows tucked under a steep gray roof. The front door was exactly in the middle, and all the tall windows up and down were perfectly matched and symmetrical. Over their heads and over the house swung the thick boughs of the great shade trees, casting an ever-changing net of shadow and sun on the ground below. Kate listened to the gentle rush of the wind whispering through leaves and branches. She felt it settle into her soul and fill some lonely place there.

The Lodge was a very ordinary square house designed to provide four spacious rooms on each floor with a hallway down the middle. The front door faced the straight hall and staircase, which began about ten feet inside it. Kate, standing on the rug, could see right through to the back door, which stood open to let in the breeze. On her left was a parlor, on her right, a dining room, open to each other by the full width of the entry. Their walls began only at the staircase.

Houses take on the character of their inhabitants. Kate's initial impression was of tranquility and tidiness. Gauzy white curtains fluttered at the large glass windows, and soft, plump chairs and sofas gathered in the rooms. Tones of green, white, and blue predominated in the upholstery, and the walls were a soft graygreen. The cushioned chairs and quiet hues spoke of peace. The crystalclear windows and perfect spotlessness spoke of industry.

Kate and Emily trailed through the house after their greataunts and saw everything there was to see, from the kitchen by the back door to the upstairs bedrooms. Prim and Celia had the two bedrooms on the left side of the upstairs hall, and the girls were given ones on the right.

Kate's room faced the front. "We did think this would be pretty for a young lady like you," said Aunt Celia. "It has Grandmother's furniture, and Prim and I could just imagine you combing your lovely hair before the glass at her dressing table."

Emily had the back bedroom. "You'll never believe how many storms we have here, dear," cautioned Aunt Prim. "Such wild country! If you wake in the night, my room is right across the hall. No need to dodge around the stairs when you're in a fright."

❧

The next several days saw the girls settle in and become a part of the rhythm of life at Hallow Hill. Some demands were placed on them, but they were free to roam their new surroundings for hours every day. It must be admitted that the two older women found their new charges quite exhausting. Whenever the girls burst out the door with a picnic hamper to go off on a long ramble, it is hard to say who of the four felt most relieved.

It took the girls a week to find the druids' circle that their cousin had spoken of. They discovered it after supper one evening, quite close behind the Lodge. The forest path they were following began climbing a steep slope. As they looked upward, they saw an evenly planted row of ancient oaks set in thick green turf. In the gaps between they could see a further row of trees, but so massive were the specimens in this double ring that they could not see past the two rows together. The enormous trunks, wider than the girls could span with their arms, formed a perfect barrier, protecting whatever lay beyond from careless eyes.

Hand in hand, the girls approached this awesome barricade and slipped between the giant sentinels. The tops of these hoary trees, so close together for so many ages, had grown into one dense, continu-ous ring. No sunlight pierced it to fall on the intruders beneath, and yet the green turf continued underfoot, right up to the great trunks.

Inside the ring, the broad crown of the hill was almost flat. They could not see beyond the trees either to the distant hills or to the woods outside. They were in a huge room walled by living plants. Above them, past the tangled branches of the oaks, stretched a per-fect circle of darkening twilight sky about seventy feet across. The lush turf formed a dense, soft carpet underneath, and small white field lilies sprang above it on long, thin stalks, like tiny stars scattered across a dark green sky.

Speechless, Kate and Emily stood and looked around. This was a silent place. No birds sang in the branches of the great trees, and Emily found no bugs crawling in the grass beneath. Slowly they wandered to the very middle of the twilit circle and dropped down onto the inviting turf.

"Do you think the druids built this place?" asked Emily.

"No." Kate knew that this was no ruined monument to a dead religion. The circle was alive and aware. It exerted a magical force that welcomed and comforted her, as if good people had arranged a place for her security and care.

"But if the druids didn't make it, who did?"

"I don't know, Em," Kate said thoughtfully. "Perhaps our ancestors did. I feel so much more at home here than I do up at the Hall. And just imagine how the stars must look from here! Let's stay a little while longer and watch them come out."

As night fell on the tree circle, the stars shone in the round ceiling of sky over their heads. Kate gazed, enchanted, at the brilliant lights hanging above her. She had always had a deep love of the stars. She sometimes felt that if it hadn't been for them, she never could have stood the loss of her parents. As long as she had the stars, she would never be alone. Even when she wasn't looking at them, she could feel their gentle radiance in her mind. They had never seemed as beautiful as they did tonight. One by one they emerged until the ebony sky was full, and the glittering net shimmered over their heads.

"We'd better go back," warned Emily, thinking about what her worried aunts would say. They crossed to the enormous trees, now black in their own deep shadows, and slipped between them to find the forest path again. It took some time before they hit upon it in the meager, dappled starlight. As they walked slowly homeward in the darkness, Kate tried to remember the beauty of the stars, but a vague presence intruded on her thoughts. She began to peer into the shadows. She couldn't hear or see anyone, but she was sure someone was there. Kate rambled in the late twilight as often as she was allowed, and she had never been afraid before, but now she held her sister's hand tightly.

"What's wrong with you?" demanded Emily. "You're pinching me. We're not lost, you know. I can find the way home."

Kate stared desperately back into the forest. "Em, something's watching us!" she whispered.

"Oh?" asked Emily, very interested. "What? Where?" She turned around and peered unsuccessfully into the deep gloom.

"I don't know," murmured her sister. "It followed us down the path. I can't see it, but it can see us. Can't you feel it?"

"No," replied Emily with a shrug. "It's probably just a fox. Come on, Kate, we'll get in trouble." And she towed her preoccupied sister across the Lodge lawn. At the door, Kate stopped and looked back. The heavy shadows under every tree seemed full of menace. Once she was in the house, the feeling left her, but it came back a little later as they talked in the parlor. The greataunts never drew the heavy curtains. Kate stared suspiciously at one gauzecovered window after another. She even rose and looked out into the dark night, but there was nothing there that her eyes could see. After a few minutes of this restlessness, her greataunts began to watch her in some surprise. Embarrassed, she excused herself and went up to bed.

Nighttime became an ordeal for Kate after this. Sometimes she would be free of the feeling until bedtime, when she would begin to pace and fret under the conviction that something was watching her. She, who had always loved the stars, began to avoid looking out the windows after dark. Even in her bedroom on the second floor, she would wake in the night, uneasy. She would lie as still as she could under the covers, peering around the room at the darkness, and she began to have exhausting nightmares. When Kate tried to explain her feeling to her greataunts, they laughed at first and then looked puzzled. Hallow Hill was so remote that no one ever came or went across its grounds. The aunts never even locked the doors.

Prim watched Kate with concern and decided that both girls needed more to do. They had been through a great deal, and they had too much time to dwell on it. She had already talked to the girls about the sorts of lessons they had learned and had found Kate to be shockingly overeducated. Kate's father, seeing in his daughter a real intellectual enthusiasm, had taught most of her lessons himself. Both father and daughter were fired with a love of literature, and they had spent hours reading and discussing books together. Aunt Prim was appalled.

"I think it's sweet that she spent so much time with her father," said Celia.

"Well, that's where her case of nerves has come from," declared Prim. "All that book reading, all that flowery poetry. It's enough to make any girl flighty and high-strung. Why, she's old enough to have a family of her own by now, and she's never been out in society. If you ask me, Celia, these girls have been neglected. No man knows how to raise proper ladies."

Prim began teaching the girls practical skills, such as how to plan meals, keep household accounts, and manage servants. Over time, she and Celia observed with satisfaction that Kate was settling down. It is true that Kate slept more soundly at night because she was busier during the day, but she continued to be haunted by the powerful feeling that something was watching her. She couldn't avoid it or ignore it, so she just kept her worry a secret from her aunts. She could tell that it did nothing but upset them.

As high summer came, Aunt Prim took Kate to pay a call on her guardian. The call, she discovered, concerned her deeply. Prim wanted Hugh Roberts to take Kate into town for the winter season. It was time, she said, for the girl to be out in society. So much had to be arranged first. Kate's guardian would have to fulfill his responsibilities.

Hugh Roberts didn't take the call at all well. He had no patience with fashions and parties. He didn't see any good reason why the important pursuits of the mature should be set aside to allow the young a chance to make fools of themselves. He paced up and down the room as he and Prim argued. At one point he turned angrily on Kate herself.

"Are you tired of country life already?" he demanded. "You can't wait to go off skipping and gossiping with a whole bevy of brainless belles?" Kate wasn't in the least tired of country life, though she did find the thought of society parties a bit thrilling. She didn't say this to her angry guardian, but maybe he saw it in her face. If so, it did nothing to improve his temper.

After the unpleasant interview, Aunt Prim hurried off to speak to Mrs. Bigelow, the housekeeper, leaving Kate to wander the Hall alone. This activity never failed to fill Kate with uneasiness. The Hall might belong to her, but it never seemed to want her. She was nothing but an intruder here.

Kate did what she often did when she was at the Hall and had time to herself. She went to the huge fireplace in the upstairs parlor to study the picture that hung above it. Two girls, both around thirteen years old, stood hand in hand before a forest landscape and looked out at her. One, black-haired and green-eyed, had a red rose tucked into the waist of her old-fashioned dress. She met Kate's gaze as if she were about to tell a funny secret, and she looked as if she were try-ing not to giggle. The other, pale and blond, gazed down at Kate with solemn dark blue eyes. She did not smile. Perhaps she had learned already those lessons in life that make smiling difficult. Kate stared back at the blond girl thoughtfully. She felt, as she always did, that there was something familiar about her.

"She looks very like you, don't you think?"

Hugh Roberts stood a few feet behind Kate. He met her sur-prised glance a little sheepishly, but he walked up beside her to study the picture, hands behind his back. "I mean the one on the left, the blond girl, Elizabeth. The resemblance is quite startling. I've thought so ever since you came here."

He paused, but Kate said nothing. She was staring at the picture. Of course! How had she not seen it before?

"Adele is the girl on the right, Dentwood Roberts's child. Her father and my great-grandfather were brothers. I am the last of an old and proud family, Miss Winslow."

Kate turned to him, thoroughly puzzled. He caught her confused look and nodded.

"Oh, yes, Elizabeth on the left is indeed your great-grandmother, but Elizabeth is related to no one in the family. For all we know, she might have fallen from the moon.

"The story goes that one spring night old Roberts went walking with his daughter. Adele was about three then. Her mother had died soon after she was born, and old Roberts doted on his only child. They paused at the druids' circle. Have you been there? A lovely spot at twilight. There Roberts sat while his little daughter ran about picking flowers. He listened to her happy prattle. He fell to dreaming and thinking of his dead wife for a few minutes. And when he rose to call his daughter to him—what do you think he saw, Miss Winslow? Not just his Adele. Now there were two little girls playing in the moonlight."

Kate felt her hair prickle and goose bumps rise on her arms. She couldn't say a word.

"And that's where Elizabeth came from," said Hugh Roberts with a shrug. "No one knows who she really was. No one even knew her name. She appeared just like a fairy child in the old tales, like the changeling that she was." Bitterness crept into his voice. "Because the two girls did not both survive, Miss Winslow. When they were about sixteen, Adele died suddenly. No one knows how. But old Roberts took Elizabeth and left Hallow Hill that very night, and neither of them ever came back.

"Dentwood Roberts had adopted Elizabeth. Now she was all he had. When she died in childbirth, he took her son to raise. He left everything he had to that son when he died: Hallow Hill and all it contained. It went to a man who had never seen it, who could never appreciate it—who never even visited it once. My family, Dentwood Roberts's brother's family, has leased the house ever since. Eliza, beth's son was your grandfather, and Hallow Hill now belongs to you. Oh, we call each other cousins, Miss Winslow," he said blandly. "But you're no relation, really.

"I wonder how the founders of this house would feel if they could learn about this strange turn of events," he mused, "that their own flesh and blood would have to pay rent just to live in their own home. Pay rent to strangers, who didn't even care about the land. Yes," he added smugly, rubbing his hands, "I'm the last of a proud line."

I'm unwanted, thought Kate in a rush of despair. Unwanted, with no family left. And my land belongs to me almost through fraud. It's worse than having nothing at all. She couldn't say a word. She turned and left the room as quickly as she could, hurrying down the stairs. Hugh Roberts watched her disorganized retreat, and his smile widened. Then he walked back to his study, whistling cheerfully.

Chapter
Two

The change in Kate was obvious to all, but no one understood it. Prim and Celia were sure Kate's restless unhappiness was due to disappointment. Prim assured her that Hugh would give in to their arguments and take her into town, but Kate no longer wanted to go. In the aftermath of her guardian's horrible disclosure, society parties had gone quite out of her head.

Kate couldn't bear for her little sister to find out that they weren't really family, so she said nothing about what she had learned, and she tried to keep up a cheerful appearance. But keeping a secret from loved ones is a heavy burden, and now she was keeping two secrets. Her nightmares were wearing her out, and her worried sister's constant questions were upsetting her. Prim noticed the pale cheeks and the dark shadows under her niece's eyes. Lips tight, she called the doctor, but neither he nor Prim could find anything wrong. Between them, they dosed Kate with a variety of strong and well-meaning remedies that did no good at all.

The weather changed with the approaching end of summer, and clouds gathered over the Hill. One breathless afternoon nothing could bring relief to spirit or body. A gray haze hung in the air, too diffuse to be called clouds, but too thick to be called anything else. The sun shone through it as a brilliant white spot, and not a whisper of wind stirred. As evening came, no thunder rumbled in the hills, and no breeze sprang up to fan their clammy cheeks. The sun was leaving without a blaze of color. The thick haze just seemed to swallow it.

"Please, Aunt Prim, let us walk up in the hills and see if we can't find some cool wind somewhere," Kate begged. "I promise we'll come back before it gets dark." Her aunt knew better than to let her go. Storms were sure to follow a day like this, even if they were taking their time building. But at last she gave consent, with all the conditions that approaching storms and nightfall demanded. They were to stay out of the woods, watch the sky, and come back at the first sign of bad weather.

The girls headed down through the orchard, intent on the rocky meadows beyond. Kate was sure that if they climbed to the top of one of those grassy hills, they were bound to find a breeze, but at the top of their meadow, they found no breath stirring. The twilight was blending with the strange, close sky to form a dark brown haze, and the grass at their feet shone with a blond shimmer, as if the few rays of light left could not rise above the surface of the ground. Landmarks even a few yards away were melting into the brown gloom. Purple lightning bloomed across the dark sky before them.

"We'd better go back," sighed Kate.

They waded through the grass back down the hillside. Ahead of them in the thick dusk stood the stone wall of the meadow, but no gate appeared as they followed the meadow's edge.

"Wait, Em, we must have gotten turned around. The gate's over there."

As their fence formed a corner with another stone fence, the gate appeared a few feet from them, white boards gleaming in the dim light. They hurried over to it as another shining purple curtain shook across the sky, and swinging the gate shut, they sped up the little road before them.

A couple of minutes later, they stopped short in bewilderment. Another stone fence blocked their path. But how was this possible? They should be at the orchard by now. The two girls climbed a slight rise and looked around in all directions, trying to make out the shapes of trees that marked the orchard. Some faint light still remained. They could see each other's faces, pale in the deep dusk, but now they couldn't distinguish the black horizon from the black cloud banks. The lightning, undulating over the swollen masses of the clouds, was distant and too weak to see by. It gleamed silently, first in front and then behind them.

"This makes no sense," Kate said firmly, thinking over the way they had come. "All we had to do was walk back down the hill, through the gate, and up the orchard path. We've missed the gate somehow. There must be two in that meadow, and we hit on the other one. We'll follow the road back and look for the other gate out of that field, the one that takes us to the orchard."

With that plan in mind, they started off confidently, but now their light was gone. They found the little road again more by feel than by sight, but it didn't lead them to a gate. It turned and skirted along another stone wall, went through a tumbled-down gap, and lost itself altogether in a narrow draw.

Again and again, Kate tried desperately to find the right path in the darkness, making them retrace their steps, but each time they did, they lost their old landmarks. Everything seemed to shift in the darkness around them. They had no idea which direction they faced or where home was. They could only tell that they were moving farther and farther from the shelter of the woodlands. The fields were flattening out, and stone fences were becoming rare.

There followed a time that was the worst in their lives. Method was gone, and landmarks were forgotten. They blundered along hand in hand through the dense blackness, following any path they crossed. Lightning seemed to be all around them now, and every white flash lit up a dreary landscape that held no familiar sight. One black field followed another. They might be one mile from home, or they might be ten. They certainly felt that they had walked a hundred.

As they stumbled along, footsore and exhausted, Emily let out an excited squeak and tugged Kate around. Far across the fields, a light was shining. It wavered, winked out, and then showed up again. The girls turned and scrambled toward it.

The light was a bonfire, blazing up in the darkness with a red-dish glow, and figures moved back and forth before it. The fire lit up no house or barn. It appeared to be built in the middle of an empty field. Kate began to watch the figures by the fire uneasily. A hunting party? Gypsies? Vagabonds? Two men stood by the fire in long cloaks, their hoods pulled down over their faces. That spoke perhaps of hunting and of the stormy weather. Two or three short people moved about as well. Children? They had to be, but there was some-thing odd about their shapes. As the girls came nearer, Kate noticed four horses standing patiently beyond the fire. They appeared to be saddled. Hunting, then, but who would be out on such a night? She began to slow down, not so anxious to walk out of the darkness toward this strange group, but Emily, clutching Kate's hand, began to speed up. Warmth, light, people—these held no fears for her. She broke into a trot, pulling her sister behind her.

The party turned, sensing their approach. One of the short figures broke away from the firelit circle and bustled toward them.

"Oh, look! Two pretty girls right out of the storm! Do let old Agatha tell your fortune, dears."

"Gypsies!" whispered Emily excitedly as Agatha hurried up. Kate stared down, astonished, at the shortest woman she had ever seen. Agatha came up only a little past Kate's waist, but her small, stocky body did not appear to be hunched or twisted. The old face was seamed into countless wrinkles, and the black eyes snapped and sparkled in the firelight. "Here," she said, capturing Kate's hand in her own surprisingly large one, "come by the fire so I can see your pretty face."

As Kate followed Agatha over to the bonfire, she glanced around nervously at the other members of the party. The two men stood nearby. One was only a little taller than she, thick and barrel-chested. The other man, of average height, towered over him. Perhaps they had been conversing before, but now they were silent, watching Agatha and the two girls. They were draped in the black cloaks and hoods she had noticed earlier, and she could see nothing at all of their faces. This was prudent, given the coming storm, but it irked Kate to be seen and not to see. She wished she had a cloak of her own.

Agatha, meanwhile, was peering intently at Kate's palm, turning it this way and that in the firelight. "Oh," she breathed. "Not every young lady has a hand like this." Kate heard chuckles from the men. "But, dear," she said, ignoring them, "I see danger in this hand. Danger from someone very close to you." Now the men roared with laughter. "Be quiet, the two of you!" She whirled on them, still holding Kate fast. "I'm very serious!"

"What about me?" demanded Emily eagerly, holding out her hand to the old woman. "Do you see danger in my hand?" Old Agatha took her small palm and turned it toward the fire.

"And such a lively thing you are, my dear!" she said to Emily. "Still a long way from marriage, aren't you? Well, that can't be helped, and one does grow, you know." Emily giggled over this odd speech, but Kate frowned. Hugging her arms about her, she stepped back from the firelight and eyed the two men warily. Now they had turned away and were talking again in quiet tones. She couldn't seem to catch what they were saying. The taller one threw back his head and laughed at something the short one said. She noticed as he laughed that he carried one shoulder higher than the other.

"Your palm speaks of tears early but laughter late," Agatha summed up grandly. "That's as good as a palm can say. You've a lovely, open nature, child."

"Oh, Kate, look!" Emily called excitedly. Kate turned to see a huge black tomcat approaching the fire. It rubbed its head against Emily's knee, its velvet coat shining in the light. Kate felt as if she couldn't breathe. Surely the cat was four times—no, six times— larger than the largest cat she'd ever seen!

"Isn't he beautiful?" squealed Emily, kneeling to tickle his chin. She loved animals of all descriptions, and her greatest regret was that the aunts wouldn't let her keep pets. The enormous cat was almost eye to eye with her. "Miaow?" he said plainly, and that is just what it sounded like: a *miaow* said by a person imitating a cat. Kate shook her head and stared hard at the giant feline as if he were a puzzle she needed to solve. Something needed explaining here. Per- haps she was just dreaming?

"Oh, scat, Seylin!" scolded Agatha, waving her big hands. "Such a nuisance you are, really! Go on!" The men walked away, heading toward the horses. A small boy came out of the shadows to throw wood on the fire. Kate thought she saw a beard on his face as he turned to look at her. Just a trick of the light, perhaps, or nerves. Enough of this! Emily stepped toward the shadows, coaxing, "Seylin . . ." Kate caught her by the arm and pulled her around, turning to the old woman.

"Thank you so much for the fortunes," she began firmly, "but what—"

"Oh, I know all about it, dears!" Agatha interrupted kindly. "Two pretty girls lost on a wild night, scared and tired, looking for the way home. You let old Agatha take care of that. We'll take you home, don't worry. Can't have you out in a storm like this, no. And the only question is, who will take whom? Let's see, where did they go? What's your name, dear, Kate? And who will take Kate home, eh?"

The taller man was leading his horse, a large gray hunter that any gentleman might be proud to own. Kate noticed that the man limped slightly. That, along with the high shoulder. Old age? His posture was unaffected, and he carried himself with dignity. He couldn't be old; he had laughed like a young man, and when he spoke, his voice was not an old man's voice. It was rich and pleasant, naturally commanding. "Don't worry, Agatha. I'll take your Kate home, of course." Amused and tolerant. Amused at what? The old woman? Their silliness in getting lost?

"Oh, Marak!" breathed Agatha delightedly, turning her twinkling black eyes on him. Kate felt again that sense of unease. Why the delight and excitement over a simple, good-hearted gesture? The man brought his horse up to her wordlessly and turned to check the saddle. She could see nothing but a black cloak. Good cloth, Aunt Prim would say. Expensive cloth, generously cut. Big, gloved hands pulling down the stirrup. Kate looked more closely. The right hand had six fingers.

"W-wait!" she stammered. "You—you don't know where we live. How can you promise to take us home if you don't know where we live?" The man paused for a fraction of a second and then continued his work without looking up. She turned quickly, hoping to see a surprised look on Agatha's face, hoping to find some answer to the riddle she was facing. But Emily blurted out helpfully, "Yes, we live in the Hallow Hill Lodge. Do you know where that is? Are we very far from there?"

"Of course we know where you live, dears," replied Agatha with a chuckle. "Do you think anyone in this country doesn't know of the pretty girls come to live with the two old ladies up in the forest? We've not got much to gossip over around here. Now, let's see. Marak, shouldn't Thaydar take the little one along? Such a receptive nature, such pluck."

"I think so," replied that amused, amiable voice. "It's probably for the best. So, ready?" And he turned to Kate, putting out his hands to boost her up onto his horse. Emily was stroking the horse's neck delightedly. He was far finer than any at the Hall.

"No!" said Kate, stepping back and treading on her sister's foot. "I—I prefer to walk, thank you." A silence swept across the little group.

"Oh, Kate!" Emily gasped.

The rider dropped his hands slowly and seemed to stare down at her from beneath his hood. He was almost a head taller than she was. "Really," he said distinctly, all amusement gone from that commanding voice. His manner was beyond cold. It was glacial.

Kate forced herself to hold up her head and face him as the blood rushed through her cheeks in a tingling wave. She wasn't sure why she had said what she did, but she would not be faced down now by strangers. Something was wrong here; she knew it. She refused to be a fool for them.

"Yes," she replied as calmly and formally as she could. "Please lead my sister and me to the Hallow Hill Lodge, where we live. If you do, we will be very grateful. I hope we are not far from the Lodge because we do not wish to try your patience too long."

The hooded man continued to stare at her for a long moment. Then he gave a short laugh. "Well, well, how intriguing! No," he continued firmly over Agatha's spluttered protests, "we will certainly humor the cautious young woman. Thaydar, I'll not need you. I believe one horse is sufficient to point out the way." He swung up into the saddle. "Now, shall we begin our walk?" he added to the two girls. "Or, that is——" he went on, bending toward Emily. "I assume that you *prefer* to walk, too?"

"I do not!" said Emily decidedly, glaring at her sister. She caught the rider's arm and let herself be swung up before him.

"Em!" shouted Kate, panicked, but it was too late. He settled her little sister comfortably and put the horse into a plodding walk. Kate stood for a second, hands shaking, unsure what she had expected. Then she had to scramble after them.

The darkness pressed in around them as they left the bonfire behind. Lightning flickered and flashed. Marak's good humor seemed to have returned, and he soon had Emily telling him all about life at the Lodge. Kate stumbled along at the horse's flank, trying to keep up. She felt like a complete fool.

"So your name is M. That's a letter, isn't it?" he asked. This notion caught Emily's fancy powerfully, and she couldn't stop giggling.

"My name is Emily Winslow, but my sister calls me Em. Or maybe she calls me M. I wonder what I stand for." Kate tripped over a root and thought Emily sounded like an idiot.

"Isn't it funny how humans name a child one thing in order to call it something else? So many names. It's like a game. M's a new one. Kate—now, that's a name everyone knows."

They were walking through a field of weeds. The weeds were up to Kate's waist, and she kept slipping on the long stalks. "Miss Winslow," she muttered through clenched teeth, but Marak heard her. He must have very good ears.

"Oh, hello, Kate, are you all right down there? Are you enjoying your walk? So, Miss Winslow. How convenient. You have one name for friends and another for enemies." Emily giggled again. He certainly was making a hit with her.

"I do not have a name for enemies," Kate answered sharply. "Polite society dictates the use of a person's name." She emphasized *polite;* she just couldn't help herself. "I am Kate within my family and Miss Winslow to strangers."

"Oh, good, Kate," came the cheerful reply. Really, this was intolerable. "I can keep calling you Kate and still be part of *polite* society. I'm family, you know. Hugh Roberts of Hallow Hill is a relative of mine. His grandfather and my mother were cousins. Their fathers were brothers."

"Really?" exclaimed Emily excitedly. "I didn't know we had any more relatives." Neither did Kate. She felt her mortification could not go further. Perhaps this man had been on his way to visit his cousin. He must have known all about the two new wards. And now everyone would know how absurdly she had acted. But why had he been so rude? Why the hood, the wordless meeting? Really, it was his fault she had made such a colossal blunder. She was upset to the point of tears.

"I'm afraid if you're Mr. Roberts's relative, you're no relative of mine," she snapped before she realized what she was saying. Oh, no! After keeping quiet all this time!

"What?" demanded Emily, and, "Really?" exclaimed her tormentor. He reined in the horse and turned to face her. "What do you mean, you're not a Roberts? I thought you were living with your great-aunts."

"Oh, Em, I'm sorry," faltered Kate, looking up through the darkness at the pale smudge that was all she could distinguish of her sister's face. "It's old news, really; no one minds. Our great-grandmother was adopted into the family, that's all."

There was a pause. Then Marak urged the horse back into a walk.

"I can't say I'm sorry," he said thoughtfully. "New blood is very good for the Hill. But which great-grandmother are you talking about?" Thoroughly cowed, Kate told the story of Elizabeth's adoption, Adele's death, and their own consequent arrival, but she was rather scandalized when Marak laughed at all the wrong places.

"That's not how my mother told that story, Kate," he said carelessly. "I wouldn't believe everything that fool Roberts tells you." Emily snorted delightedly, but Kate was bewildered.

"Do you mean you think he lied about the adoption?" she asked, struggling along by the horse's side.

"Oh, no. That's the only thing I do believe, but what a thing to tell you. Poor Kate!" he teased. "I don't think Roberts likes you at all."

If he calls me Kate one more time, thought Kate, I'll do something horrible. Then she thought about the several horrible things she had already done that evening and subsided into misery again.

"We don't like him, either," confided Emily heatedly. "He's just hateful, with his long words, and his *hallow hill,* and his *hollow hill,* and his linguistic persistence of ignorance."

"What?" The rider seemed highly amused. "He's been explaining everything for you, has he? Tell me, what did he say about the Hill?" Emily went into a somewhat confused rendition of their cousin's speech on the place-names, and this time Marak laughed at all the right places.

"Well, Letter M," he announced, "almost every bit of that is wrong. Completely and thoroughly wrong. Pigheaded. Would you like to know why it's really called Hollow Lake?"

"Yes!" exclaimed Emily.

"It's called Hollow Lake—because it's hollow." There was a momentary pause.

"Now, what does that mean?" Emily burst out.

"It's just hollow, that's all."

"How is it supposed to be hollow?" demanded Emily. "You're just being silly!"

"No," the man replied pleasantly, "I assure you I never lie. Now, that's a funny thing, lying. If you notice, M, most humans can't do without it. They consider it an essential component of—how shall I call it?—*polite* society." Kate felt the sting in his words and set her teeth. She wondered when this interminable journey would end.

"Humans lie to each other constantly. They mean to. They think it best. They tell you what a clever child you are when they mean someone should muzzle you, and they tell one another how hand/ some they look when they think they look absurd. They believe they're doing the world a favor by lying. Why, take your sister as a case in point."

I won't say a word, Kate promised herself stoically, and Emily rushed to defend her sister against her newfound favorite.

"Kate doesn't lie!" she said indignantly.

"Oh, doesn't she?" answered Marak, sounding much amused. "Well, M, I'm sure she doesn't lie often, but such is the frail nature of humans that she simply couldn't help herself. Imagine"—he low/ ered his voice dramatically—"as she stood by the bonfire tonight, she saw outlandish and otherworldly sights, and when I came toward her to lift her onto this horse here, she knew—she just *knew*—that if she let me put her onto this horse, she'd be galloped away beyond the world we know into some strange, shadowy underworld." His voice dropped to a whisper. "And not one of the mortals on this earth would ever see her again."

Emily went off into gales of laughter. Kate felt a swift chill run through her. How could this stranger know what she had felt? She hadn't even known it herself. But that was it exactly, down to the last detail.

"And so," continued Emily's storyteller cheerfully, "what on earth could your sister say? Could she say, I think you are about to steal me for what awful ends I know not? No, she is a human. She fell back on the *polite* lie. And so she said"—and here he took on a haughty tone—"'I prefer to walk.'"

Kate forgot her promise to keep quiet. "You must think that I am a perfect fool!" she exclaimed.

"Oh, no," the rider assured her. "You are a woman of rare perception. Not one woman in a hundred—maybe a thousand—would have realized in time. I find myself wondering," he added thoughtfully, "just how you managed it."

Kate tried to puzzle out this strange speech. Another riddle for her to solve. It sounded very important, but she was too tired to make any sense of it. If the walk continued much longer, she was afraid she would collapse. She felt as if she had never done anything else but stumble through blackness.

"And here we are," concluded Marak. They came up a rise. The orchard trees loomed out at them. Gravel crunched underfoot. And in another minute, there stood the Lodge itself, solid and comforting, with golden light streaming out of all the downstairs windows. The rider swung down from the saddle and lifted Emily to the ground. "Off you go," he told her. "I stay here."

"But won't you come in, Mr. Marak?" begged Emily. "I know the aunts would love to meet you."

"Oh, I know them," he answered carelessly. "I remember when they first came here. A pretty young thing the blond was then, I assure you! But newly widowed. That was a real pity," he added feelingly. "No, I'll come in another time."

"Good-bye, then, and thank you for the ride!" Emily wrung his hand and dashed up the path. He turned to Kate, who stood hesitating, almost too tired to walk farther. Now that they were back in the light again, she found his cloak and hood insulting. She could make out nothing about him, and he seemed to know everything about her.

"Kate, you look terrible!" he said sincerely. "You're completely exhausted. Well, you won tonight, and I'm not a good loser. I'm not used to it. But until next time"—and he held out his six-fingered hand.

Kate shook her head and put her hands behind her back. She glared up at him, beside herself with indignation. She said firmly, "I hate to appear rude—"

"Yes, you do, don't you." He laughed. "Oh, I know what's bothering you," he teased before she could turn away in disgust. "The cloak and hood. It's been on your nerves all evening. You've been imagining all sorts of horrors, I'd guess."

This is just another way to goad me, Kate thought grimly, but he was absolutely right.

Marak tugged back his hood and examined her stunned expression. He watched her cheeks grow pale, her lips bloodless. He grinned in delighted amusement.

"You imagined all sorts of horrors. But maybe not this one." And he swung back into the saddle and rode away.

Chapter
Three

"Mr. Marak brought us home," Emily said from Aunt Celia's arms. "He's so nice, he let me ride his horse, and it was such a beauty, too! We should invite him over to say thank you."

Aunt Prim knelt before the fire, heating water for tea. Never mind that it had been steamy all day; with the thunderstorms around, the air at the Lodge had turned gusty and chill. Besides, Aunt Prim believed in treating any case of accidental contact with inclement weather as if the victim had just been dragged out of a snowbank.

"Who's Mr. Marak, dear?" asked Aunt Celia, yawning and smoothing back Emily's tumbled hair. It was one o'clock in the morning, and both aunts had been too frantic to sleep.

"Oh, you know, Mr. Roberts's cousin. He knows all about you. He said you were a pretty young thing, Aunt Celia, when you first came here."

"How nice of him to say that, dear," she answered, "but I can't place who he would be."

Just as Emily opened her mouth to explain, the door slammed loudly. They looked up, startled, to see Kate standing against it, a Kate they had never seen before. It wasn't just that her clothes were damp, filthy, and torn. It wasn't even that her hair straggled wildly about her dirt smudged face. It was the ghastly color of that face and the glittering eyes full of unshed tears. She stared back at them for a few seconds, her chest heaving as she struggled for breath. Then she burst into loud sobs and collapsed onto the floor.

"Draw the curtains! Draw the curtains!" was the first thing she managed to say. Emily ran to comply. They hustled her to the couch, pulled off her shoes and stockings, and piled blankets on her, but when Aunt Prim brought her a cup of tea, she could barely hold it, her hands shook so much. She gasped and shivered and alarmed her aunts extremely.

The worried Prim wrapped Emily in a blanket and made her drink a cup of tea, too. "But, Aunt Prim, there's nothing wrong with me," protested Emily. "I don't know what's wrong with Kate, I really don't. She and Mr. Marak were quarreling a little, but I think that's really her fault because she was rude to him. What happened to you, Kate? You look like you've seen a ghost."

Kate let out a quavering little laugh. I suppose I do, she thought. The memories of the bonfire and the journey whirled around in her head like fragments of a dream. She gulped the hot drink, feeling its warmth spread through her, and looked at the cozy room. Everything here was so real, so solid. Outside she could hear rain lashing the windows, thunder rolling and advancing, the wind howling in the trees. The storm had finally struck.

"Emily," said Aunt Prim. "I want you to tell Celia and me everything that happened tonight. And, Kate, I want you just to listen. Start right at the beginning and go on till the end, and don't leave anything out."

Emily had been waiting practically her whole life for such an invitation. She had a world-class story and a perfect audience, and her sister was not to say a word. Emily started at the beginning and went on till the end. She didn't omit a thing. She didn't even forget to tell them that their nephew was a pigheaded fool.

"Well, Kate, I can certainly understand your being tired and upset," Celia said cautiously. "But—did anything else happen, dear? That Emily's left out?"

"Yes," Kate said, taking a breath. "After Em left, Mr. Marak said good-bye to me. No—he said—he said until next time." She thought about that for a second, and her eyes grew large. "And then I wouldn't shake hands with him because he'd been so rude. So he laughed and said I was just upset because of his hood, that I'd been imagining all these horrors. And then"—she raised her frightened eyes to theirs—"then he pulled back his hood. And he said I might have imagined other horrors, but not this one. Because—because— he wasn't human. He just wasn't human! Oh, Em, you were on that horse with him! I can't believe you're still alive."

The three listeners exchanged amazed glances. Emily was the most startled of all. She stared blankly at her sister.

"I thought he was nice," she said.

"Now, Kate," asked Prim, "when you say this Mr. Marak wasn't—human—what exactly do you mean? Do you mean he didn't look human?"

"He, well . . ." Kate trailed off, looking around at their expec-tant faces.

"Well, what?" prompted Emily. "Did he have three eyes?"

"No, just two, but they were so strange," she answered. "Dif-ferent colors. Light and dark."

"Kate," said Aunt Celia kindly, "that is quite rare, but it's not unheard of."

"I know," Kate replied, "but that wasn't all. His hair was all wrong, too. It was part white and part black, like a horse's mane, and it was long, and loose, and it wasn't like hair somehow." She looked helplessly at their puzzled faces.

"For heaven's sake, Kate, he was an old man," snorted Emily. She had secretly been hoping for empty eye sockets or no head.

"No, you're wrong, Em, he wasn't old. Oh, he must be old, but he looked, well, not young, but . . . not old. But so ugly and bony, and his skin was so pale! And his eyebrows were all thick and bushy, and his teeth—there was something awful about his teeth." Emily started to giggle. "Stop it, Em! I just can't explain it." She glared at her sister. "You wouldn't be laughing if you saw him, too. He was just—all wrong somehow."

"Well, Kate," said Aunt Prim sympathetically, "he doesn't sound like a nice old man at all. He sounds like quite an eccentric all the way around. He certainly set you up for a shock, wearing a hood and talking about horrors and ghostly rides. I suppose if you saw him neatly trimmed and brushed by daylight, you would have thought he looked odd, but you were tired and unstrung, and he wanted to give you a scare. Your nerves weren't ready for it, that's all. You haven't been yourself these last several weeks."

A short time later, Kate lay in bed listening to the rain against the windows and the ominous rumble of the thunder. Flashes of light ning lit the sky. She stared up into the darkness overhead, dreadfully tired but too upset to sleep. She was contrasting the terrifying mem ory with the humiliation of trying to describe it. She wasn't sure which one was worse.

Her door creaked open in the darkness. A small figure padded in and snuggled down next to her.

"Kate, are you awake?" came a whisper. "I'm sorry I made you mad. If you don't like that man, I don't like him either, but it was splendid to hear him call Mr. Roberts a pigheaded fool."

"Yes, I suppose it was," Kate whispered back. She hugged her sister and smiled a little at the memory.

"I've thought of something," Emily whispered. "I'll bet he was a ghost. Did he shimmer a little? Do you think he was a ghost?"

"I don't know," Kate murmured sleepily. "Maybe he was. Maybe his skin shimmered. It certainly looked odd."

"Did he look as if he'd been dead a long time?" Emily asked.

"No," came the drowsy reply.

"Well—how about a little while?" Emily prompted hopefully. She waited. "Kate? Had he been dead a little while?" But no answer came. Her sister was asleep.

Kate's nightmares left her no peace. A man in a black hood kept dragging her from the house. She caught onto chairs, banisters, door frames, anything within reach, but he was stronger than she was and just laughed at her. She couldn't see his face, but his eyes gleamed brightly from beneath the hood. When dawn came, she was glad to get up.

The house seemed very quiet with all the windows closed against the rain. Kate stood at the parlor window and watched the wind tossing the tree branches. Thick, dark clouds hung low in the sky. Aunt Prim came back from the Hall after lunch, bringing Hugh Roberts with her. They hurried up the steps together as large drops began to fall, and in another moment the rain cascaded down in silvery sheets.

Hugh Roberts came into the parlor and warmed up at the fire. He hadn't seen much of his charges in the last couple of weeks, and he was surprised at the change he found in Kate. Prim was right. The girl looked really ill. The big man rubbed his plump hands together as he toasted them in the heat.

"Your aunt has told me quite a tale of adventure," he announced to them. "Do you have any idea how far you were from here? What land you crossed last night?"

"Em, you were on the horse," Kate said. "Did you see any lights or landmarks? I was too busy trying to keep my footing," she added resentfully.

"I couldn't see anything at all," Emily said. "It was as black as a pot out there. I don't know how the horse kept from tripping over his own feet."

Her guardian frowned at her critically. "If it was as dark as that," he observed, "I don't see how anyone could have possibly brought you home. Didn't you carry a light?"

The two girls looked at each other, surprised. Neither had thought about this. "No," answered Kate, "he didn't carry any light at all. I was walking right by the horse, and I kept tripping because I couldn't see. I don't know how he knew where he was going."

Hugh Roberts looked from one to the other of them. "Your great-aunts didn't see this gypsy," he remarked.

"He stopped just past the orchard and said he wouldn't come in," Emily said carelessly.

"And he rode back the direction he came," said Kate with a shudder.

Their guardian rubbed his chin thoughtfully, surveying them both. "And you say this man was my cousin?"

"That's right," said Emily. "He said he was family. He said that your grandfather and his mother were cousins."

"Yes," added Kate, "and that their fathers were brothers."

Hugh Roberts put his hands behind his back and began to pace slowly. "Now, that's a nice little puzzle," he told them. "And if you work it out, you'll find that such a cousin would be the child of Dentwood Roberts's daughter Adele. But Adele Roberts, as you know, Miss Winslow, died as a child. She left no children of her own, and her playmate's son inherited the estate."

Adele again! Kate was dumbfounded. She called to mind the picture from the Hall parlor. Black hair and green eyes, laughing. Adele, who had died so that Kate could own Hallow Hill.

"Let's examine this rationally," Hugh Roberts suggested, ticking the points off on his fingers. "You get lost within sight of your own house. You meet a hooded man who claims he's the son of Adele Roberts. You walk home without so much as a candle through a pitch-black night, and then you raise a fuss because he's some sort of ghastly monster. Really, Miss Winslow!" he concluded in irritation. "Don't you think I'll see through a story like that?"

Kate stared at him, confused. "Why do you think we would invent such a thing?" she asked.

Emily jumped up in a fury. "We really did get lost last night," she declared, "and your cousin Mr. Marak really did bring us home. He knew all about Aunt Prim and Aunt Celia, and he knew about you, too. He knows lots of things about this place that you don't know, and he assured us that he always speaks the truth."

Hugh Roberts failed to look either mollified or convinced. "Miss Emily," he replied heatedly, "if you can introduce me to this monster cousin, I'll be happy to believe you. Otherwise, let me just remind you that you're dealing with an educated man who knows the difference between fact and superstition." He glared over his spectacles at Emily, who glared right back.

Kate hurried to say something more helpful. "I know it sounds unbelievable, Mr. Roberts," she said. "I can't explain how we got lost, but Mr. Marak certainly is no creation of ours. He's the most unpleasant man I've ever met. He deliberately scared the wits out of me."

Hugh Roberts studied her narrowly, clasping and unclasping his hands. Her pale, worn face and earnest voice made it obvious that she was sincere. "So you really believe in that story you told?" he demanded in surprise. "You didn't invent that monster? You didn't just make it up for a thrill?" Kate shook her head without a word. Her guardian noticed again how thin and sick she looked.

"Children, run up to your rooms for a few minutes. I'd like to speak to your aunts alone."

Hugh Roberts left in the dogcart half an hour later. Noticing her aunts' frightened eyes, Kate wondered in irritation what on earth he could have said. They soothed Kate and fussed over her like two old hens. They didn't let her sew or read. They wanted her to rest. And every time she said something—anything—they exchanged furtive glances.

Emily fared little better. At suppertime she tried to bring up the strange rider again, and Aunt Prim snapped at her.

"Don't tell stories," she said sternly.

"Stories!" Emily cried. "I never do! Kate—"

But Aunt Celia interrupted. "Leave your sister out of this," she said sadly. "Kate's nerves aren't strong, but we expect you to know the difference between facts and falsehoods."

"Well, I like that," Emily stormed a few minutes later as she stomped back and forth on the wooden floor of Kate's bedroom. "We tell them what someone else says, and we get blamed for lying. I'd like to see them face a ghost. I think your nerves are just fine." She flung herself down on the bench at Kate's dressing table. Looking in the tall, old mirror at its back, she made a disgusted face at herself.

Kate lay on her bed, not really listening to Emily's tirade. She was staring up at the canopy, trying to puzzle through to the truth of last night. It did seem very much like a dream, like the nightmares she had been having. Maybe she had exaggerated. Maybe she had been half asleep and hadn't really seen enormous cats or children with beards. Maybe she hadn't really seen that strange caricature of a face. Facts and falsehoods. Weak nerves. She closed her eyes, terribly tired.

"Come look at this." Emily's voice rang out loudly, blaring like a bugle call through Kate's foggy brain.

"Oh, Em, what?" she begged. She opened her eyes and turned toward the dressing table. Nothing. Sitting up grudgingly, she found her sister standing by the window, staring out at the rainy trees beyond.

"Now they can't say I'm a liar!" Emily declared triumphantly. "This is great! Shall I call Aunt Prim?"

Level with the window but a dozen feet away, a cat crouched disconsolately on a dripping tree limb. It turned its golden eyes toward them, ears flat against its head, and shifted uncomfortably from foot to foot. It was very wet, very unhappy, and very, very large. It was the big black cat from the bonfire.

"Poor Seylin! He's so miserable," Emily said sympathetically. "Kate, don't you think we could call him down and bring him inside?"

"No!" yelped Kate more forcefully than she had meant to. "No, Em. We have to think this through. If that man who brought us home last night is a ghost, then his friends can't be much better, can they?"

"But I petted Seylin!" Emily protested. "He's perfectly solid and not in the least terrifying. And he's out in the rain. You can see how much he hates it."

Kate went to the window and pulled back the lace to get a better look. The huge cat stared at her steadily.

"No, Em," she said at last. "I don't like it. He may be a normal cat, but I'm not willing to find out. Aunt Prim would never let a cat into the house, anyway, much less a wet one as big as that. And I don't think it'll do any good to tell the aunts he's the same one we saw last night. They don't want to hear about last night at all."

Emily went grumbling off to bed. Kate spent another minute staring out at the cat. Then she dropped the sheer lace and pulled the long, thick curtains over the window. The rainy evening was fast becoming a rainy night. She lit the candle on her dressing table and changed hurriedly for bed.

She fell into a restless slumber, but even in the confused shreds of dreams, she knew she wasn't safe. In her sleep, she was telling Emily all about it. "Then I heard a click as the window opened," she said, and in that instant Kate was wide awake. The click hadn't been a dream. She craned her neck to see over the footboard. The heavy curtains still covered the window, but they were billowing gently outward as they caught the breeze.

Kate crawled to the bedpost and ducked behind the thick, gathered curtains of the bed. The open window let in all the sounds of a drizzly night: the gentle dripping and tapping, the wind sighing. Another unmistakable sound joined them: slow, heavy footsteps by the window. They wandered in an unhurried fashion down the room as if the unseen caller were looking casually around. They came closer and closer. They were right beside her bed.

Kate let out a scream. "Get out of my room!" Then she ducked down farther and held her breath. Nothing happened. The stillness was profound. She scrambled up and peered into the darkness, but she couldn't see anyone there. The window was closed now, and the curtains hung limp. No footsteps sounded in the room beyond, no movement, no breathing. Long seconds crawled by.

"I'm not in your room," announced Marak's pleasant voice.

Kate froze in horror. Her first instinct was to leap to the door and run away, but he was bound to follow her. If she ran to Emily's room, he might hurt her little sister, and if her great-aunts ever saw such a monster Kate was sure they wouldn't survive it. She stared feverishly into the blackness but saw nothing at all. Where could he be?

She slipped out of bed and crept to her dressing table. Her hands shaking, she struck a match, but her candle blossomed into golden light before the match even caught. She whirled, examining her bedroom by its friendly glow. The room, lit by the single candle flame, seemed full of shadow and menacing beyond words.

"You told me to get out of your room," noted Marak's voice behind her. "Look in the other room, the one you see in your mirror."

Kate turned to face the tall mirror on her dressing table. What she saw could not possibly be. She put a hand on her bedpost to steady herself. The reflection reached out a hand and clutched its bedpost, too. A hand with six fingers. Marak stood facing her in the old tarnished mirror. Kate's own image was gone.

What Marak was, Kate didn't know, but he couldn't be a human, not with that big, bony head and tough, wiry body. The slightly bowed legs and large, knotted hands conveyed the idea of strength without grace. He was wearing a black shirt, breeches, and boots, but he had left the riding cloak at home, and his high, twisted shoulder showed to advantage. His face and hands were a ghastly pale gray, and his lips and fingernails were dark tan—the colors, Kate thought, shuddering, of a corpse pulled out of the water. His dull, straight hair fell, all one length, to his twisted shoulders. Most of it was a very light beige, but over one eye a coal-black patch grew back from the forehead, the long black wisps overlaying the pale hair like a spider's legs. His ears rose to a sharp point that flopped over and stuck out through that rough hair like the ears of a terrier dog.

Most striking of all were Marak's deep-set eyes. The left eye was black; the right, emerald green, and they gleamed at her as if lit from within. Marak's dull hair drifted into his face where the cowlick didn't push it out, so his black eye shone through a pale curtain.

This grotesque vision rendered Kate incapable of action for a minute. As her wits began to return, a grim resignation came with them. Em and the aunts were weaker than she was. She would have to face him alone. She took a step toward the frightful image and groped for the bench, seating herself unsteadily before the mirror. The monstrous reflection moved as she did, sinking down upon its own bench. Those odd eyes watched her attentively and shrewdly, and Marak grinned at her. Kate stared in fascinated revulsion. His teeth, small and even, were a dark silver-gray, and they were sharper than proper teeth should be.

Everything about this creature was inhumanly freakish, inhumanly ugly, and she was very grateful that it was not in the same
room with her. The mirror was between them. Or—was it? Suppose he could just grab her with those corpse's hands? She held her
breath and reached out to feel the mirror, and the figure beyond
slowly reached out its hand as well. They came closer and closer
together until Kate felt something cold brush her fingertips.

A second later she was on her feet by the bed, gasping for air, the
overturned bench hitting the floor in front of her. Marak sprang
up to copy, but he failed in the pantomime. Instead, he clung to the
bedpost, whooping with laughter.

"You should have seen your face!" he hooted. "I had no idea that
touching glass could be so alarming!"

Kate drew long breaths, her fright giving way to indignation.
Yes, that was this creature's other characteristic, she remembered
with disgust. Inhumanly ugly and, as far as she could tell, inhumanly rude.

"I never saw anyone move so fast! You should have seen
yourself!"

Kate eyed him balefully, furious at being laughed at. This is the
last time, she vowed firmly, that I give him that satisfaction. She
righted the upset bench as calmly as she could and sat down shakily.
Marak moved to do the same, not bothering to copy her this time. He
just pulled the bench up and sat down as if they were across a normal table instead of across magical dimensions. Then he propped an
elbow on his dressing table and leaned his cheek on one big, knotted
hand, looking out at her expectantly.

"Yes, I should have seen myself," said Kate, finding her voice
with an effort. "I'm looking in a mirror, aren't I? I want my reflection
back where it belongs."

"I'll be your reflection," Marak teased. "You'll come and sit
before me, and I'll tell you how beautiful you are. I'll tell you that

there's no woman in the whole land to compare with you, just like magical mirrors are supposed to."

Kate decided to ignore his impertinence. It was the only ladylike thing to do. "Why did you come here?" she demanded angrily. "Why are you bothering me?"

"I'm here tonight for the same reason that I was here last night," he replied. "Are you sure you really want to know why? You look a little upset." He crossed his wiry arms and leaned forward to study her carefully. "There's no insanity in your family, is there?"

The irony of this question coming out of the mouth of a grotesque illusion left Kate speechless for a few seconds. Insanity? Not until he came along. She shrugged, looking blank.

"No insanity," Marak concluded in relief. "That's good. You do keep surprising me," he admitted. "I thought I had you sound asleep. Then there you were, sitting up and shrieking like a teakettle. Really, Kate!" he reproved, shaking his bony head at her. "What if someone had heard you?"

"Are you a ghost?" Kate asked quickly before she could lose her nerve. Suppose he did something dreadful!

"No," he answered. "I am alive, just as you are."

"Then you're a devil?" she guessed.

"How wicked do you think I am?" He chuckled. "You think I'm evil incarnate just because I irritate you? There must be a special place in hell for people who use your first name without permission." He threw back his head and laughed loudly at his own joke.

Kate glared at him in embarrassed rage. "Then what are you?" she demanded.

Marak considered her shrewdly.

"I'm a goblin," he replied and grinned at her. Kate shuddered. Those frightful teeth! She stared at him, completely at a loss. She tried to think of everything she had ever heard about goblins, but it wasn't much.

Marak watched her with interest, waiting to see what she would say next. "Just what is a goblin?" he prompted the confused Kate. She rallied before he could make fun of her.

"Something rude," she stated emphatically. He was helpless with laughter.

"Oh, Kate, I do like you," he confessed. "You're quite a welcome surprise. So you don't know what a goblin is. I'll tell you, then. It is a creature of the race begun by the First Fathers, made with their magic as they drew on the strength of all the other creatures to produce their children. And the goblin you see before you is Marak, the King, the direct descendant of the Greatest of the First Fathers of our race.

"In each generation since the very beginning," he said, "the King's Wife has borne only one child, and that child is always a son. Each son has become Marak in his turn. The King is the guardian and source of the magical gifts of our race. Without the King, the race is lost." He paused and considered her thoughtfully.

"But this King's first wife has died without leaving a son," he told her.

Kate eyed the grotesque goblin uneasily. What should one say to a monster who has lost his spouse? Her upbringing had not prepared her for moments like this.

"Shall I tell you what your mirror sees?" Marak went on. Kate frowned and looked away, expecting more teasing. "I see a young human woman who is astonishingly beautiful," he said. Surprised, Kate eyed him warily. "And who has demonstrated a courage, intelligence, and resourcefulness that I did not at all expect. In short, I see an ideal King's Wife."

It took Kate a few seconds to comprehend, and then her blood froze in her veins. She couldn't move or speak, though she was vaguely aware that the ugly creature was watching her with concern. The room began to grow dim around her.

"Kate," said that commanding voice, "you are having a horrible nightmare." She heard him over the roaring in her ears. It was the only thing he had said that made sense. "Lie down now." Kate put her head down on a pillow. A blanket came over her. She felt its warm touch against her cheek.

"Sleep well, with no more nightmares," concluded the voice. "When you wake up, you will be refreshed. But you will remember everything that has happened tonight in perfect detail."

The candle snuffed out, and the mirror went blank, but Kate didn't notice. She was already sleeping soundly and peacefully, carrying out the goblin King's orders to the letter.

Chapter
Four

"Wake up! Are you going to sleep all day?"

Kate opened her eyes and blinked drowsily. Aunt Prim pushed back the curtains and unlatched the window as Emily sat down next to Kate. A fresh, cool breeze flowed into the room. Outside, Kate could see green leaves glowing in the bright morning sun.

"How are you, dear?" asked Prim cautiously, coming over. "Emily said she heard you crying out and talking in your sleep. I'm sorry I didn't hear you. Are you feeling any better?"

"I feel wonderful." Kate smiled up at her. "I slept so well that I'm completely refreshed." She frowned. "But then, I had to, didn't I?" she added bitterly. Emily and Aunt Prim exchanged puzzled glances.

"Well, dear," Prim said anxiously, "we're going down to the Hall for the day, but I think perhaps you should stay home and rest."

Kate climbed out of bed. "Oh, no," she declared. "I don't want to miss a lovely morning like this. Mrs. Bigelow is bound to have a wonderful meal planned for us at the Hall. I'll be ready in just a few minutes," she promised, and shooed the two of them out the door.

Feeling bold, she hurried to her dressing table. She sat for a moment and examined her reflection closely, but the mirror behaved in every respect like a good mirror should. It reflected a cozy, personable room and the glorious day outside. There was nothing to indicate the strange happenings of the night before. Nothing, that is, beyond her own peculiar expression. One cannot look entirely ordinary, she considered, after such a horrifying event. Or, although she failed to realize it, after being told one is astonishingly beautiful. She did linger just a minute longer than usual before the glass, turning her head to catch a view of her profile. Then she remembered the goblin's proposal to flatter her whenever she came near the mirror and jumped up in a huff.

Kate dressed hastily, splashing her face with cold water to bring the color to her pale cheeks. She brushed her hair at the mirror and tried not to think about what she had seen there, but her strange visitor's every gesture, every word came clearly to mind. She could practically relive the night's events. What had he said? "You will remember everything that has happened tonight in perfect detail."

Good spirits waning, she went to the window to clear her thoughts. No giant black cat waited outside, but a dingy gray squirrel crouched on the tree limb by her room, right where the cat had been. It was facing her window, and Kate had the distinct impression that it was watching her.

She came out to the waiting carriage with a brave smile for her worried aunts, but when a small squirrel came leaping down to the gravel path beside her, she brandished her fist at it and chased it away. She turned back to find all three occupants of the carriage staring at her in bewildered alarm.

"Heavens, Kate!" reproved her sister. "Bullying a squirrel!"

"Hush, Emily!" Prim scolded sharply as she and Celia exchanged anxious glances.

They arrived at the Hall, and the aunts swept in, greeting Mrs. Bigelow. Kate straggled behind, uneasy and irritable. At the door, Emily paused and looked back. She caught Kate's arm with a grin and pointed at the carriage.

There on the roof crouched the squirrel. It sat up, chattering, and waved its tail at her. Kate had a vision of herself chasing it headlong down the gravel track, yelling like a banshee. No, perhaps she'd better not. She gathered the shreds of her composure about her and stepped through the door. If she shut it behind her with more force than necessary, she was unaware of it. Occupied with her own thoughts, she didn't see the shocked glances of her aunts as she walked past them to take her place in the dining room. Mrs. Bigelow sat down with the family and summoned the staff to begin serving the meal.

Kate picked at her food. If God is so good, she considered unhappily, why won't He make this horrible creature go away? But the Romans hadn't asked permission before hauling the Sabine women away to be their wives, and the ancient tribes were always taking women captive. God gives His creatures freedom to act, her father had taught her, and it is our responsibility to use it correctly. But what if a magical goblin has no intention of using his freedom correctly? I suppose it's my responsibility to stop him, Kate concluded pessimistically. As well as I know how.

That raised another point. What did she know about how to stop goblins? Nothing whatsoever. She had heard the term applied to mischievous children, and she thought she remembered a story about goblins from her nursery days, something about ugly little creatures with big round eyes who caused trouble to farmers. Kate felt a sense of indignation. Her education had obviously been inadequate. She must learn more, but not from the goblin himself. Kate was sure she wouldn't escape another encounter with him. Perhaps she could find out something useful from Mrs. Bigelow. She had lived there all her life and was bound to know something about goblins. Maybe she could tell Kate what to do.

The meal was dragging on in awkward silence. No one had been able to think of much to say. Perhaps this was because Hugh Roberts

ate without his usual book, paying close attention to the conversation. Kate didn't know how her aunts felt about this abnormal
behavior, but it made her rather uncomfortable.

"Mrs. Bigelow," she said to the housekeeper as carelessly as she
could, "Mr. Roberts told us once that there are lots of folktales about
Hallow Hill. Do any of the stories mention goblins?"

Hugh Roberts leaned his large bulk forward and looked at Kate
over his spectacles.

"Who has told you about goblins, Miss Winslow?" he asked.
"And please don't try to tell me that it was my cousin." This was
a nice mess, decided Kate, taken aback. She couldn't possibly
answer him.

"I was just curious," she said.

Her guardian turned to the housekeeper. "Did you tell her?" he
demanded.

"Of course not, sir!" that good woman gasped, her pleasant face
wrinkled in concern. "I knew you wouldn't want the young ladies
hearing those old stories."

"So there are stories about goblins!" exclaimed Kate in relief.
"I'd very much like to hear them."

"Don't you think you've heard enough of them already?" her
guardian asked her knowingly, but when Kate gave him a puzzled
look, he gave her a puzzled look in return. "All right, Mrs. Bigelow,"
he sighed, "we'd better hear the stories again. Maybe then we'll get
somewhere."

"Well, now," began the housekeeper hesitantly. "Now, you girls
know that I've never breathed a word about goblins to you. But the
truth is, my own grandparents and the folk they lived among would
have sworn to you that there were elves and goblins in these hills.
Why, when I was a child, there wasn't a single one of us girls allowed
out of the house after sunset. All because the magical folk, you see,
they be creatures of the nighttime, and they can't see in the day.

"The old folks told us that the goblins would steal a girl if they caught her out wandering in the twilight. They'd drag her away to their caverns under the Hill to be a goblin bride. Her hair would turn white, and the color would fade out of her, and she'd become like one of them creatures herself, nursing some squalling goblin brat in those dripping holes down in the Hill. They always did want the pretty ones, the girls who hadn't been married, so once we were married, you know, we didn't have to worry about them anymore."

Kate remembered Marak commenting on how pretty Aunt Celia had been in her youth, but she had been a widow. "That was a real pity," he had said emphatically. Now she knew what he had meant.

"No one ever did see the goblins or the elves," Mrs. Bigelow continued, "or if they did, they didn't let on to have seen them. They be terrible secretive creatures and powerful with magic, and it didn't pay to cross them at all. Sometimes, old folks said, they'd hear hunting horns at night, and sometimes sounds of battle, but the wise folk barred their doors and pulled their shutters. You see, the elves and the goblins were here in this land long before us, and folks respected their ways."

"But what were you girls supposed to do if you did meet a goblin?" asked Kate. "Sneeze, or throw salt in its eyes, or say the Lord's Prayer?"

"There's no right way to meet a goblin, dearie," said the housekeeper. "Staying inside at night was all we could do because they'd not take notice of us then. If a girl was to get stolen, well, she was stolen, is all. Sneezing and salting wasn't going to help."

"Did you know any girls who got stolen?" asked Emily hopefully.

"Well, no," Mrs. Bigelow admitted. "Not that there wasn't the occasional odd bit of news. A girl might go out for a walk and never come back, and her family would never know what had become of her. But there is one story from my grandmother's day that always scared us young girls into staying safe indoors, and that was the story of Miss Adele Roberts.

"You see, my grandmother said Miss Adele was as bold as any general, and to tell her not to do a thing was the same as to see her do it. Her playmate Miss Elizabeth was a timid little thing, and it may be that encouraged Miss Adele in her outrageousness. If it was riding the half-broken colt or walking a cliff's edge, Miss Adele would do it, half for the fun of the thing and half to hear Miss Elizabeth's frantic screams begging her to stop. But they went everywhere together, and for all her frights and shocks, Miss Elizabeth couldn't bear to be left at home.

"When they were just about old enough to be thought young ladies, folks warned them to stay safe at home at night, and that right away fired Miss Adele's ambition. She swore she'd be the first to walk into the goblin caves right through their own front door. She'd catch a goblin with her own bare hands or perish in the attempt. And so, evening after evening of those pretty summer days, she was ranging about the woodlands and fields in the twilight, calling for those goblins to come out and show themselves.

"Then came the night the old folks had been waiting on. Miss Elizabeth came running into the house, screaming and crying, and Miss Adele was nowhere to be seen. It seems Miss Adele had been marching up a wooded path with a stick in her hand, whacking at the tree trunks and calling on the goblins, when all of a sudden a whole crowd of creatures leapt from the shadows around her. Then a tall man in a black cloak and hood stepped to her side. He lifted her up in his arms, and the whole crowd melted into the shadows and was gone, with only the sounds of Miss Adele's screams left behind them to show where they had been.

"Old Roberts stood up looking pale as death, and he called for his master of hounds. The two of them went off with lanterns and the pack on a leash. And when they returned without her in the wee hours of the night, old Roberts called the staff together, and he bade them all good-bye. 'My daughter is dead,' he told them, 'and don't think you'll see her again.' Then he took Miss Elizabeth into the carriage with him, and two good strong lads for protection, and they rolled off into the night. And that was the last Hallow Hill ever saw of the old master or his daughter."

"Then it's true!" cried Kate in horror. "Adele did become the King's Wife!" The entire group turned toward her, stunned. "The goblin King's Wife," she hurriedly explained. "Adele had to marry the goblin King, and that creature is her son. He wasn't lying to us after all, Em."

Her dinnertime companions couldn't have looked more astounded. Even Emily gave her sister a baffled look. Hugh Roberts took off his spectacles and polished them with his napkin.

"What on earth are you talking about, Miss Winslow?" he demanded.

"I'm talking about terrible danger," insisted Kate urgently. "Please, you have to send me away from here! They got Adele," she said with a shudder, "and who knows how long she survived down there, but they're not going to get me."

"You think goblins are trying to get you?" asked her guardian in surprise.

"I know he is," answered Kate firmly. "He told me so." Hugh Roberts put his spectacles back on and stared at her over them. Then he turned to her sister.

"Miss Emily, you went on that adventure, too. Do you know anything about this?" His younger charge shrugged and shook her head.

"Of course she doesn't," said Kate. "He told me last night. He said his first wife died childless, and I'm ideal. But they can't see in the daytime," she added, planning rapidly. "If I leave now, maybe I can travel beyond their reach by nightfall." She began calculating how long it would take to pack and what she would need to bring. The others at the table exchanged apprehensive glances, their meal quite forgotten.

"Prim? Celia? Nighttime callers?" demanded Hugh. They looked at him and sorrowfully shook their heads. "Miss Emily?"

"She had a nightmare," whispered Emily. "She was talking in her sleep. I heard her."

"No one else saw him," declared Kate impatiently. Really, they were wasting her time.

"How convenient," murmured her guardian dryly.

"Oh, for heaven's sake!" exclaimed Kate. "I know it seems impossible, but you just have to believe me. Adele's your own relation, after all. Haven't you learned anything from her story?"

"Miss Winslow," remarked Hugh Roberts distantly, "we don't concern ourselves with old gossip. We live in the nineteenth century now. Not even Mrs. Bigelow really believes her goblin tales."

Kate glanced, surprised, at the housekeeper, who was watching her anxiously. The pleasant woman gave an embarrassed shrug and looked away. Kate paused, deeply frustrated, and looked around the table at the others. They all looked as if they wished they were somewhere else. She took a deep breath and tried again.

"I understand your doubts," she said reasonably. "I can see why you thought we invented our walk home the other night. There are parallels to Adele's story, of course. It would be easy to think that we had heard it and decided to make up our own, but I promise you that we didn't. I would be happy to show you proof if only I had it. But please believe me," she insisted as calmly as she could. "I'm in terrible danger. I'm not lying to you."

Her guardian rose and began to pace the room slowly, his hands clasped behind his back. He turned to look at her several times. Kate looked back as sincerely as she knew how.

"I do believe you," he remarked finally. "I can see that you're not lying."

Kate let her breath out in relief. "Then you know I'm in danger," she concluded. "You'll send me away."

"No, Miss Winslow," countered Hugh Roberts. "I do not know that you're in danger, but I do know that you're sincere in your delusions. It's obvious that your nerves have given way and left you in a frantic state. You've made some sort of break with reality."

Kate rose to her feet, astounded. "Are you saying that I've gone mad?" she demanded.

Her guardian looked dismayed. "There's no need to use so harsh a term," he protested. "But we felt even before this strange outburst that your nerves were showing severe strain. You must admit, Miss Winslow, that you've given us cause for concern."

Kate stared at each of them one by one. Mrs. Bigelow, fiddling anxiously with her fork and knife. Aunt Celia, face hidden behind her handkerchief. Aunt Prim, staring at the pattern on the platter with the most intense concentration. Emily, pushing a few stray peas around and around with her fork. Kate looked back up to meet her guardian's pale-eyed stare.

"You've certainly given me cause for concern, too," she remarked bitterly. She turned on her heel and walked out of the room.

⌒

After a half hour of frantic searching, Emily caught up with Kate. Her sister was lying in the middle of the tree circle, staring at the white clouds overhead. She sat up as Emily approached and began gathering the small lilies that grew within her reach.

"Oh, Kate, I'm so sorry," Emily wailed miserably. "I do believe you! I do! You're not really mad, are you?" she quavered. "I mean, I understand if you want to be. . . ."

"Don't be a complete goose, Em," said Kate disgustedly. "The rest of them are bad enough." She told her sister about the events of the previous night. Emily hugged her knees and listened carefully, not saying a single word.

"Oh, Kate," she breathed when her sister was finished. "Your very first proposal." Kate stared unbelievingly at the round, solemn eyes and flopped onto her back, laughing loudly. When she recovered, she attacked her little sister and tickled her unmercifully.

"How dare you," she choked, "call that travesty a proposal! I simply can't believe it! What an idiotic thing to say!"

"Well," her sister sheepishly amended, brushing grass off her dress, "it was sort of like a proposal, anyway. Do you think he loves you?" she added, wide-eyed again.

"Please," groaned Kate, lying back to look up at the clouds. "He's not even human! He's a grotesque monster! Weren't you paying attention?"

"But he's royalty! And he can do magic," her sister pointed out excitedly. "Think how handy if you can't light your candle in the dark."

"And that's exactly where I would be—in the dark." They both sobered up, thinking about Mrs. Bigelow's tale of the dank caves under the Hill. Kate shivered. "Imagine!" she said. "Poor Adele, shut up in a hole like that. I'd never survive it, Em. I'd die, I just know I would." Emily took her hand and squeezed it affectionately.

"I'm sorry," she said sympathetically. "It does sound terrible. But I'll help. What do we do?"

"I don't know," Kate replied gloomily. "I've been trying to think of a plan. I know good and well that they won't let me near the horses, and if I try to take the dogcart, they really will think I'm crazy. We'll just have to find some way to convince Mr. Roberts and the aunts that the goblin is real."

"I don't know why they don't believe you," commented Emily. "It makes perfect sense to me."

"We live in the nineteenth century now," Kate mimicked her guardian in a lofty tone. Then she giggled.

"If he knows that, why's he still wearing a wig?" demanded Emily. "I wonder if he's completely bald without it."

"Don't you dare ask him," warned her sister, standing up. "We'd better go home now and face the whispering aunts. We'll stay together in your room tonight, and maybe I can find some way to convince them tomorrow."

But even this simple plan proved impossible.

"You want us to do what?" Kate gasped to Prim. That dour woman held a letter out to her.

"I want you and Emily to take this message up to the Hall for me," Prim replied defensively. "You'll stay with Mrs. Bigelow tonight."

"But Aunt Prim," spluttered Kate, "you can't possibly mean it! It's already dark out there!"

"I certainly do mean it," her aunt said forcefully. "Kate, I know you're afraid of—of the dark—but Hugh suggested this, and I think it will help. You need to face your fears."

"What?" gasped Kate. "You actually expect me to walk out this door—and *face* them?"

"Kate, get hold of yourself!" the old woman said firmly. "We simply can't have another day like today."

"Oh, you won't!" cried Kate, snatching the letter from her. "You won't have any more days like today ever again!" The two girls stumbled out into the night.

"This is just splendid!" snapped Kate, clutching Emily's hand tightly. "This is simply perfect!" She stopped short at the gravel path. "Now what on earth are we going to do?"

"Run?" suggested Emily uncertainly.

"Oh, for heaven's sake, Em! They have horses."

They entered the forest. The moon, almost full, climbed a nearly cloudless sky, and Kate gathered courage from its pale rays. Bright moonlight dappled the path before them with silver spots, but under the trees, the shadows were black and ominous. After only a couple of minutes, they heard just what they had been afraid to hear: the creaking of saddles and the ringing of hooves on stone. Voices behind them began to laugh and howl.

"Come *on!*" Kate cried, and they did their best to run. They stumbled over roots and caught their clothes on branches. Kate lost a shoe and ran on in her stocking. The horses were almost upon them. She dragged Emily off the path into the deep shadows beside it. The horses trotted by.

"Quick!" gasped Kate. "They missed us!" She jumped to her feet with her sister in tow and ran across the path into the woods beyond. About ten feet off the path, a clearing opened up. A little woman worked in the moonlight, filling her basket with herbs and humming melodiously.

"Help!" panted the girls, dashing up. Old Agatha's broad face and snapping black eyes turned toward them.

"Oh, look!" she cried, clapping her hands and dropping her herb-filled basket. "It's my two pretty ladies! Now, help from what, my dears?"

Kate stopped short in horror, but Emily burst out, "Agatha, save us! The goblins are coming!" This was a rather silly speech to make, but the little woman took their trembling hands kindly enough.

"Not yet, dears," she soothed. "Who's been chasing my ladies?" As if in reply, they heard hooves on the path again. Kate pointed mutely toward the sound.

"Oh, that!" Agatha chuckled. "They're no goblins! Just a couple of clodhopping humans out for a moonlight ride."

"But they're after us!" cried Emily. Kate nodded vigorously. She tried to swallow the lump in her throat, but it stuck fast.

"Not for long," declared the little woman. "Just stand still now." She reached into one of her capacious pockets and pulled out some sort of powder, carefully patting it down into the hollow of her hand. The horses were almost upon them. Agatha took a deep breath and blew the powder toward them. The air was filled with the sound of terrified neighing and plunging, riders' confused shouts, and snapping branches. The two horses tore off down the path to the house as if demons were after them, their riders clinging to them more by accident than skill.

Old Agatha watched them go, chuckling with satisfaction. Then she bent and retrieved her basket and went on with her work. The girls stared after the horses in amazement. The exhaustion of the sudden fright and quick run caught up with them, and they stood speechless for a moment, drawing in shaky breaths.

"We're so excited about the wedding, dear," Agatha assured the petrified Kate, her nimble fingers working in the weeds at their feet. "And a prize you are, to be sure, after the King's last wife. What a dull, drab thing she was, poor mite! He certainly didn't deserve that. And a fine King he is, too, my dear, though I should say it, who was his old nurse, you know. He's the best magician we've had in many a generation, though there do be some who say he's too elf-pretty to be a proper king."

"Mm," said Kate stupidly, too horrified to reply, but Emily was quite interested in the little woman's speech. She had no difficulty, as usual, in thinking of things she wanted to know.

"What do you mean, elf-pretty?" she asked the busy Agatha. "And why doesn't the King just marry another goblin? Doesn't anyone at home want to marry him?"

"Oh, they couldn't, dear, you know," old Agatha replied. "Goblin women don't bear well. Many goblins marry outside for to bring in fresh blood, you see. And the King, always. It's the ancient way of our race. Elves and humans for the King, though there's been the occasional dwarf," she added proudly. "And that's the way it's always been for us. The high families marries the elves and dwarves or a pretty human girl, and the beast folk marries whatever of the animal folk they fancies. The cat tribe, the dog tribe, eagles or bears, anyone who'll be a good mother to goblin young. That's why gob/lins look like everything on earth."

The two girls pondered this extremely peculiar statement. Emily was not to be thwarted, however.

"What do you mean, elf/pretty?" she asked again. Agatha stopped her work and stretched.

"The Kings tended to marry elves, back when the elves still lived. They're all gone now, the elves. I saw the last when I was a child. She was this King's grandmother, and he's like her in ways. He's hardly got a single animal trait about him, and that's odd in a King. No wings or claws, no feathers or fangs, and that makes folks call him elf/pretty. Oh, they were our cousins, you know, the elves, though there was no love lost between us. They were pretty to look at, but we were the stronger race. We captured their women when/ever we pleased, and the goblins learned their magic. This King, now"— she nodded to Kate—"he knows all about elf magic. It's a powerful good to the goblin folk to have a strong King."

A strong King. That was just the problem. "Yes, well," Kate said, managing to find her voice at last, "Emily and I had better be going now. Thank you for your help."

Old Agatha's black eyes twinkled up at Kate shrewdly. "Don't thank me just yet, my dear," she said.

"Well, good/bye, then," Kate answered. She took Emily's hand and turned to go. Then she let out a gasp. Her feet! They were glued to the spot. She tried to tear them free, but they seemed to have grown roots.

"Agatha!" she wailed. She and Emily struggled fruitlessly and then stared at each other in panic. The goblin woman calmly carried on with her work.

"We're so excited about the wedding," she repeated. "We've got everything all ready. And I'm in charge of the women's part. It's quite an honor, you know."

Kate thought she could hear distant hoofbeats over the drumming of blood in her ears. "Agatha," she pleaded futilely.

"Now, now, dear," the old woman said soothingly, "you've no need to carry on. He'll make a good husband for you, you know. He was that kind to his other poor wife, and she was just as mad as a spring hare."

Yes, that must be hoofbeats, Kate thought desperately, and she knew how that poor mad wife must have felt. But somehow, she knew just what to do.

"Agatha," she said winningly, not even sure what she was saying, "you don't want the King's new wife handed over like a sack of potatoes. Everyone will hear of it. What a dull, drab thing I'll seem." The little woman paused in her work, her bright black eyes on Kate.

"And isn't it good to see the King so busy," Kate chatted on. "Something new to plan for every day. It's good for him, you know," she added persuasively. "He always does get things his own way."

Agatha burst into a chuckle and patted Kate's hand. "Oh, go on with you," she said indulgently as if she were sending them out to play. "Go ahead and get a little head start; it does make it sporting. He'll be here soon enough."

"Thank you, Agatha," Kate gasped, snatching her sister's hand and dashing from the clearing. On the path, they both froze, listening. The horseman was very near.

"To the tree circle!" called Kate. "He's already at the house." Then she saved her breath for running. As they tore up the little slope that led to the tree circle hill, the hoofbeats drummed out loudly behind them. The horseman was catching up.

"Don't look back," Kate begged, but Emily couldn't help it. As they raced toward the first circle of trees, she glanced over her shoulder to see the gray horse break from the woods behind them. His master held him at a gallop, riding low, black cloak streaming back in the wind and one arm reaching out to snatch the sisters. Then Kate was dodging between the massive trees, dragging Emily behind her. They heard the horse plunge and slide to a stop as they ran to the center of the clearing.

The stars hung huge and low over them, and the almost-full moon shone down, but a crackling ring of purple lightning split the sky. It arced and danced in the trees, blinding their dazzled eyes, and a fierce wind whipped up, whirling and tearing at their clothes. The sisters threw themselves on the ground and huddled in terror, their arms clutched tightly around each other. The wind whistled and sang in their ears, and the constant cracks of lightning picked out patterns on the insides of their tightly closed eyelids. Emily sobbed aloud in fright. Kate waited in a state beyond fright for the hands that would drag her away. When they didn't come, she began to grow impatient. What was he waiting for?

"Stop doing that!" she called out loudly. "You're frightening my sister!"

Complete calm reigned instantly. No lightning crackled, and the wind puffed down to a gentle breeze. After a few seconds, the girls raised their heads and looked about them, expecting to see destruction and chaos, wildfires and uprooted trees. Instead, the stars hung huge and low, and the silver moon shone down. The clearing looked exactly as it had before.

"Kate," called Marak's pleasant voice from beyond the huge oak trees, "it's time to stop this foolishness now. Come out before you make me do something rash."

Kate felt her blood turn to ice. She stroked the grassy turf for a second. The feel of it gave her confidence. She looked around at the stars, the moon, the trees. These were things that she could count on.

"You can't come in here, can you?" she shouted back. "This is a magic place."

"Don't be ridiculous," the goblin answered reasonably. "Of course I can come in. It is a magic place, and I'm magic."

"Oh, no, or you'd already be here," Kate shouted exultantly. "Your magic doesn't work here. You can't do anything to us, I know it!"

Marak walked into the clearing, stopping just inside the circle of trees. Emily gave a gasp of dismay and scrambled to her feet. She was getting her first good look at the goblin King.

Marak grinned, showing his dark teeth. "Kate, you're a treasure," he declared. "I don't know how you know things, but you do. You're exactly right. I can't do anything to make you leave this place. Anything magical, anything actual. All force is completely forbidden here because this is the elves' and goblins' truce circle." He sighed. "And once again, I just wish I knew how you know it."

Kate struggled to her feet, wild hope making her giddy.

"We're safe here," she told her sister. She turned triumphantly to face the goblin King. "And you might as well leave. We'll be staying here all night where you can't hurt us."

The wiry goblin smiled at her. "Now, who ever gave you the idea that I would hurt you?" He shook the striped hair out of his brilliant eyes. "No, force is not allowed at all within this circle. You are free to do whatever you want to do. Or whatever you're persuaded to do. Elves and goblins aren't susceptible to persuasion spells, so there's no protection against them." He leered at the two sisters. "Let's see, Kate," he suggested. "I think what you really want to do right now is walk over to me."

Kate stiffened at once, her confidence evaporating. "I certainly do not!" she gasped. Marak's big, bony face wore an amused grin.

"No?" he asked coolly. His voice dropped, becoming quiet and gentle. "Walk toward me, Kate, first the left foot and then the right. You want to come away with me." He continued in a steady murmur, the pleasant voice almost a singsong. Kate felt her resistance begin to fade. He was so convincing. It all sounded so easy. She found herself taking a step.

"Em, help!" Kate cried out in dread, but before her sister could come to her aid, Marak's voice quickened a trifle.

"And M, you want to sit right down and watch her," he went on smoothly. Emily plopped down on the grass. "You just wonder what all the fuss is about." His even voice continued, rising and falling, almost without words. Emily watched Kate tottering step by step toward the edge of the circle, her teeth gritted, hands clenched, desperately trying to stop herself. And Emily wondered, indeed, what all the fuss was about.

Kate was almost to the first circle of trees. The goblin King kept up the quiet rhythm, stepping away from her back between the oaks. His smile was triumphant as he reached out to her. Kate gave a strangled cry. As he disappeared from view, she felt the magic pull weaken just a little. It was her only chance. She turned and bashed her head as hard as she could against the trunk nearest to her. With a sigh, she crumpled at the foot of the tree. The moonlit world winked into darkness.

Chapter
Five

Emily came to her senses. Feet flying, she dashed to her sister's side, but Marak reached Kate first. He rolled her over, a stream of foreign words issuing emphatically from his lips. Emily flinched, afraid of magical lightning or some other powerful result, but no spell was underway. Marak was just venting his sorely tried feelings in the capable goblin tongue.

"Leave her alone," Emily cried. Marak paid no attention. He snapped his fingers in the air, and a small silvery globe appeared. It was not as bright as a candle, but it shed a soft light. Marak moved it to a spot about three feet above Kate's face. When he released it, the shining globe hovered obediently in the air.

By its silver light, Emily could see a large, shallow wound across her sister's forehead. Blood was running in a dark stream into her hair and across her closed eyelids, and a shadowed bruise was already spreading under the skin around her eyes. The goblin murmured something under his breath, pressing his fingers into the wound. He pulled them away and wiped Kate's forehead with his cloak. The wound stopped bleeding. Emily watched it closely, but no fresh trickles flowed from it to join the dark tracks congealing in Kate's hair.

The goblin walked away, licking his bloody fingers, and came back a minute later with a small bag in his hand. He knelt again by Kate. Loosening the bag, he scooped out a small quantity of cream and carefully smeared it across the open wound. As he did so, the wound bubbled, flattened, and formed a sudden skin. Within a few seconds, it had healed without a trace.

Emily stared openmouthed at the goblin as he applied minute dabs of cream, frowning with deep concentration, his coarse, striped hair falling over his bony face. As he smoothed the salve down the side of Kate's nose and underneath her eye, the bruise melted back into fair skin. He took a somewhat generous dollop and pressed it onto her forehead over the spot where the wound had been, murmuring something under his breath. Emily watched the cream vanish as if he had driven it through the skin.

Kate began to groan and twitch. Marak quickly caught her face between his hands. He laid all six fingers of his right hand on her brow, and she relaxed again into slumber.

"You really can work magic!" breathed Emily, staring at her weird companion in awe. Marak flicked her a glance from those gleaming bicolor eyes and then went on with his work. He ran his fingertips speculatively over Kate's eyes and nose. He ran them along her temples and down her neck. Emily sat back, hugging her knees to her chest, and studied the busy goblin King. Kate was right: He did look pretty frightful. His pointed ears poked out through his shaggy hair like a dog's. In fact, he looked about as ugly as anything she had ever seen, but Emily was ready to forgive a great deal in someone who could work magic. He didn't seem so ghastly, really. She mulled over what Kate had told her that afternoon and what Agatha had said in the clearing.

"Kate says you want her to be your new wife," she began.

"That's right," he murmured, applying salve to a bloody knee he had found. Emily watched in excitement as the scab bubbled away. In a few seconds the knee was whole and undamaged. Real magic, right before her eyes.

"But she doesn't want to be your wife," she pointed out. Marak had reached the filthy, ragged sock on the foot with no shoe. He pressed his knotted hand on the bottom of her foot and sighed in exasperation, reaching for the salve.

"That doesn't really matter," he remarked inattentively. "The King's Wife is always a captured bride."

"I think that's the most vile thing I ever heard," declared Emily forcefully. So what if he could work magic! "How could you suggest such an awful thing? No wonder she doesn't want to marry you!"

Marak paused, cradling the foot in one gray hand, and looked up sharply. "So Kate doesn't want to be my wife," he said, and grinned, showing his sharp, dark teeth. Emily flinched and decided that he was rather ghastly after all. "Well, young M, just what do you suggest I do? The goblin King can't marry his own kind. Should I go about holding hands and making sheep's eyes at farmers' daughters till some girl decides to give goblin life a try? And what if she balks at the first sight of her subjects or panics halfway through the ceremony? Do I peck her a fond kiss farewell and start all over again?" He gave a short laugh at the thought. "A long life my race would have if we Kings behaved like that. No, the King's Wife is always a capture. It's the only prudent way." He went back to his ministrations on the torn-up foot.

Emily considered that this was the most splendidly evil speech she had heard in her whole short life. She was lost in admiration of its appalling wickedness. Then she frowned again, stabbed with a sudden concern.

"But Kate loves being outside under the moon and the stars," she said. "If you marry her, couldn't she at least come out sometimes?"

"No," said Marak flatly. "But she'll settle in. They always do."

"Did your first wife settle in?" asked Emily. Marak fixed her with a glare.

"My first wife went mad," he said abruptly. "She didn't believe in goblins." He went back to his work. "I found her by the lakeshore one evening, picking flowers, and I took her home there and then. But it seems the fool's mother had gone mad, and she was always waiting her turn. She fainted during the wedding ceremony, and we never had another lucid word out of her. She believed we were just some sort of dream she was having, a delusion in her mind. I studied magic tirelessly after that, trying to find a cure, but I found nothing, absolutely nothing, that would touch pure human madness." He shook his head, sharp teeth bared and a look of disgust stamped on his pallid face.

Emily watched the strange creature silently for a moment, thinking about that poor stolen woman. "Kate says she'll never survive it," she insisted anxiously. "She says she knows it'll kill her."

"Is that so?" remarked the goblin, failing to sound impressed. He had concluded the search for injuries. He pressed his long, bony fingers on Kate's forehead again. "And what is she going to die of, exactly?"

Emily told him Mrs. Bigelow's story about the cold, dank caves under the Hill. She told him about the hideous things that lived there and about the poor goblin brides, their hair turning white and their skin growing gray, nursing their squalling goblin brats in the dripping caverns far from the sun.

Marak threw back his head and laughed. Reaching up, he extinguished the little orb. Then he turned to Emily. "And you believed her, did you?" he hooted. "Really, M, what a tale!"

"But you live underground, don't you?" she persisted.

"We live under the Hill, yes," he affirmed.

"And is it—really awful—in those caves underground?"

"It is more beautiful than you could possibly imagine," he said impatiently.

Emily pondered this statement. More beautiful than she could imagine. She considered the dank backdrop of her gaunt, white-haired goblin bride and added some sparkle to the cave walls. More beautiful still. She put in a subterranean stream and shiny rock formations. More beautiful than that. She sighed and gave it up.

"If you steal Kate, would you steal me, too?" Her voice trembled.

Marak was studying the sleeping Kate. He glanced up and grinned at her. "A little young, aren't you, to be a goblin bride?" he teased. "All ready to have your hair turn white in those dripping caves underground?"

"But you said—" Emily began as Marak chuckled. "Anyway," she concluded unhappily, "she's all the family I have. I just don't want to be left behind."

The goblin stopped laughing. "Agatha's right," he remarked. "You have a lot of pluck." A small silence reigned. He was watching the unconscious Kate narrowly, the way the cook watched rising bread or baking pies. Emily wondered what he was looking for. She thought about the dwarf woman and what she had told them.

"Agatha says there aren't any more elves," she told him sadly. "Did the goblins kill them all?"

Marak didn't look up from the sleeping Kate. "They destroyed themselves," he answered absently. "They didn't want to survive. We goblins stole elf brides, of course, but that was a good thing for the pretty elves. It gave them unity, something to strive against. Otherwise, they were likely to just wander off in all directions. They always were a little too good for this world." Somehow this didn't sound like a compliment.

"Their last King didn't bother to find a new wife when his first wife died childless. Then he died unexpectedly, and that was the beginning of the end. My great-great-grandfather met with the elves on this very spot and offered to take them in with us. There's a colony of dwarves like that who live under my command. But they said no." Marak snorted. "Catch an elf living underground," he said scornfully.

"We hunted the elf women tirelessly after that, to get the good of the blood before it was all gone. Oh, an elf would tell you quite a tale of woe, with sadness written all across his pretty face. But it wasn't our fault they died out. They did it to themselves. Batty stargazers," he added with relish.

Emily stared around in amazement. Elves and goblins had met right here. She tried to imagine them, beautiful and ugly, tall and short, noble and frightful. No wonder she loved this magical place. The goblin King watched Kate closely, laying his big hands on either side of her face again. He turned in abrupt decision.

"What I want to know is—" Emily began, but Marak leaned forward swiftly and put his six fingers on her brow. Then he caught her as she toppled and laid her down gently in the grass.

"What you want to know is almost everything," he remarked to her sleeping form. Then he turned back to her sister.

<hr/>

Long, dreary hours passed while Kate tossed in unhappy dreams. Finally she sat up in bed with a jerk, jarred out of sleep. She stared around futilely at the thick blackness of the room. Not one ray of light crept in past the curtain. Kate stumbled through the gloom, clutching the furniture, because the room was so dark that she couldn't see where to step. She tried to light her candle, but not even a spark broke the inky darkness around her. Moving by feel, she quitted her room and edged down the hall. She crept into Emily's room and shook her sleeping form.

"Em, wake up!" she begged, shaking and shaking, but Emily just flopped limply in her arms like a giant doll. Another fruitless attempt to light Emily's candle and another hideous trip through the dark. She thought she heard a chuckle as she stumbled across the hall. She wrenched open Prim's door and slammed it shut behind her, but Aunt Prim lay like the dead in the darkness, not even breathing. Kate stood in indecision, afraid to touch her. Was that tapping at the window? A twig, or fingers? Kate fled the dark room, leaving her aunt's body behind in the night.

Out in the hall again, she was sure she heard a whisper. It came closer and closer, but no footsteps came with it. Kate began to sob in panic and strike out against the blackness. Clinging to the banister, she sank down on the stairs. The whisper was coming close again, and she couldn't get away. She hid her blind face against her arms and huddled on the stairs, a hunted, trapped animal, all alone in the dark.

"Kate, look at me," Marak said in a commanding voice. He took her hand in his, kneeling beside her. Kate closed her eyes tightly in dread, throwing out a hand to catch at the banister and drag herself away from him. Instead, she felt soft grass, a tree trunk. She opened her eyes. White moonlight flooded in, and the blackness was gone, but the nightmare was still very real. He was bending over her. He had caught her at last.

"Look at me," Marak ordered again, and Kate looked up into those odd-colored eyes. He knelt close by her, holding her hand in his strong, knotted fingers. Kate closed her eyes to block out the horrible sight, drawing in shallow breaths.

"And did we have a pleasant sleep?" he inquired sweetly. "Nice dreams?" Kate shivered and kept her eyes tightly shut. "No, not a nice dream," the goblin remarked with satisfaction. "So you spent a little time stumbling around in the dark. And no worse than you deserved, either, for smacking yourself into a tree. What a fool stunt, Kate."

Kate's breathing slowed, and she began to remember where she was. She sat up a little unsteadily, pulling away from him. She was free of the nightmare, and her mind was beginning to work. She frowned as thoughts began to connect themselves.

Marak studied the sullen face. "No gratitude at all?" he asked. "Not one kind word for patching you up after you tried to batter your brains in?" Kate's hand rose to her forehead, and she felt about for a bump. Then it traveled to her hair and encountered the dried blood. She retraced the track of blood. No break in the skin. No pain, no soreness. She stared at the goblin, eyes round with surprise.

"Kate," he told her seriously, "that was a stupid thing to do. What if I hadn't been here? What if you had died? I lie awake worrying about what's happening to you out here. You could be falling down a well, or breaking a leg, or catching a fever. What if you need my help, and I can't come in time?"

Kate continued to prod her forehead, feeling rather foolish. If he hadn't been here, she certainly wouldn't have run into the tree. Need his help? Why would she need his help? She couldn't imagine want-ing him anywhere near her, broken leg or not.

"And what were you doing, anyway, wandering around the woods at night? I wasn't expecting that," he admitted. "I thought you'd be barring yourself in your room or maybe locking yourself in a wardrobe." He chuckled at the thought. "What happened?" he asked, grinning at her. "Did you come looking for me?"

"Of course we weren't looking for you," Kate said warily, mov-ing a little farther away from him. She spied Emily lying in the grass, and her heart almost stopped.

"What did you do to her?" she cried.

"I answered her questions," Marak said carelessly. "Almost all of them." He leaned back contentedly against a tree trunk. As Kate began to shake her sister, he added, "Leave her alone. She'll wake up when I tell her to." He laughed. "Did you know that she wants to be stolen by goblins? She actually asked me."

Kate's heart sank. The world was going horribly wrong. A few weeks ago she had been sitting with her sister in this very spot under the stars, perfectly happy. Now a grotesque monster was haunting her and menacing her with a terrible future. Poor Em lay motionless, locked in his magical control. Kate looked down anxiously at her sleeping face. They had to find some way to escape.

"We found out what really happened to Adele Roberts," she said quietly.

"Oh, really?" asked Marak, interested. "Well, don't look so tragic about it," he smirked as she raised her sad eyes to his. "My mother's life was happy enough."

Kate gloomily thought about the unlikely possibility of Adele having had a happy life. What terror and loathing she must have felt, captured by freakish monsters and locked away in a dark cavern far below the earth! An airless tomb, thought Kate in horror. A living tomb from which that bright, brave girl was never able to escape.

"I'm not going down there!" she cried desperately. "I won't go down into those dark caves away from the light, away from the stars. I won't live underground in some ghastly hole, sealed off from the air under mountains of rock."

The goblin King crossed his arms comfortably and smiled in wry amusement. "Kate," he remarked, "your ignorance is colossal."

Kate stared. How typical! He was just making fun of her. He was threatening the loss of everything she loved, and he didn't even care. He closed his eyes, leaned his head back, and continued calmly, "If that's what you think my kingdom is like, I certainly know not to ask you to come."

Hope swept through her. "You won't?" she gasped.

Marak opened his eyes again and frowned at her eager expres-sion. "Of course not." He shrugged. "I'll just take you there. No sense in asking."

Kate felt her stomach lurch. Her pulse began pounding in her temples.

"No!" she declared emphatically. "I won't let you take me away."

The goblin put his head to one side and grinned at her through his rough hair.

"You won't let me? How are you going to stop me? After all," he teased, "you can't bash your head in every night. What if you're too far from a tree?"

Kate jumped to her feet and began to pace, beating her hands together. "There's a way out, I know there's a way!" she cried. "I have to find out what it is."

Marak watched her attentively. "Sit down, Kate," he said.

"After all," she observed, stopping and pointing a finger at him, "you don't have me yet." She sat back down on the grass nearby, not even noticing her own obedience. "You haven't been able to catch me," she declared excitedly. "I've stopped you so far."

Marak shouted with laughter.

"You stopped me?" he whooped. "Stopped me from doing what? Did you lead yourself home when you were lost? Did you tell yourself to go to sleep from the other side of the mirror? You haven't stopped anything. I stopped myself. I didn't want to upset you too much. Human minds are fragile. They don't come back from that kind of shock."

A feeling of despair washed over Kate. She looked down, struggling against tears.

"I could have put you kicking and screaming on my horse that very first night," he pointed out cheerfully, "but I'm very glad that I didn't because you interest me. You're so terribly determined. I never know what you'll do next."

"So this is all just a joke to you," she cried savagely. "A cat-and-mouse diversion. I never heard of anything so cruel!"

"Careful," the goblin advised, holding up a bony hand. "Don't forget logic. If I'm cruel to be patient, what would I be if I had put you on the horse that first night? Compassionate?" He chortled. "Kindly?" Kate glared at him.

"I think you're hideous," she said forcefully. "You're mean and hateful, making a game out of someone else's misery."

The goblin King stopped laughing and studied her pale face. "Do you know, Kate, I believe you're right," he declared. "I am being cruel to you. You seem to be taking this very hard. You're starting to lose sleep and fret about the future, and you're listening to all sorts of ridiculous tales. This kind of delay isn't good for you, either. The sooner it ends, the better."

Kate paused, alarmed. This was not the point she had been trying to make. She didn't seem to be getting anywhere. In fact, she was making things worse.

"But I don't want to marry you at all!" she shouted.

"Of course not," Marak agreed. "I never thought you did. There aren't any volunteers to my kingdom, but we try not to let it discourage us." He rose and walked slowly to the center of the tree circle, studying the clear night sky.

"I hope it won't offend you if I leave you now," he remarked pleasantly. "Several matters still need my attention tonight. Since you consider us enemies, I'll guarantee your safe arrival at the Lodge, and since I consider us engaged, I'll provide you with an escort. I'm not going to let you come to harm while you're still outside." He knelt by Emily's sleeping form. As he took her hand in his, she sat up, speaking.

"—how it got to be a truce place, anyway." She looked around. "Oh, hello, Kate's up."

"Yes, and I'm leaving now before she heads for another tree," Marak teased. "I'll tell you about it some other time. Seylin will see you home." Then he was gone between the huge black oaks. They heard him give a quiet whistle and speak in a low voice. They heard his horse coming unhurriedly toward him, blowing out its breath. Then came the creaking of leather, the jingle of metal, and hoof-beats moving away.

Chapter
Six

Kate realized that she had been sitting in the same position for some time. She climbed stiffly to her feet, terribly tired.

The huge black cat moved silently through the trees to join them. "Hello," he piped in a thin, reedy voice. "The King says I'm to walk you to the Lodge." Kate jumped and gasped, feeling abruptly that she did have weak nerves, but Emily yelped in delight.

"Oh, Seylin!" she cried. "You clever cat! You can talk!"

The large feline sat down. "Well," he said in an abashed tone, "I'm not really a regular cat." He turned his round eyes with their huge black pupils on Kate. "Are you ready to leave now?" he trebled politely.

Kate swung her arms, hesitating. It was still nighttime, or at any rate very early morning. She hated to leave the safety of the tree circle.

"I don't know, Em," she said cautiously to her sister. "Maybe we should stay here until the sun comes up."

"You don't need to worry," Seylin assured her earnestly. "I just look like a big cat, but I can protect you with magic. The King wouldn't have made me your escort if he didn't think I could handle the job." Kate detected a note of pride in this last statement.

"Yes, well," she demurred, trying not to think about the extreme peculiarity of debating courses of action with a giant cat. "I'm not questioning your ability to protect us from ordinary dangers. I'm more afraid of your King than of anything else out there."

"Oh, you didn't hear him say he was going back to the Hill?" said the cat. Kate had a swift mental image of Marak sitting on some rough-hewn rock throne, maybe with spears crossed over it, presiding over a drunken revel of hooting goblin warriors.

"But what if he didn't really mean it?" she said warily.

There was a tiny silence. The huge cat's pupils contracted in surprise, the round golden eyes full on her.

"You think the King lied?" Seylin asked in a horrified squeak.

Startled, Kate opened her mouth to answer and then shut it again. She thought of her goblin tormenter as her own private nemesis to rail against and loathe, almost like a monster she had invented herself. The idea of his having an outside existence, a reputation, and loyal friends had simply never occurred to her. She felt very peculiar.

"I—I—well, why don't you lead?" she stammered apologetically, and then fell into an embarrassed silence as they walked away from the old oak trees.

Emily walked beside the huge cat, admiring his thick black fur. "I had a cat where we lived before," she chattered, "a big tabby one. He was wonderfully fluffy, like a soft winter blanket. I miss him terribly. He had green eyes. I hope he's happy with the cook. She always gave him butter because she said it was good for a cat's coat. Is it? Could you always talk? Do all goblin cats talk?"

"I think butter's good for everybody," Seylin avowed seriously. "I have a cat, too, a white one with blue eyes. She spits at me when I try to talk to her in cat. Cats can't really talk, at least I can't understand them when they do, except when they say things like 'feed me' or 'get away.' Some of the real cat goblins act like they can understand more. Oh!" he said as Emily tripped on a tree root. "I forgot you can't see well. Here"—and rearing back on his hind legs, he made a motion with his right paw. Kate was amazed to see a small silver orb appear in the air. It cast its faint radiance like a captive moonbeam on the shadowed path around them.

"Oh, Seylin, you can do it, too!" Emily cried, enchanted with the reappearance of her favorite trick. The cat reared back on his hind legs again and gently batted the shining globe from one paw to the other, clearly enjoying the attention. The light threw silver ripples down his thick, sleek coat as it bobbed back and forth in the air.

"That's elf magic," he said proudly. "The King taught me how to do it, and nobody in the whole kingdom can do it but me and the King. Isn't it pretty? It's a little moon. Of course, it's not good for much when the moon's just a sliver because it's a sliver, too, and you don't get anything at all when the moon is new. That's how elf magic generally is. It's pretty to look at, but it doesn't really get you anywhere. I know lots. Do you want to see some more?"

At Emily's enthusiastic confirmation, he winked out the globe, and black shadow swallowed up the path. "I did that because this looks better in the dark," he explained. The huge cat held out his paws and swiftly tapped the path before them, shrilling out a few words of command. Nothing happened for a second. Then a soft glow emanated from the ground at Seylin's feet as a tiny silver plant broke through the earth. Gracefully unwinding and arching through the air, it grew rapidly into a bush with shining silver leaves. Buds formed at the ends of its delicate branches and blossomed into a mass of shimmering golden lilies. The leaves rustled musically in the night breeze, and as the lilies swayed to and fro they tinkled like a carillon of tiny bells. Kate and Emily stared openmouthed, completely captivated by the plant's beauty.

"That's my best one yet," piped the cat. "The King says I do it even better than he does, but they don't always turn out this good. It must be because the moon's close to full. Elf magic generally strengthens with the moon. That's sort of silly if you think about it because you can't really count on the moon." The cat waved his paw through the unearthly apparition, and the glorious plant disintegrated into a sparkly snowfall. In a few seconds, its shining particles vanished with a quiet whisper, and they were in darkness again. The cat relit his tiny moon and started down the path, the silver globe bobbing along just above his right shoulder.

"I can do more than elf magic, of course," he added, padding along. "I'm good at goblin magic, too. It's lots more practical, like if you need to fight somebody or open a locked door. But I can't do any dwarf magic. Dwarf magic depends on stones, and they can tell if you're not dwarf. I'm not dwarf at all. The King can do some even though he doesn't look dwarf. Agatha does dwarf magic a lot, and the real dwarves do it without even thinking. It's how they carry their loads and do their building and making. They're such little people, but they can do more with stone and metal than any giant ever could. They can just make the earth do anything." Kate remembered Agatha bolting them to the ground, sticking them into place as if they had grown roots.

"Couldn't you teach me how to do a little magic?" Emily begged as she trotted to keep up with the cat. Seylin laid his ears back a little.

"I don't think so," he said apologetically, "not if you're just human. Humans don't have any magic. Agatha says they don't need it. They live just like cattle, chewing up the land and raising herds of babies. Everybody knows they're God's favorites; they already get everything their own way. Elves and goblins got their magic from the First Fathers, and dwarves say they're related to rocks, so they just know how to ask rocks to behave. Agatha says there's some humans who talk with the devils and get them to do things, but she says that's not magic, that's stupid, because devils always make sure they get paid better than they work."

The trees began to thin as they came within sight of the Lodge. All its windows were dark. Seylin immediately put out the little moon.

"I'll be right here if you need me," he told them. "I'm glad it's not raining anymore. I have to look just like a regular cat all the time when I'm outside. We're not allowed to attract attention. Humans would think it was funny if they saw a dry cat sitting in the rain."

As she thanked the cat politely, Kate felt her head beginning to hurt. She was a little overwhelmed by all the help she had received that night from goblins. There was something deeply wrong in these unnatural monsters rallying around her, if only because the most urgent help she needed was some means to escape them. It made it very hard for her to decide how to battle them when they kept rush-ing solicitously to her aid. It was beginning to make her feel rather ridiculous.

Emily was feeling no such qualms. Tonight was without ques-tion the most thrilling evening she had ever had. Of course, she could understand Kate's outraged feelings about being a potentially captured bride—after all, who wanted to be a bride?—but goblin life obviously had its advantages. Pets, for instance. Even Seylin was allowed to have a cat, and for heaven's sake, he was one himself! And he could work magic, too. Emily felt a pang of envy. All she could do was embroidery. A lot of good that would do her if she ever had to open a locked door. Nor could she imagine people stand-ing around marveling at a display of needlework.

Considering her lack of magical abilities, Emily decided it was a good thing that the Lodge doors were never locked. Kate and Emily slipped inside and tiptoed up the stairs. Kate felt like lying down on her bed without even changing clothes, she was so tired, but instead she involved Emily in a whispered council of war. Emily told her what had happened while Kate was unconscious, and Kate told her about the goblin King's decision to bring things to a swift conclusion.

"This is it, Em, I know it," she said urgently. "This is my last chance, and we have to make it work. We haven't tried to escape on foot. We might make it."

Emily thought about this for a second. Then she sighed, thinking of her soft bed.

"All right. Where are we going to go?" she asked gloomily.

Kate shot her a swift look of gratitude. "I don't know yet. We'll just go as far away as we can. Maybe we can get off goblin land in one day if we start early."

Emily looked extremely skeptical. "We can't even walk as far as Hollow Lake in one day," she pointed out, "and the goblin King said he stole his wife by the lakeshore."

Kate shivered at the thought of the poor mad bride. "We'll go the other direction, away from the Hill, and we won't bring anything but a picnic basket so we can avoid attracting attention. Go tidy up, Em, and put on a clean dress. We can't walk down a country road with blood and dirt all down our fronts. But don't light a candle, or Seylin will call the others. And don't wake up Aunt Prim!"

Emily slipped out, and Kate changed quickly, wadding up the old dress and stuffing it under her bed. Then she put on clean stockings and picked out another pair of shoes. She remembered losing one of her favorite pair in the woods. This was the second dress in a week, too, that she had destroyed in midnight scrambles. She surveyed the meager choices left in her wardrobe and sent bitter thoughts in Marak's direction. Then she splashed water into her washbowl and combed the blood out of her hair. By the light of the setting moon, she surveyed her uninjured forehead in the mirror. Try as she might, she could find no sign of the large wound Emily had described.

Emily tiptoed back in, carrying her shoes. She made a face when she saw Kate.

"Why are you wearing that nasty blue thing?" she wanted to know. "It's all faded, and the sash makes you look five years old."

Kate felt that this was just the sort of comment calculated to undo her resolve. "I have far more serious things to consider than the condition of my dress," she declared a little tragically. "I'm really beyond those sorts of petty concerns right now."

"That's good," said Emily. Then she brightened. "I know. If the goblin King sees you looking like that, maybe he'll change his mind." Kate didn't see any reason to honor this with a reply. She grabbed her shoes and headed down to the kitchen. She pulled out a small wicker basket and piled some provisions into it.

"Let's go," she whispered. "It's already dawn. We'll leave by the front door. If Seylin's still where he said he would be, we can keep the house between us."

In a few minutes, they were hurrying down the gravel track through a rustling, dewy meadow, the forested hills to their backs now and the fields before them. Somewhere on these fields, Kate remembered with a sinking heart, the goblins had kept watch around their bonfire. She wondered just how far their magical king-dom extended.

The exhausted girls stumbled along the pebbly track, stepping on their long shadows as the red sun rose over the Hill behind them. Kate's shoes were cracked at the toes, and her feet began to ache. She tried to turn over the events of the night in her mind, but it all began to run together and change. She was arguing with Marak. She was yelling at him, and he was laughing. Agatha came and looked at her palm, telling Kate to be careful. "I see danger in this hand," she said, her black eyes huge, "from someone very close to you."

Someone very close. Kate came out of her doze with a start. She heard the clopping of horses' hooves coming along fast behind them. Swiftly she grabbed the sagging Emily by the arm and glanced around for cover. There was none to be had. They were in the middle of a mowed field with not so much as a rock wall in reach. Kate's heart pounded as she whirled to face her enemy. What right, she thought furiously, did he have to be out during the day?

The dogcart bowled into sight over a slight ridge. The old mare stopped a few feet from them and dropped her head, blowing heavily. Hugh Roberts climbed down from the seat, his wig askew and his round face brick red with anger.

"Miss Winslow," he remarked heatedly, "you are quite beyond our ability to handle."

He drove the girls to the Hall in silence. Emily fell asleep on the way.

"Come with me, Miss Winslow," he ordered, leaving the cart at the door. Kate climbed down and looked back at her sleeping sister, a lump in her throat. I've lost my last chance to escape, she thought. I won't see Em again, and now I can't even say good-bye.

Her guardian led her down the hall to one of the bedrooms. "I'm leaving you in here," he told her. "Ring if you need anything." Kate stared aghast at the elegant bedroom. It was on the ground floor, facing the dense forest of the Hill, and it opened out onto the shaded terrace via a pair of pretty double doors. Almost the whole wall by the terrace was window, covered with lacy curtains.

"How long will I be staying here?" she demanded anxiously. Her guardian paused in the doorway.

"I don't exactly know," he said ponderously. "I feel you are now a danger to yourself and to your sister. You'll have to stay in here until we can decide what to do about you. Prim and Celia cannot deal with you at the Lodge."

Kate could just imagine a whole coterie of monsters assembling in the woods outside those double doors. At twilight they would come bursting in and haul her away, their weird goblin chieftain in the lead.

"Mr. Roberts," she begged, "please don't leave me in this room! At least put me on the second floor or in a room that doesn't face the forest. There must be bedrooms that are safer than this."

"Safer from goblins?" Hugh Roberts asked sardonically, and Kate knew that the argument was over. She heard him lock the door as he left.

Exhausted and frustrated, Kate flung herself down on the bed to think. Ever since she had asked for her guardian's help, things had gotten worse and worse. He had practically accused her of insanity in front of her aunts, he had instructed them to throw her out of the house after dark, and now he had locked her up in a room perfect for goblin attack. Short of delivering her tied up to the goblins' front door, Kate couldn't think of anything worse he could do. Of course, she concluded miserably, he would say that he just wanted her to face her fears. She was pretty sure that was exactly what she would be doing once twilight came again.

Kate devoted some time to escaping, but the large, opulent room thwarted her attempts. She could find no way to pry open either windows or doors. The windows were nailed shut, and they held many small diamonds of glass cemented together by lead strips. She wasn't sure she could batter her way out with a chair even if she could risk the noise. The doors onto the terrace fastened together with a heavy bolt that slid between them, and the key was gone from the lock. Yet she knew that her solid prison posed not the least problem for the goblin King. Even his magical cat knew how to open locked doors.

The day passed very slowly. Kate tried hard not to think about what twilight would bring. Restless and lonely, she wandered about and studied the various diversions the room had to offer. Outside was a beautiful day. She stood for a long time at the window, watching the sun dapple the terrace. It's my last chance to see sunlight, she thought miserably. My very last chance.

When her guardian brought lunch, Kate refused to speak to him. She was finished giving him ideas on how to make her face her fears. If he was too well educated to believe in goblins, she wasn't going to change his mind. Tired out from worry and all the late nights, she lay down on the bed and fell into a doze. When she awoke, the room was filled with the shadows of twilight. Kate jumped up in a panic. What was it she had said to Agatha? Handed over like a sack of potatoes. She couldn't bear it. She had to do something, she just had to!

How would the goblins attack her? They wouldn't hesitate to invade the house if they could do so undetected. They would doubt-less make sure that she was unable to raise an alarm, and the easiest way to do that was to make sure that she was asleep. The goblin King controlled sleep with a magical ease. Kate doubted she would even wake up until she was underground.

How could she raise an alarm if she were asleep? Kate looked about for inspiration. A large crystal lamp stood on a table by the hall door. If she could pull the lamp down as she was being taken out, it would make a substantial crash.

Kate quickly went to work. Her light was going fast, and the shadows beneath the trees were getting thicker and blacker. She hastily ripped from her dress the sash that had so offended Emily's taste. It made a cloth rope about six feet long. She tied one end tightly around the base of the crystal lamp, then dropped the sash over the side of the table and pulled it underneath. She brought a pillow from the bed and lay down next to the hall door. Then she tied the other end of her makeshift rope to her ankle. Now if she moved away from her spot by her end of the table, the lamp would be tugged off its resting place and crash to the floor a few feet away.

Kate pushed her dress hem down to hide the knot and huddled in a furious pitch of suspense for the attack. She was as far as she could be from those ominous double doors, and she felt well rested and alert. Maybe she could raise the alarm before the doors were even open. When they came, she thought excitedly, they would find her ready to meet them.

Go to sleep, Kate. And that was that. One minute she was wide awake, waiting for the first hint of trouble. The next minute she was locked in a profound slumber. The doors swung open to let in the quiet sounds of the deepening twilight, but Kate slept on, trapped in a dreamless darkness beyond any possibility of action.

A loud knocking sounded on the door right above her head.

"Miss Winslow," said Hugh Roberts through the door, "a visitor has just arrived and is anxious to meet you. I'll give you a few minutes, and then I'd like you to join us."

Kate opened her eyes and stared straight into the unmatched eyes of the goblin King. Marak crouched over her in the dusky gloom. He already had his arms around her, about to lift her from the floor, and his pale hair brushed her face. He froze, glancing toward the door as her guardian delivered his message. Kate tensed to scream, but Marak absently laid a finger across her lips, and she found herself unable to make a sound. As she twisted her head from side to side, trying to find her voice, she saw the goblin grin in amusement. Kate glared up at him frantically and jerked her foot as hard as she could, yanking the lamp to the floor just beyond them. It hit the stone with a terrific smash, spraying his back with crystal shards. He turned, startled, to locate the source of the sound.

"Miss Winslow, what are you doing?" Hugh Roberts called through the door. "What's happening in there?" But Kate was still unable to yell for help. Marak tightened his grip on her. This is when he drags me away, Kate thought feverishly. In another second, he'll have me unconscious, and I'll wake up underground. She struck at him as hard as she could, clawing and fighting to break free.

"Miss Winslow, answer me. What's going on?"

The goblin had a number of solutions at his disposal, but it is hard to think or work magic while under attack. Kate yanked his hair. When he peeled her hand loose, she twisted and got an elbow into his chest. She threw out an arm and banged the door. As he raised his six-fingered hand to touch her forehead, she sank her teeth as hard as she could into his thumb.

"That's it, Miss Winslow. I'm coming in there."

Marak pushed Kate away and sprang to his feet. She scrambled to sit up and banged into the door, throwing her head back to look at him. The goblin's face was twisted in a snarl of fury, his sharp teeth were bared, and his eyes blazed in the twilit room with an unnatural brightness. He raised his arms in front of him, the eleven fingers pointing out rigidly, dark drops clinging to his bleeding thumb. Kate ducked her head instinctively, bracing for the lightning, or worse, that would follow. She felt the hall door push against her, but she couldn't move for terror. The enraged goblin flicked out his hands, the fingers pointing away from her, and moved them apart in a slow, deliberate circle of the room. Pictures sprang from the walls. Knickknacks and vases leapt from the furniture. Bookshelves overturned. The washstand upended. The room was filled with the sound of smashing, splintering, and crashing, and the air was filled with flying debris. The goblin King glared down at Kate, his pallid face haughty, as she cringed and shielded her eyes from the exploding fragments. Then he spun on his heel and walked rapidly from the room. As he passed through the open doors, he made a casual gesture. The doors slammed shut behind him with an unearthly force, and the glass from the whole expanse of window fractured and fell in.

Kate staggered to her feet and watched him disappear into the shadow of the trees as the hall door swung open behind her. Dazed, she looked around at the wreckage. Twisted picture frames and powdered ceramic covered the floor. Books cascaded out of broken shelves, and bits of window glass spangled the Oriental rug.

"Extraordinary!" she heard a voice murmur behind her. Kate turned to find two men standing in the doorway, staring at the scene before them with open mouths. Her guardian, his plump face blood-less, clutched the door frame with both hands. As her gaze fell on them, he made an attempt to push himself upright.

"Miss Winslow," he said, his voice unsteady, "meet Dr. Stanley Thatcher, head of the Westcross Asylum."

Kate turned around again and looked out at the black forest, delighted and amazed. She had faced the goblin King alone and had beaten him! She had been set out like bait in a trap with no friends, no weapon, and no magic, and she was still standing free in the moonlight while he headed back to his horrible caves. She wanted to whoop and shriek, to yell insults into the darkening night. Instead, she demurely turned around and faced the two men.

"There's been some kind of explosion," she said, studying the doctor with cool curiosity. "Look, the windows blew in. Do the rooms next to this one have broken windows, too?"

Hugh Roberts didn't seem to have heard the question. He had wandered a few steps into the room and was staring around in shock. Kate felt a smug amusement. If her pompous guardian found a little thing like this so upsetting, she could just imagine the look on his face if he saw the goblin King himself.

"I don't think we know," said the doctor briskly. "Mr. Roberts, why don't we check the other rooms for damage?" Her guardian glanced around distractedly and followed the doctor out. As soon as they left, Kate bent and untied the knot from her ankle. She was just standing up and surveying the ripped sash when Mrs. Bigelow appeared in the doorway.

"What happened?" she gasped. Kate retied the damaged sash over her dress.

"I don't know, Mrs. Bigelow," she said calmly. "Some kind of explosion. The men were just checking on things."

The housekeeper's face sagged. She turned frightened eyes on Kate.

"It's *them,* isn't it, that did it?" she whispered darkly.

Kate patted the torn sash into place and strolled past the house-keeper into the lighted hall.

"I really don't know what you're talking about," she replied.

⌒

Later, sitting in the study, she sipped her tea and surveyed her new combatants with serene assurance. She had just defeated a goblin with her own bare hands. The head doctor of a lunatic asylum couldn't possibly frighten her now.

Actually, Dr. Thatcher didn't look very frightening. He didn't look as if he would want to be. A fit, white-bearded man of fifty, he had an agreeable, fatherly face and seemed interested in everything. Kate would have loved to tell him about her fight with Marak. Dr. Thatcher would have found him fascinating. But she had no desire to be locked up in an insane asylum, so the truth would have to wait until she was alone with Emily.

"The other rooms weren't damaged in the slightest," Dr. Thatcher was saying. "Have you any idea what might have caused it, Miss Winslow?"

"None at all," Kate answered readily. "I went to the door to respond to your knock. Then there was a devastating crash, and I hid my face and tumbled to the floor. Could it have been a prank, do you think? One of the stable boys playing with gunpowder or coal dust? Goodness, I hope no one blew a hand off!"

Kate's guardian polished his spectacles. "I don't know," he said unsteadily. "I'd rather not discuss it now. Miss Winslow, I've been to see Dr. Thatcher about you, and he very much wanted to meet you. He's interested in your goblin visitor."

"Oh, do you study goblins?" Kate asked.

"I'm afraid I don't know much about them," admitted the doctor with a smile.

"Then we'd better call Mrs. Bigelow," Kate suggested. "She can tell all sorts of wonderful tales about them. Did you know that her grandparents actually believed goblins existed? Elves, too. Isn't that charming?" She smiled at the men. They stared back, a little nonplussed.

"Now, wait a minute, Miss Winslow," said Hugh Roberts with a frown. "I just heard a story from your sister this afternoon stuffed chockfull of goblins. The goblin King was coming to drag you away."

Kate fixed her guardian with a surprised stare. "And you believed her?" she asked in astonishment. The doctor turned his interested eyes from her to Hugh Roberts, whose pale cheeks flushed a bright pink.

"Miss Winslow," Hugh said firmly, "you yourself said you were in terrible danger, and you begged me to send you away. You said the goblins were coming to drag you off, just like Adele Roberts in the story."

Kate shrugged. She wished that Marak were there to see her. If lying was for humans, then by all means, let her lie.

"But I never thought you'd believe it," she said artlessly. "I thought grown men knew that goblins couldn't exist."

Her guardian rose from his chair and began pacing the floor. "What about that strange creature you saw the night of the storm? What about your hysterical dash through the door? Prim and Celia practically had to revive you."

"I certainly didn't invent that," Kate assured him. She turned to Dr. Thatcher. "My sister Emily and I got lost in a stormy night, and we stumbled onto a camp of Gypsies. An old woman told my fortune for me, and a Gypsy guided us home. He told us all kinds of terrible stories as we walked through the night, and he was entirely muffled in a black cloak and hood. When we arrived at the house, he pulled back the hood so I could see his face. Now, Aunt Prim says that if I saw him during the day, I would have thought he looked strange, but after that frightening walk and all those stories, I was ter‑ rified. It seems funny now. In fact," she added bitterly, "I know he enjoyed scaring me into fits." She smiled at Dr. Thatcher, who chuckled. Her guardian looked thunderstruck.

"But what about the nightmares?" he demanded angrily, pacing before the fireplace. "What about staying out all night? What about running away from home?"

"I can't deny the nightmares," Kate answered. She turned to the doctor. "I know they worried my poor great‑aunts. They're quite unused to the trials of parenthood. All three of my guardians are new to children, you know. And it's true that we were away from home late last night. My aunts and Mr. Roberts decided it would be good for my nerves to walk from one house to the other in the dark. Of course, we protested quite tearfully. You have to remember the shocking Gypsy we'd met just a couple of nights before. He could have been roaming the woods. And as a matter of fact, we were chased."

"By the goblin King," suggested Hugh Roberts, looking over his spectacles meaningfully.

"No!" insisted Kate, frowning at him as if he were a slow pupil. "We were chased by a couple of clodhopping hu—I mean, farm boys, out for a moonlight ride. They must have been playing a joke on us. Maybe they knew you and the aunts were going to send us out on a ghost walk." She looked at her guardian, and Dr. Thatcher did as well. Suddenly and inexplicably, Hugh Roberts's blush deepened to a dull, unhealthy red.

"We lost them at the tree circle," continued Kate, "and we rested there to catch our breath. It was so beautiful and peaceful there under the moon and stars." She paused, remembering the unholy purple lightning and whipping winds. "I'm afraid we just fell asleep. When we woke up, it was so late that we went back to the Lodge because it was closer, and the aunts were already in bed. But I don't know why you thought we tried to run away. We were just heading out on a ramble with a picnic basket."

Dr. Thatcher turned to her guardian. "They had only a picnic basket?" he asked. "No clothes, no belongings?"

Hugh Roberts looked as if Kate had personally insulted him. "Miss Winslow, I warn you," he said, gasping with rage. "I know you're lying, and you know it, too. You know you believe in goblins, and you know you aren't rational about them!" He glared at Dr. Thatcher. "She isn't! She isn't rational! She's insane!"

Kate stared at the big man in complete amazement. She had never seen him so angry before. He'd been worried that she was making a break with reality, but he didn't seem at all pleased that she'd rejoined it. She fell silent, unwilling to embarrass him with any more lies. Dr. Thatcher looked from the enraged man to the astonished girl, and his gaze turned thoughtful.

"Mr. Roberts," he said soothingly, "I'm very glad you've asked me to come tonight, and I'm enjoying the conversation immensely, but I think it would help my examination of your ward if we had a few moments alone."

Hugh Roberts subsided and left the room. Dr. Thatcher turned his kind eyes on Kate.

"Miss Winslow," he said thoughtfully, "your story does make a certain sense, but Mr. Roberts mentioned other factors that are hard to explain as high spirits and pretend games: poor sleep, loss of appetite, and a feeling of being watched. In spite of your cheerfulness, you do appear rather thin and pale. I can see that your guardian would be a little difficult to confide in." He chose his words with care. "Is there anything that you would like to tell me about? Anything that's been troubling you?"

Kate squirmed a little. It was one thing to lie to Hugh Roberts, whom she disliked. It was quite another thing to lie to this friendly, likable man. But he was a doctor who worked with insane patients. If she told him about Marak, he would decide that his asylum was the best place for her to be. Kate looked into his sympathetic eyes and wished with all her heart that he were her father.

"You know I lost my father a few months ago," she began.

"Of course," Dr. Thatcher said gently. "It must have been a terrible shock, and yet they tell me that when you first came here, you were doing very well. Your problems didn't start until later."

"Did my guardian tell you that he's not really related to me?" she asked sadly. "My sister and I are the result of an adoption several generations back. We supplanted Mr. Roberts's side of the family, and he's quite bitter about it." She sighed. "He probably didn't think it was important when he told me that story, but my nightmares and poor appetite started then. It hurt to find out that my sister and I have no real family left."

Dr. Thatcher leaned back and nodded gravely. "I was afraid of something like this," he said. "It explains a great deal. Miss Winslow, I don't think you need to worry about insanity. You seem to be facing your problems very well. I can't help feeling disappointed, though," he added, smiling ruefully. "When I saw the wreckage in that bedroom tonight, I really thought I was on to something."

"What do you mean?" asked Kate.

"I help people who are insane," he declared, "but I do look for special cases. You see, there's so much about the mind that we don't understand. Sometimes, in great stress, people do things that are well beyond their physical powers, and sometimes insane people do them, too. It's as if, not knowing what reality is supposed to be, they can go beyond those limits that we accept for ourselves."

"Do you mean they can work magic?" Kate wanted to know.

"Well," chuckled Dr. Thatcher, "I suppose you could call it that. I would say that they can do the extraordinary and inexplicable because they accept it as part of their world. For instance, we have a woman in the asylum who thinks she's a rabbit. I have had specialists study how far she can jump. It's amazing to watch. Another patient thinks she's two completely different people. She crushed her foot one day, and we found her walking around on this badly damaged foot normally and without the least sign of pain. Why? Because she claimed that the other of her two selves had broken her foot. The person she was at the moment was perfectly well."

Kate smiled, her fancy tickled by the stories. "So when you saw all the broken glass and torn-up furniture, you thought that I had done it," she said. Dr. Thatcher nodded. "I'm sorry to disappoint you. I didn't do it, and I don't think I could do it, either."

⁓

Several hours later, Kate snuggled down comfortably in bed. Yes, she was still at the Hall, and yes, her indignant guardian had locked her in again. She was once more in a ground-floor bedroom with double doors leading onto the terrace. The designers of the Hall's fashionable newer wing hadn't exhibited much creativity from one room to the next. But she and Dr. Thatcher had talked until early in the morning, and a new day was not far off. She had vanquished two different enemies on two very different fields of battle. Neither one was gone for good, but that was a problem for tomorrow. Today had been simply glorious, and she would take care of tomorrow when it came.

A knock at the door roused her in the late morning, and Hugh Roberts entered the room. But this was not the pompous man she had infuriated the night before. His eyes were large and grave, and his manner was uncertain.

"Miss Winslow, I'm terribly sorry," he said hesitantly. "I realize now that I should have believed you. You said you were in danger, but I never dreamed it might be real." Kate sat up, alarmed.

"I'm afraid it's your sister," he explained awkwardly. "Emily has completely vanished."

PART II

Lamplight

Chapter
Seven

Hugh Roberts had expected Kate to cry at the news, and cry she did. She lay on her bed, face in the pillow, and refused to look up. But he had also expected her to talk. That Kate refused to do.

"You have to help us find her," he insisted. "You must know something about the creatures who took her. Dr. Thatcher and I will go out with the men and see if we can't bring her back." Kate just shook her head, mute. Hugh Roberts awkwardly stood by, not sure what to do.

"Don't you want out of this dangerous room?" he asked. "I'll let you out if you'll talk to us. For heaven's sake, I'm her guardian! I can't just let her disappear like this!" Silence from the bed.

"I'll send you away from here right now," he promised. "I'll send you someplace where you'll be safe. Miss Winslow, please. Don't you want to be safe from those creatures?"

Face in the pillow, Kate considered. Did she want to be safe? What difference did being safe make now? How could the heartless beast have done it, how *could* he? She knew the goblin had been furious when he left last night, and he had said once that he was a poor loser. But how could anyone—even someone inhuman—have threatened her little sister? Poor, dear Em, all alone in those hideous caves, surrounded by howling monsters. But surely they wouldn't hurt her. Surely they wouldn't turn her into a goblin bride. She was just a child! The goblin King had said so himself. It must be his way of getting even with Kate. She remembered him laughing, saying, "Do you know that she wants to be stolen by goblins?" It was all very well for Mr. Roberts to talk about bringing Em back to the daylight, but Kate knew that he would never succeed.

Kate paced her room that day like a tormented soul. When Hugh Roberts came several more times to plead with her, she remained absolutely firm. She knew exactly what she had to do. She watched the terrace outside her window closely. As twilight fell, she saw the familiar face of the big black cat peering out from the shadows and called him over to her with a gesture. Looking first left and then right, the cat cautiously approached her. She waved him down to the terrace doors, which didn't shut properly. There was a small gap between them.

"Seylin, where is the King?" she asked, speaking softly for fear of being overheard.

"He's in court now," piped the cat.

"I need to see him right away."

The cat looked at her through the glass of the double doors. His round golden eyes grew rounder.

"You do?"

"Yes, but don't call him, Seylin. I need you to take me to see him."

The cat's eyes were huge now.

"You do?" he squeaked. "All right. I'll take you." He paused for a second. "The King will surely be surprised."

"Good," said Kate grimly.

The cat laid his paws on the doors, and they swung open. How easy, thought Kate disgustedly. How childishly simple. She stepped quickly across the terrace and into the darkening forest, the black cat in the lead.

Half an hour later, they were standing in front of a cliff face. Seylin reared up on his hind legs, balancing quite easily. "Here, take my paw," he said. She did so. "It might help if you close your eyes."

Kate closed her eyes. "Now, five steps forward." This is it, she thought. Drippy caverns. Darkness. She felt dizzy. She counted off five steps, then opened her eyes and blinked in astonishment.

She was not in a drippy cavern, at least not yet. Instead, she felt as if she had walked into the middle of a kaleidoscope. Mirrored surfaces faced her on all sides. Even the floor was a fractured mirror. She and the black cat were reflected hundreds of times, each time at a more drastic angle. She began to feel rather seasick. Black-cloaked guards approached them from many directions. It was a few seconds before she realized that this was only one guard reflected many times.

"Oh, do you have your eyes open?" asked Seylin. "I'd close them again. This can be confusing if you've never seen it before. It's sup-posed to make it hard for enemies to find the next doorway." She gratefully shut her eyes as Seylin talked to the guard. They walked forward. Now the drippy caverns, she thought.

But no, they were in a long, straight corridor of polished black stone, lit by globe-shaped lamps hanging from brackets on the walls. Goblin guards of various sizes and shapes walked about the corri-dor. Some of them took Kate's breath away. They all appeared to be wearing a variation of Marak's normal black attire, and this com-bined with the black stone of the corridor made them difficult to see. Kate realized how appropriate such a uniform was for creatures who would only be out during the night. No wonder humans seldom saw a goblin!

At the end of this corridor was a huge door several times higher than Kate. It appeared to be solid iron. She looked around, waiting for another guard to emerge and let them through. Instead, a deep, hollow voice rang out. It seemed to come from the door itself.

"Hello, little Seylin," said the voice.

"Hello, door," piped the cat.

"Didn't I just let you out?" asked the door, sounding puzzled.

"I need to see the King," Seylin said earnestly.

"Who is the pretty woman?" asked the deep voice.

"She needs to see the King, too," said Seylin.

"Are you sure I should let her in?" The door seemed rather doubtful.

"The King wants to see her, too," Seylin assured it.

There was a pause. "He could see her out here," the door suggested.

"He's in court. Come on, door, I'm in a hurry," complained the cat. The door slowly swung open, and they walked through. Kate stopped on the other side, feeling rather overcome.

Ahead of her lay what she knew must be a vast cave, but it didn't resemble one at all. She seemed to be looking across a narrow valley under an intensely black night sky. She stood on a wide street that dipped down to the shallow valley floor and then rose up again beyond it. Beside her, rows of trees filled with colored lights marched down the slight incline. Along the very bottom of the valley ran a small river, and the street crossed it on a low, arched bridge before climbing upward again through elegant formal gardens.

On the far side of the valley, the street became the entrance steps to a palace so wide and so massive that it completely blocked their view of whatever lay beyond. Story upon story of colossal square windows shone out onto the park. The architecture reminded Kate of ancient Greece or Egypt—that is, if a titanic ancient temple could rise so high into the sky. No, not the sky. No friendly stars winked down at her. Kate squeezed Seylin's paw in a flurry of panic and pictured the stars that were just coming out in the sky beyond this cave. They settled into their proper places in her mind, their silvery light mingling with the rising full moon, giving her the courage to face whatever lay ahead.

"Do you want to go back out?"

"Oh, no, I'm sorry, door," answered Seylin. "We were just look-ing around."

"Because I don't know if I'm allowed to let you back out," said the door gravely.

"No, no, thanks," replied the cat, and started down the street toward the palace.

"I'll have to wait for orders," the door said stubbornly as they walked away.

"It's really so stupid!" fumed the cat in a shrill hiss. "They're all like that. The King says they're just supposed to delay an enemy long enough for the rest of us to find it and kill it."

They were passing the rows of glimmering trees. These looked like graceful saplings perhaps three times Kate's height, but she could see that they were entirely artificial. The slim trunks and branches gleamed like solid gold, and throughout their crowns, huge, jeweled flowers bloomed. From the boughs hung colored lanterns, casting a faint light that illuminated dark green stone, not grass. The garden paths between the rows were mosaics of pale, polished rock.

As they walked, the delicate flowering trees gave way to thick summer growth, the rich green stone leaves almost paper-thin. Soon they passed dark bronze trees loaded with stone foliage in polished reds, oranges, and yellows and came to Kate's very favorites, the trees by the river. These had trunks and branches of silver, the slender boughs loaded with delicate, tinkling clear crystals. Beneath them shone snow white paving stones. The crystals caught the pale light of the lanterns and refracted it in delicate rainbows onto the stone below.

"We need to hurry," Seylin urged as Kate lingered to look at the beautiful trees. Tugging her along, he crossed the river. The shallow water foamed over rapids carefully composed of small cubes of rock sticking up from the shallow riverbed. Water in Kate's world would catch the moonlight, but this river needed none. The many bubbles of foam appeared to shine with their own soft light.

Now the pair was climbing toward the steps of the palace. Beds of fanciful jeweled flowers alternated with musical fountains, and lamps of all colors lined the paths. Kate felt again that the light was rather faint. How beautiful these gardens would be in the daylight, she thought. Then, with bitter disappointment, she realized that it would never be day here. She was seeing the gardens not at night, but as they would always be.

The palace had no doors. Kate and Seylin stepped into an entrance hall several stories high, its outer wall pierced by huge windows. The enormous chandelier needed no candles because the crystals themselves shone. In their dim light, a huge double staircase curved up before the pair. On the wall between the wide flights of stairs, a mosaic of glass tiles sparkled with all the colors of a sunset.

Seylin pulled her down a corridor to the right. Kate felt rather giddy. She could absorb her surroundings only in snatches—here a hall with walls and floor of polished jade, there a hall of burnished lapis lazuli. While there was artwork everywhere, none of it represented anything she could understand. The smooth floor sparkled with scatterings of brilliant mosaic tiles in complicated, almost random patterns, and the walls were inlaid with horizontal bands of contrasting stones. They turned a corner and whisked by a tiny feathered creature rather like a yellow mop head.

The big black cat led Kate through a deep arch, and she gasped. She stood on a broad landing between two wide, curving staircases under an enormous dome. Below her lay the circular floor of this vast round chamber. The room was dimmer than Kate found comfortable, but she could see at a glance that it was bustling with monsters, all of them stylishly—not to say foppishly—dressed. Seylin towed her down the staircase, bumping through the crowd, and Kate felt that she would never draw breath again.

The first sight of Marak had been enough to send Kate into a tearful panic, and Marak himself had mentioned the possibility that a girl would want to run back home after a glimpse of his goblin subjects. Kate stared at the jumbled assortment of huge ears, strange limbs, fur, feathers, and hair, unable at first to sort out anything of what she saw. Then she began to form scattered impressions. The girl in the yellow satin evening gown with her hair in a tall coiffure would have been pretty except for her extreme resemblance to a cat. Her small round face, huge eyes, and tiny nose were startling enough, but the little split cat mouth and the foot-long whiskers made Kate feel queasy. Then there was the burly man in the elegant red coat. His left arm was normal, but his right was huge, brown, and furry, and it ended in four-inch-long claws. And there were all the little creatures in the crowd, many no taller than Kate's knees. Some of them stood on rolling metal platforms and were wheeled about by liveried servants.

Monster piled on monster in her field of view: the eight-foot-tall, unbelievably thin man with a long, long gray face; the woman with the dog's paws and large, floppy spaniel ears who looked quite elegant in a rose-colored dress of shirred silk; the figure with high stiltlike legs who wore the most remarkable deep blue trousers. Goblins obviously favored wigs, lace, ribbons, bright colors, and extravagance. Even those creatures who had fur or feathers wore something rich and vibrant, if only a jeweled turban or a hat with a long plume.

Everywhere, turning toward Kate from the crowd, were pale goggle eyes, huge cat eyes, glowing red eyes, bright bird eyes, as the creatures caught sight of the one thing that did not usually appear in goblin court: a pale-faced human girl. A whispering, growling, hissing sprang up as she walked by. Kate became painfully aware of her smudged, tearstained cheeks, her tumbled hair, her cracked shoes, and her crumpled blue dress with the ripped sash. She and the goblins stared at each other in mutual horror. Kate had never in her life seen such frightful deformities, and the goblins had never seen such a hideous dress.

Seylin stubbornly towed the near-fainting girl across the huge expanse of floor to the throne, an elaborate affair that resided under an embroidered canopy on a broad circular platform of stone. And on that raised circle, his back to her, stood the King, talking to two other goblins as they looked together at some manuscript spread out on a golden stand. He was elegant in a suit of dark green cloth, his striped shock of hair neatly tied back with a black velvet ribbon. Over the suit's tailored coat, he wore a short black cape painted with strange golden symbols. He wore no boots; his dark green breeches buckled at the knees, ending in fine black stockings and low shoes. Her own father, greeting important visitors, had never been more formally or fashionably dressed.

As they approached and the King turned, Kate realized in a flash what it meant to be elf-pretty in a goblin world. Once she had burst into tears at his inhuman appearance. Now she almost did so again at the strangely welcome sight of his familiar, somewhat human face amid the monstrosities and deformities of his goblin subjects.

Seylin stopped before him and swept into a deep bow. Kate looked at the big cat and didn't know what to do. Should she curtsy? If she tried, would her knees collapse and simply dump her onto the floor? Before she could decide, Marak stepped forward and captured her hands in his.

"Kate!" he shouted. "What in the name of all you call holy are you doing here? You are the last person—the very *last* person—that I expected to see!"

All day Kate had imagined her defiant glare as she spat out her little speech, but now that the moment came, she could barely pronounce the memorized line. It was a good thing Marak had excellent hearing because most of it came out in a whisper.

"I have come here of my own free will to say that I agree to marry you if you will release my sister unharmed."

There! She'd said it. Kate braced herself for his triumphant laughter. Instead, she saw the King stare and then glance sharply at Seylin. Her heart stopped. Had she come too late?

Marak noticed her shattered expression. "Of course, Kate, of course," he hastened to assure her. "I'll do it gladly."

Kate let out the breath she had been holding. A wave of relief swept over her and left her shaky. Em would be all right. That was the important thing. It didn't matter what happened to her.

"Now," said Marak briskly, "tell me all about it. How did it happen? Do you know where she is? Who's holding her?"

Chapter
Eight

Kate found her voice. "What do you mean, who's holding her?" she demanded. "You are, of course!"

"Me? Certainly not." The King frowned. "Seylin?" he inquired.

"I don't have any idea," squeaked the cat in surprise. "She never told me why she wanted to see you."

"But . . . but," babbled Kate, "you know you took her." Marak gave her hands an impatient shake.

"Kate," he said reasonably, "why would I want to steal your sister? I'm having enough trouble with you. Not that she hasn't offered," he added with a chuckle.

"But you took her to get back at me," insisted Kate mulishly. He looked at her sullen face and chuckled again.

"Revenge is an honored goblin pursuit," he said cheerfully, "but we do tend to save it for our enemies. So! We've established that I'm to release your sister and that you have no idea where she is. Locating her is the first thing. We can save your theories of goblin strategy for another time."

Marak released her hands and unfastened his short cape. An improbable-looking black hairy creature with short legs shuffled up behind him, its head barely higher than the King's knees. It reached up incredibly long, skinny, apelike arms and plucked the cape from his shoulders. At the same moment, a goblin in livery boomed out something in a loud voice. Kate heard a rustling and turned to see the entire crowd sink into a low bow. Marak didn't appear to notice. He was already talking rapidly in his own language to Seylin and the two goblins who stood with him. The cat darted off, racing on all fours through the crowd. Marak caught Kate's hand again and walked through a small door behind the throne. She found herself back in the great entrance hall.

"What I want to know," he said seriously, "is why you even think M is missing. You've been locked in for two days except for that one badly timed interview last night. Where are you getting your news?"

"Mr. Roberts came this morning and told me Em had vanished," she said. "He wanted me to tell him all about you so he could start a search for her. But I wouldn't talk to him," she added gloomily. "I knew it wasn't any use." Marak shot her a penetrating look, but she was staring at her feet and missed it.

"Kate," he said, "tell me everything that happened from the time I left last night until the time you came away with Seylin. I've not been paying enough attention to your human friends." He paused. "No, on second thought, tell me everything that happened from the time you woke up. That'll give you a chance to talk about chewing on my thumb." He laughed. "I expect you'll enjoy that."

As Kate talked, they walked along hallway after hallway and up staircase after staircase, always climbing. The lovely polished stone gave way to rougher surfaces and plain doors. Marak listened attentively and asked a number of questions. When she finished, he remained deep in thought. He absently tugged the ribbon from his hair, combed his fingers through it, and shook it out, still pondering. Then he turned toward her, his strange eyes gleaming with excitement.

"So you just walked in the front door unannounced to trade your life for your sister's," he said. "By the Sword, Kate, I'm impressed!

It's almost unbelievable. What a King you'll bear!" he said admiringly. "A better one than I, there's no doubt." Kate could think of
no possible reply to this statement, but Marak expected none. He
stopped in a dark passage at a large, wide double set of doors. "Your
first dank cavern, Kate," he chuckled, pulling one door open.

Kate stepped into a big, empty cave of native rock lit by the
familiar globe lamps. A large, flat wall at the far end appeared to be a
dark mirror, a gentle rustling sound coming from its glinting depths.
As they approached it, she jerked Marak's hand in an attack of ver-
tigo. The wall was a sheet of calm black water, gently lapping the
roof and floor. It looked just like the surface of any pond or lake
except that it was vertical. Amid the gentle ripples, she could see her
startled reflection and the goblin's amused one. She reached out and
dipped her hand into the wall, stirring the cool water, and then
pulled it out wet and watched it drip onto the cavern floor.

"That's enough," Marak laughed. "You're making waves. Back
up a few steps so we can see what we're doing. And you don't need
to hang on to my hand like that. If you don't jump in, you're not
likely to drown. Now, let's see where your sister is," he continued
meditatively. "It'll be a lot harder if she's already far away."

Their reflections faded from the water's surface. In their place
appeared a low, cluttered room full of boxes, old furniture, and sacks
of various descriptions. A candle burned on a three-legged table,
and on a musty couch lay the small, thin figure of Emily. She was
bundled into some kind of restraining jacket, and her eyes were
tightly blindfolded. Her mouth was muffled by a voluminous gag.
Not only were her ankles bound with a wide scarf, but several turns
of rope over the couch kept her from rolling to the floor. Kate was
absolutely speechless with horror.

"I'll admit it," said Marak brightly. "Your sister certainly does
need releasing. Do you recognize this place?" Kate shook her head.
"Let's back up, then."

The image changed, and Kate saw the familiar shape of the Hall under a lovely full moon. Marak pointed at a faint golden light coming from one of the basement windows.

"That's where M is," he said calmly.

"I don't understand!" cried Kate.

"Oh, but I do," the goblin assured her. "Now, let's see. Who else is in the house?"

Kate jumped as several goblins walked quietly up to join them. Two were the goblin men from the dais. One had long white fangs and eyes like a cat's, and the other was so hideous that Kate couldn't bear to look at his face. Marak didn't turn around to acknowledge the newcomers. He was looking into the study at Dr. Thatcher and Hugh Roberts. They appeared to be arguing. The scene dissolved, only to be replaced by the Hall kitchen. Mrs. Bigelow sat alone at the big wooden table, her wrinkled face wet with tears.

"Is that all?" mused the King. "Where are the others? Let's see— where's John, the stable boy?" Again the scene dissolved and was replaced, this time by a view of a path through the moonlit woods. A whole party of servant men was walking along with several hounds on leashes. "There are the men. But the women? Where's the cook? Oh, he's used them to send a message to the Lodge," he remarked, studying the shifting images. "My guess is that each and every one of them refused to make the trip alone." Kate stared unhappily into the parlor at Hallow Hill Lodge. Her aunts sat weeping on the couch, surrounded by the maids, the Lodge cook, and the Hall cook.

The King turned away from the water and began talking to the two goblins from the throne room. The hairy black creature who had taken his cape trotted up with a bulky bundle of clothing balanced on a stool, forming a mound so high compared to its diminutive stature that only its eyes were visible above it. As it turned toward Kate, she noted in alarm that its eyes were large and brilliant orange in color. Beside it trotted another, smaller creature of similar shape, carrying boots. This creature had orange hair and black eyes instead and so was the reverse of its larger twin.

The black-haired one plopped the stool down before the King and gathered up the clothing. Marak sat down, deep in conversation with the goblin men, who were apparently his lieutenants. The small orange goblin wedged the King's shoes off deferentially and handed him thick socks, which he absently pulled on. It handed the King first one black boot and then the other.

Seylin trotted through the door. Behind him, a huge yellow-eyed ape swung in on his knuckles. Kate was surprised to find that he was covered with dark gray feathers. Another one swung in after the first, identical except that his feathers were dirty white. If Kate had seen the next two goblins a week ago, she would have gone into fits. As it was, she gave a small squeak of alarm and moved a little closer to Marak, who looked up at them as he pulled on his boots and exclaimed in satisfaction. The new arrivals had skinny, stiltlike legs longer than their King was tall and similar long, polelike arms. Their bodies and heads were quite tiny by comparison, resembling round, fat barrels with knobs on the top. Each held a large paint-brush in one hand and a paint bucket in the other. As the King rattled off orders, they glided about restlessly on their long folding legs and put their arms out sideways, bending and straightening them. They reminded Kate sickeningly of spiders.

Marak rose and went back to the water mirror. The two tall, spi-dery goblins followed him. Hand out, the King called up the image of the search party. They were at the shadowy cliffs of the Hill now, lanterns swaying, standing and arguing. The search party became smaller as he backed the mirror away from the scene. In a few sec-onds, Kate saw tall black trees crowd the foreground.

Now Marak cupped his hands, frowning into them in concen-tration. A white smoke lapped over his fingers and began drifting to the cavern floor. He held his hands out toward the mirror and blew gently. Tatters of smoke floated into the surface of the water. Kate saw mist begin to rise among the trees and shimmer in the moonlight. The goblin King watched the mist gathering force for a moment, lapping into hollows and wafting up toward the moon. Then he beckoned the spidery goblins. They moved forward on their long limbs and walked straight into the wall of water. In another second they were gliding down the foggy forest path.

Kate stared at the bizarre creatures moving beneath the moonlight. One applied his paintbrush to the dead tree at the head of the path. A moment later, the tree had vanished completely. The other dipped his paintbrush into his bucket and began swiping it in the air. A thick bush began to appear in the middle of the path. They next erased a large rock, only to paint it in again a dozen feet away. Within a couple of minutes, the path was unrecognizable. Paintbrushes at the ready, the creatures glided rapidly off in the direction of the arguing search party.

Marak turned away, and the mirror went dark. The rest of the waiting goblins resumed preparations, but Kate remained where she was, staring at the lapping water. She was remembering the night when she and Emily had met the goblins at their bonfire. Gates had moved, and roads had shifted. Now she realized with a shudder that she and Emily hadn't been alone. These lofty monsters must have glided right beside them, changing the landmarks as they approached. She jumped when Marak stopped beside her. He noticed her horrified expression and nodded in understanding.

"You're right," he said calmly, just as if she had spoken out loud. "They led you straight to where we were waiting." And then, with a sharptoothed grin, "You only thought you were lost."

The hairy black monster reached up its ridiculously long arms and laid Marak's riding cloak around his twisted shoulders. As the King pulled it about him, the furry black fingers worked carefully, freeing his pale, coarse hair from the cloak's confining weight. Kate watched, still shuddering. Marak studied her thoughtfully as he fastened the catch.

"Come with me, Kate," he said. "I'm going to check on a few things I might need."

A few minutes later, she was sitting on a tall stool, feeling a little better. She looked around her at the stone room they were in, a cross between a library and a laboratory. Books and manuscripts filled an entire wall of bookshelves, another wall was covered with cabinets full of shelves and drawers, a writing desk occupied a space by the door, and she sat beside a high, broad worktable with star charts and diagrams fastened to the wall above it. Glass bottles, pottery jars, and metal boxes ranged across the cabinet shelves, and bunches of herbs hung from a rack. Utensils and bowls of various sizes were stacked neatly at the back of the worktable, and a mortar and pestle stood by her hand. She watched the pallid goblin as he prowled the room, lost in thought. He pulled out a deep drawer and rummaged through it, one finger holding a place in a small leather-bound book that he had plucked from the shelves.

"This is where your magic comes from," Kate observed, looking about with interest.

Marak was amused. "My magic comes from me," he corrected. "This is where I keep my tools." He found the object he had been after, checked the book again, and dropped the object into a pocket of his cloak.

As the goblin King browsed his magical tools, Kate mulled over the events of the day. She was in the last place she had wanted to be, and she had promised to marry a monster. Now she knew that Emily had been in the basement all the time. She thought about her guardian's accusation that she was insane and needed to be locked away. She remembered him trying to persuade her to talk, to tell them all about the creatures who had stolen her sister.

"He lied to me," she said, feeling completely discouraged.

"He's a human," the goblin agreed. "Of course, you lied to him, too, but I don't see that he left you much choice about it."

"Or maybe you did it," she accused him. "You could have put Em down there to make me think it's Mr. Roberts's fault, to make yourself look better."

Marak peered at her through his rough hair. "To make myself look better?" He laughed. "No, Kate, I know how I look. I've scared, upset, and offended you, but I haven't lied to you."

Kate subsided, miserable. She had made her promise, and it was too late. He would never let her escape now. She pictured her guardian as he'd been last night, yelling at her in front of Dr. Thatcher. She'd had no idea he was capable of such a thing. She looked at the black-cloaked goblin as he stood, deep in thought, drumming his six fingers on the cabinet in front of him.

"I thought I only had to worry about you," she said bitterly.

For once, Marak didn't laugh. "You don't have to worry about me," he said. "I do wish you'd stop. It would make both of our lives much easier." She shrugged and looked away. Marak studied her with a frown.

"Don't you think it's funny that he calls himself your guardian?" he asked. "Your guardian, your protector." He paused for a second, eyes narrowed. "I think it's the funniest thing I've ever heard."

As he pulled down another book and gathered more things from drawers and cupboards, Kate began to grow very sleepy. She fell into a doze. Then she shook herself and jumped down from the stool.

"You're enchanting me, aren't you!" she exclaimed. Marak was studying the book again. He didn't look up.

"But I want to come, too," Kate said stubbornly. The goblin poured the contents of his pocket out onto the worktable nearby and checked through them as if he hadn't heard. "After all, I came here by myself," she pointed out. He swept the assembled items back into his pocket, satisfied. "I promise to come back," she added hesitantly. It wasn't an easy promise to make.

Marak glanced up then, a shrewd look in his eyes. "My pretty bride," he said with a wry smile. "I finally have you underground where you belong—after quite a battle, too. And you want me to let you out again?" He shook his head in disbelief. "Oh, you bravely hurled yourself to the monsters when you thought it was the only way to save your sister. But"—he walked over and bent down to look into her eyes—"I think that if you knew she was safe, and you realized that I wasn't going to hurt her, you'd forget all about your promise to your poor goblin husband. And you'd bolt if you had even half a chance."

Kate tried to meet his steady gaze but failed. He was absolutely right. Marak stood in thought for a moment, watching her miserable face.

"You don't mind if I reinforce your pledge with a little magic," he suggested. She looked up, hopeful again, and shook her head.

"But if I take you with me," he warned, "I want you to promise only to watch. I don't want you to talk to Roberts."

"Why not?" asked Kate.

"Because I haven't formed a very favorable impression of my cousin. If you and he argue, I'm liable to do something I'll regret."

"All right," she promised.

He laid her right hand palm up on the worktable and covered it with his left hand. As he murmured quietly, she had the frightening impression that the two hands had grown together into one. When he lifted his hand and turned away, she snatched hers up quickly and probed at the palm. It felt completely normal. Marak watched her, grinning.

"Walk to the door," he told her, and she complied. Then he stepped away slowly, holding up his hand. Kate's hand jerked toward him. She tried to restrain it, but as he backed up, she was pulled forward. It felt as if a rope stretched from his hand through her palm into her arm. Marak threw back his head and laughed at her startled expression.

"The Leashing Spell gives you about ten feet," he said. "And I'm bigger than you are, so don't try dragging me around. Time to go." He grew serious. "They'll be waiting by now."

The band of goblins by the water wall had been joined by two grooms holding five horses. The horses were saddled and bridled, but no one made any move to mount. Marak walked to the mirror and called up an image of the Hall through the trees. The huge feathered apes promptly swung into the water. Kate felt an almost physical shock at the sight of them moving down the forest path a second later.

"They're Hulk and Bulk," Marak told her, nodding after them. "Hulk's the dark one. My mother named them."

Seylin jumped through the water barrier. Marak's fanged lieutenant took a pair of horses from the groom and stepped through next. Kate realized, seeing him in his black cloak, that this was Thaydar, the burly man from the bonfire. The other groom led his three charges snorting into the water. Marak gave a few orders to the bystanders in the cave, then pulled a rather dubious Kate into the picture with him.

She felt as if a large, cool bubble popped against her face. The next second she stumbled on the uneven rocks of the same path she and Seylin had taken from her bedroom that evening. The full moon shone through the branches, and Kate felt her heart lift at the sight of the stars through a break in the trees. She dragged her feet, looking up at them longingly.

The band of goblins gathered under the trees behind the Hall, and the groom led the horses away through the woods. The rest walked, padded, or swung onto the quiet terrace. Kate could just imagine what Mrs. Bigelow would say if she saw them.

Marak stepped up to the study window and stared into the lighted room without moving a muscle. Through it, Kate could see her guardian and Dr. Thatcher deep in intense discussion. The next second both men were asleep. Dr. Thatcher's head rolled against the back of his chair, and her guardian flopped forward, chin on chest. Marak turned away and took her hand, a pleased smile on his pallid face.

"You see, Kate," he remarked quietly, "how easy it is with everyone but you. You've been such trouble, you make me doubt my own abilities. Half the time, I suspect you of enchanting me." The absurdity of this statement almost made Kate smile, and she remembered her delight in besting him. Marak beckoned to Seylin, and the three of them moved toward the kitchen. As they passed a patch of moonlight, she looked up. It would be so hard underground, she thought wistfully, but maybe it wouldn't be unbearable.

They approached the kitchen window, and Marak gestured. "Seylin," he said in a low voice, "you handle this one." The big cat bounded to the window and froze, looking in. Marak and Kate walked up just in time to see Mrs. Bigelow slump forward, twitching slightly, her cheek on the kitchen table. "That's very good," said Marak appreciatively as the cat looked up. "You won't get that twitching, though, if you stay with them just another couple of seconds."

The group filed into the entrance hall, the two large feathered apes turning sideways and hunching to fit through the doorway. The sight of such bizarre creatures in such ordinary surroundings almost took Kate's breath away. They entered the study to find the men snoring gently as they dreamed in their chairs. Bulk, the light-colored ape, took his station right by her guardian. Thaydar stood on the other side of the chair, blocking access to the window.

The King reminded everyone of their duties in the goblin language. Seylin and Hulk went off down the hall. "—And I want you to stand here, Kate," added Marak, pointing. "Don't move too far from the hearth. That way, no matter where I step, I won't pull you down or drag you over a table." Kate rubbed her palm unhappily as he spoke, remembering that her freedom was only an illusion.

Marak went over to Hugh Roberts and gave him a stinging slap across the face with his six-fingered hand. "Wake up, cousin," he said.

Kate remembered her own nightmare as Hugh Roberts slowly awoke. Perhaps he, too, had been ordered to have bad dreams. He blinked about groggily, putting a hand up to adjust his wig. As he focused on Marak, the color drained from his round face and left it an ugly gray.

"It's always nice to meet close relatives," observed Marak pleasantly. His odd eyes glinted, and the candlelight in the room emphasized the muddy color of his lips and fingernails. Hugh Roberts gasped for breath and began to look as if he had been ill for several days. Turning his head slowly, he located the large feathered ape right beside his chair. Bulk gazed dolefully at him with his patient yellow eyes. Hugh gave a muffled groan. His dull gaze wandered around the room to Thaydar, and he let out a shriek. Kate glanced at the burly goblin in surprise. Except for those cat eyes and fangs, Thaydar didn't look so bad for a goblin. She turned back to find her guardian staring at her. He began to move his lips, but no words came out.

"Don't you dare speak to her," Marak warned. "She's not even related to you." The goblin King crossed his arms, smiling down at Hugh and showing his pointed teeth a little. "No, you want to talk to me, your own flesh and blood," he said encouragingly. "You want to tell me where little M is tonight. Kate came and told us that you thought we had her. But we don't." In spite of his shock, Hugh Roberts was listening closely, his lips working and his eyes fixed on Marak's face. Kate decided that he had gotten over his disbelief in goblins very quickly.

"Do you know where M is?" Marak asked. Hugh Roberts shook his head. The goblin's expression didn't change, but an angry gleam lit his eyes. "Then it's a good thing I do."

Hulk came sidling through the doorway, Emily in his arms. He laid the girl carefully down on the couch across from her guardian as Kate hurried over, exclaiming in dismay. Seylin padded in and sat down on the floor by the couch, round golden eyes fixed curiously on the quivering, gray-faced man.

"How's the letter?" asked Marak, kneeling next to Kate. Emily grinned at him drowsily. "M, someone's been using human magic on you—by which I mean a sleeping potion." He ran his fingertips over her temples and down her neck, then checked her wrists and ankles.

"Are you going to put any salve on me?" asked Emily in groggy anticipation. Marak smiled at her.

"No, someone's been very considerate," he replied. "No one would ever know you'd been tied up." He reached down a hand and helped Kate to her feet. "I hope you don't mind, M, but your sister can't stay here. She's"—he paused, then chuckled—"guarding the fireplace." Kate shot him a venomous look.

"Now," he said meditatively, drawing Kate back to the hearth and walking past her to the gray-faced Hugh, "this does raise a question. You're M's guardian, not I, but I'm the one who's having to guard her tonight. Do you have any idea what M was doing tied up in your basement?" Hugh Roberts stared at the carpet and shook his head.

The goblin King let out an exasperated sigh and reached into his pocket. Thaydar stepped to his side, grinning broadly. Marak handed him a small set of tongs, which he clicked a couple of times in anticipation. The King produced a rod of red sealing wax and a small bronze seal. Bulk shuffled a few feet sideways and clamped his gigantic hands over Hugh's arms. When the big man opened his mouth to yell, Thaydar bent down and seized his tongue with the tongs. He grinned in delight at the indistinct yells and cries coming from the frantic man, but Marak, on the other side of Hugh's chair, frowned in concentration. His lips moved silently as he held the rod of sealing wax above Hugh's open mouth. It softened and dripped without the aid of a flame, and a large red blob landed on the extended tongue. Marak quickly stamped the seal into the blob of melted wax and studied the impression with satisfaction. He turned away, putting the wax and seal back into his pocket, as Thaydar reluctantly released his grip on the tongue. At a nod, Bulk shuffled back a step. Hugh Roberts bent forward in his chair, choking and spluttering.

"Now," Marak said, "I'll ask you again. Do you have any idea what M was doing tied up in your basement?"

"Of course I do!" snarled Kate's guardian. "I tied the little witch up myself." Then he let out a terrified squeak and clapped his hands over his mouth. The goblins howled in amusement at his dismay, and Marak grinned at Kate's dumbfounded expression.

"It's the Stamp of Truth," he explained. "It makes the receiver answer the complete truth to every question." He turned back to Hugh Roberts. "And why did you tie M up in the basement, cousin?"

The man struggled for a second, his hands over his mouth. Then he dropped them, breathing heavily. "Miss Winslow had lied so well that the doctor wouldn't take her away. I was determined to make her tell the truth about her goblin obsession. If Miss Winslow thought her precious Em was stolen, I knew she'd admit everything, and her sister, doped and tied up, wouldn't be able to find her and tell her otherwise."

"It's so refreshing," Marak remarked to Kate. "It really brings a goblin quality to human speech, don't you agree?" A strangled sound caused him to turn. Hugh Roberts glared up at him, pale eyes frantic, a dribble of blood running from the corner of his mouth. "You're a smart man, cousin," Marak cautioned, "so I'll explain something to you. The Stamp of Truth is only ceremonially applied to the tongue. It works on the whole person. You can bite your tongue out and cut your hands off, and you'll still scribble out the truth with a quill pen clutched between your toes. I'm afraid that you'll have to adjust to life as an honest man. So tell me, honest man, why did you want the doctor to take Kate away?"

"She doesn't have any business here," hissed Kate's guardian. "She or her sister. This has been Roberts land for eight hundred years. I can show you the records."

"I know whose land it was before that," declared the goblin, "and I can show you records, too. So you wanted them gone because they were taking your land. Then why did you offer to be their guardian?"

"I had to," growled Hugh Roberts, shifting from side to side as he tried to fight the spell. "Otherwise, whoever did would have thrown me out and moved into Hallow Hill with them. Besides, being their guardian would give me certain opportunities." He glared at Kate rather desperately.

"You had plans, then?" asked Marak, frowning.

"Of course I did," snapped the gray-faced man. "Ideas, mainly. I thought about poison, but I couldn't make up my mind."

"And why's that?" asked the goblin.

"I have a horror of hanging," said Hugh Roberts with a shudder.

"What compassion!" hooted Marak. "You're always thinking of others. Did you have any more ideas?"

"I just decided to see what opportunities arose," said Hugh

reluctantly. "I had three years before she would come of age, and lots of things could happen in that time. Sure enough, she started show-ing real nervous strain, and I did all I could to encourage it. I even persuaded some village boys to play a trick, pretending to be goblins. She tried to run off the very next day. I knew she wouldn't take her sister's disappearance without a fight. I had the doctor right here to listen to her arguments when the search party brought her back from the woods."

"I see," mused Marak, watching Kate become more and more indignant. "You were well on your way to getting rid of the older sister, but what were you going to do about M?"

Hugh rocked back and forth furiously and ground his teeth. It was no use. "I would have had ten years with that one," he spat out finally. "Almost anything can happen in ten years. I was sure, if the older one was gone, that I could handle the younger one."

Kate let out a shriek of rage.

"Yes," agreed Marak heartily, "I think we've had all the truth out of you that we can stand. You've made it quite clear what kind of guardian you are. The only thing now is to decide what to do about it. Kate has already made her decision. She came down to my kingdom tonight and agreed to marry me in exchange for her sister's safety."

"Oh, Kate, really?" asked Emily excitedly, sitting up. "What was it like? Was it horrible and dark? Was it very beautiful?"

"I don't know, Em," Kate replied, trying to harness her scattered thoughts. "It was—very beautiful, yes. I think," she added slowly, "that some parts were horrible, too."

"You won't leave me behind, will you?" begged Emily. "Please take me with you. I don't want to stay here with him," she insisted, pointing at her guardian.

Marak gave Kate a shrewd, assessing glance. "I'd be happy to steal you, M," he said sorrowfully, "but I'm afraid your sister wants you to stay behind. She thinks humans make much better companions for a young child than we monsters do. After all, M, your own race is bound to love you best." He met Kate's astonished stare with a rather wicked smirk.

"How could you!" cried Emily as Kate opened her mouth to protest. "I don't think humans are nice at all, and goblins are a lot more fun."

"But, Em," said Kate sadly, "what about your great-aunts?" She tried to think of other things that tied her lonely little sister to the world she herself would have to leave. "And what about Hallow Hill?"

"I don't want Hallow Hill without you," said Emily appealingly. "Who would go on rambles with me? And I don't want to live with the aunts. They snapped at me, and they won't let me have a pet. You let Seylin have a pet," she told Marak. "Would you let me have one, too?"

The goblin King chuckled and gave Kate a triumphant look. "Have a pet?" he said winningly. "Why, M, you'd *be* a pet! You'd go about the kingdom playing with the goblin children, and the old ones would weave ribbons into your hair, which is especially soft and beautiful by our standards." Emily stroked her straight brown hair wonderingly. "And the dwarves would make jewelry just for you, rings and bracelets and pretty necklaces. They're always disappointed, the dwarves, that the King's Wife can't wear necklaces."

"Do come, Em," piped Seylin, putting his paws up on the couch. "I'll show you all the magic I know."

"That's fine as far as it goes," interrupted Kate sternly, "but you'll have to marry one of those goblins someday, Em. You're just saving them the trouble of stealing you." And she glared indignantly at the arrogant goblin King.

"Your sister is right," Marak said to Emily. "I'll bring you into my kingdom under two conditions. First, you do have to marry a goblin when you're old enough. But you can marry any goblin you like; I'll leave you the choice. And second, if you come, no changing your mind later. You won't be allowed to leave."

"I don't mind marrying a goblin," promised Emily with all the blithe disregard of a child for the future.

"You know perfectly well Em's not old enough to understand what she's losing," Kate cried angrily. "How dare you try to lure her underground after I made my promise to you! You know I intended her to stay up here and—and be a human!"

Emily started to argue, but Marak stopped her with a gesture. He came to Kate's side and took her hands soothingly. "By all means," he agreed, "we can leave little M behind. And in whose care are you willing to leave her?"

Kate ran quickly through the available choices. Her great-aunts? No, they had already failed her. Besides, after this horrible experience, Kate wondered whether they would even take Emily back in. Father's nephew had already declined. If pressured, Kate suspected that he would do it, but he certainly wouldn't love her.

"Surely you don't think," said Marak, "that your guardian is particularly unusual? A young human girl alone, with land, is going to be quite a target. Or are you proposing that I sally forth every few years to rescue her from whatever new menace she encounters?"

Kate looked up. The goblin's pallid face was calm and cruel. He knew she had no choice. He must have realized right away that he could rescue Emily and still get to keep her. Kate jerked her hands free. As he let her go, she saw the brown wound on his thumb. That had probably been the only moment of her entire life when she would get the better of him.

"Don't you realize what you mean to M?" added Marak more kindly. "If you love her enough to give up your world for her, don't you think she would want to do the same for you? She wants to be with you, and it won't be as hard for her, I think. She'll have a happy life with us. We'll appreciate her."

Kate nodded reluctantly and looked away. Her eyes met her guardian's, and she felt a rush of anger. She forgot her promise not to speak to him. "This is your fault!" she cried, helpless and furious. Her guardian glared back at her. He didn't look particularly contrite.

"Indeed it is, Kate," Marak agreed. "It's time to plan your revenge. Goblins just adore revenge." He grinned. "Do you have anything in mind?"

Kate was taken aback. "Revenge is wrong," she told him solemnly. "Vengeance belongs to God."

The goblin put his head to one side and watched her through narrowed eyes. "You won't even give God a little help?" he asked softly.

Kate thought about what her guardian had done. He had made her promise to lose her freedom and marry a monster. Hallow Hill belonged to her, but she would never live here now. She'd never even see it again. But it was hers, and no one else's, so it wasn't wrong to demand this one thing.

"I don't want him living here," she said firmly. "I want him off my land."

"Oh, good," Marak said with relish. "I thought of that one, too." He walked over to her guardian. "It seems Kate doesn't want you on her land," he announced cheerfully. "And I'm bound to say, cousin, that I don't want you here, either."

The big man stared up at him in alarm. "I didn't do anything!" he insisted. "I never even touched her, and her sister's fine."

"It's true that you didn't kill or imprison her," agreed Marak, "although I don't think you deserve much credit for that since you were certainly trying to. But no, we'll set that aside. Kate's revenge is for what you actually did do.

"Kate isn't at all like her sister. She has no desire to be a goblin's pet. She tried everything she could think of to stay out of my reach, and she did quite a remarkable job. She went to you for protection, for the help that you had promised to provide, but not only did you not help her, you actually drove her to me. Kate is the first King's Bride I know of who had to promise away her own freedom in exchange for the goblins' help. Thanks to you, she'll be lost to her own race and locked away from this land that she loves. She'll never see the sun or stars. She'll never be outside again. She'll raise just one child now, and he'll be a goblin; she'll cry for days after her first sight of him. And she'll be married to a creature she finds so frightful that I have to leash her to me with magic to keep her from running away even now."

A profound silence fell over the study. Kate stared down at the carpet, so overcome with homesickness and grief that she didn't understand how it could fail to show. There should be a physical injury to cause such pain, some wound over her heart, gushing blood. The goblin King studied her grimly. Then he turned toward Hugh with a philosophical shrug.

"It's not my problem," he said. "I have to protect my people. Kate's suffering is the price paid for the goblin race to continue. But," he added sternly, "you were supposed to protect her. You chose to become her guardian, and that makes her suffering *your* problem.

"I don't think you'll spend much time on Kate's land, anyway. The Stamp of Truth is a permanent charm. The doctor, here, will wake up never even knowing he was asleep. He'll ask you why you look so upset, and you'll tell him all about it. It's going to be very amusing, your descriptions of us all."

Hugh's anxious eyes widened as he realized what this would mean. Kate looked at the sleeping Dr. Thatcher. He was far too well educated ever to believe in goblins, especially goblins right in the room with him and somehow escaping his notice. She imagined his interested look as her guardian related his incredible tale. Hugh Roberts would soon be in the asylum himself.

"But when Kate ordered you off her property," concluded Marak, "I don't think that she wanted to wait, so from this moment forward, you are forbidden to set foot on her land."

Hugh Roberts stared at him, completely baffled. "I'll do my best," he promised shakily. "I give you my word."

"Oh, I think you'll surprise yourself," the goblin King murmured absently. "Bulk?"

The great ape seized Hugh by the head and arm. Thaydar came up and caught the other arm, stepping down firmly on Hugh's feet. Marak reached into his pocket and pulled out a tiny jar. Kneeling, he held it close to the floor, upside down. He removed the stopper, but nothing dripped out. Then he positioned the bottle below Hugh's arm and turned it quickly upright. A drop splashed upward onto the man's arm.

Before Kate's astonished eyes, the terrified Hugh began to tilt. As Thaydar stepped back, Hugh's feet slipped out from under his chair and flipped up over his head. In a few seconds, he was entirely upside down, balancing in the air, screaming and twisting. Bulk still held the other arm. He extended his own feathery arm as far as he could, pushing the man higher and higher into the air. Then he let go. Hugh whizzed through the air like a great bat and flopped grotesquely onto the ceiling.

Marak crossed quickly to Kate, who clutched the fireplace in an attack of dizziness. He put an arm around her and stared up at Hugh Roberts crawling about on the ceiling like a wasp. The big man pushed himself upright, feet stuck on the ceiling plaster and head pointing straight down. He stood swaying, goggling down at them, his round face frantic with terror. His wig didn't even fall off.

"You're not allowed to set foot on Kate's land," Marak reminded him evenly. "Well, actually, any land. Now, I understand that the doctor here is fascinated by preternatural forms of insanity. Kate tells me he believes the mind can perform impossible feats when it gives way to madness. Things not explainable in the everyday world." He paused, watching as Hugh Roberts scrabbled about above him. "You should exceed his wildest expectations."

The big man gibbered down at them, clawing at the walls, and then, making a rush across the ceiling, he tangled himself in the chandelier. Kate couldn't bear it any longer. He looked like some huge cockroach. She put her head down and stared at the floor as Marak shepherded her from the room. The quiet goblins filed out of the house, Hugh Roberts's screams echoing down the hall behind them.

Chapter
Nine

The goblins left by the front door. Kate stumbled, dazed, down the wide steps, Marak's protective arm holding her upright. She could still hear her guardian's screams behind them, and she put her hands over her ears to block out the sound. The chilly night breeze revived her a little as they crunched along a gravel walk. They were filing down one of the tree-lined edges of the Hallow Hill green, leaving the Hall and forest behind.

Kate glanced up at her strange companion's implacable face. He knew exactly how miserable she was at the thought of the life he had planned for her. He even knew how miserable she was going to be about things she hadn't thought of yet. She shivered, thinking of a hideous goblin baby. She wondered if Adele had cried for days at her first sight of him.

The goblin King knew all this, and he could just shrug it off, completely pitiless, but he could exact an appalling price for her misery from a human who he thought should have tried to prevent it. Kate cautiously pulled her hands away from her ears. She couldn't hear her guardian's screams anymore, but she had a swift image of him flopping about on the ceiling, and she shivered again. Marak paused in their walk, frowning, to pull his cloak around her slight shoulders.

But then, Kate considered, her father would say to be fair. It was true that the goblin King had been trying to capture her, but it was also true that he hadn't succeeded. She had walked in unannounced and promised to be his wife, and she had set the condition herself. He had immediately marshaled his forces to meet the terms of the agreement. He had taken her along to watch him accomplish his part, and she had promised to go back when it was done. She had even picked the revenge herself, although she'd had no idea what her simple statement would become in the hands of a magical monster.

They came to the end of the gravel walk. On the field beyond the green, the goblin groom waited with their horses. Kate stepped out of the shadow of the trees into bright moonlight. As she tilted her head to look at the full moon, she felt the grief of her loss sweep through her again. The goblin King had said she would never be outside after their marriage. Kate didn't think she could endure it.

Marak was issuing orders. Seylin raced back toward the house, and Hulk and Bulk climbed onto two big draft horses and trotted off. Emily wandered over and took her hand. Kate looked down at her little sister. Her thin cheeks were flushed, and her eyes were bright with excitement. With Emily's love of drama and of animals, she would enjoy every bit of goblin life. It was all so exaggerated, from the bright colors and rich decorations to the deformities of the creatures themselves. At last, life would hold all the variety Emily wanted.

After several minutes, Seylin came back at a run. "They both woke up well," he reported to the King. "The man woke up in the middle of a sentence, and he looked around for a minute before he could find Roberts on the ceiling. Then I had to go wake up the woman. The bell was already ringing to call her to the study, so I don't think she'll notice that her tea was cold."

They prepared to ride home. Kate noted that it was all happen-ing pretty much as it would have a few days ago, and she wondered drearily if the extra time had been worthwhile. Thaydar boosted

Emily up and then swung up behind her. Seylin sprang on behind Thaydar and wrapped his paws around the burly goblin's waist.

"Listen to me, you occasional cat," growled Thaydar, "there'd better be no claws this time, or you walk home! I don't care if you fall off—I won't be a pincushion."

"Ready?" asked Marak, and he boosted Kate up onto his gray hunter. For a few seconds, she was alone on the horse. She wanted to seize the reins and dash away, but she realized that the magical bond that tied her to the King would pull her from the horse's back. By the time she thought of this, he had already mounted behind her.

"Really, Kate, my own horse!" said the goblin reprovingly, just as if she had been speaking out loud. "I don't think he'd have done it, but I'm glad you couldn't try." He glanced down at her face, raised in silent appeal to the moon. She didn't seem to notice him at all. She couldn't see anything but the moon and the stars near it, calling her across the vast gulf of darkness. They seemed to know her name, she thought sadly. If only she knew theirs.

Marak took one sharp look at the white face of his bride and urged his horse into a gallop. The horses raced through the silvery fields, running flat out. They cleared fences and crashed through bushes, throwing up a cloud of dust and small rocks in their wake. Emily, clinging to Thaydar, thought they were going to die, and Seylin forgot all about the warning not to use claws. But Kate knew nothing of the hair-raising ride. She saw nothing but the moon and stars. They seemed so close. Surely they could help her. She could almost hear words like the chimes of bells as they told her what she needed to do. She could see the moonbeams reaching down to her like silver hands, catching at the fleeing horse. Marak leaned down low, pulling her with him, and called for more speed.

Kate felt them shift as if the horse had stumbled. She took her eyes off the pursuing moon and glanced ahead. They were on a level field, but the horse's racing feet were sinking into it as if it were quicksand. He was not slowing his gallop; if anything, he was running faster, his legs invisible below the earth. In another few seconds, Kate's feet were gone, too, and just as if the field were a mist or sea, only the horse's head plowed along above it. Waving grass stems and dirt clods raced by the edges of Marak's black cloak. Now the horse's head was gone, and the ground was rising up around her, lapping at her without waves until it reached her chest and then her neck. She screamed in terror, the goblin's arms clamped tightly around her as she threw back her head for one last glimpse of the moon.

Total darkness surrounded them. Kate closed her eyes and hid her face in the goblin King's chest, preferring to deal with a blindness that she caused and understood. After a few more seconds, the horse slowed down. Soon he was cantering and then walking, blowing from his run. She could feel the goblin relax, too, straightening up and loosening his hold on her. Kate cautiously opened her eyes. Polished rock walls and hanging lamps met her frightened gaze. She was back underground.

They came to an iron door just like the one she had come through with Seylin, though this one opened for the King without any questions. Beyond it was a wide room lined with horse stalls. Thaydar swung down from the saddle, cursing in goblin at Seylin, who had shredded his waistcoat. Emily could hardly stand up, so frightened had she been by the trip underground, but she was already asking questions. Marak lifted Kate to the ground, and their steaming, lathered horses were led away.

They emerged in a palace hallway. On one side was a line of doors; on the other, tall windows without glass displayed a spectacular view. They were high above a wide, bowl-shaped valley far larger than the one through which she had originally come, its space defined in the darkness by thousands of twinkling lights. Past the windowsill, she could see what must be the back of the palace, forming a straight wall down for several hundred feet. A large town nestled at the bottom of the palace, and across the valley, more towns were defined by other gatherings of lights. Between them were open areas crossed by lighted roads or canals.

Emily and Seylin leaned out a window farther than was safe, asking and answering in a chatter that wearied everyone but themselves. Marak walked over to the unlikely pair. "Seylin," he said, "take M to get something to eat. I don't think she's been fed at all today." Kate immediately felt guilty for not having thought of this herself. "The cooks will be at the ceremony, so you'll need to find something on your own, and then you can bring M back up to the pages' floor to pick an apartment. There should be some with windows free, and she'd better have one with a really good writing area like yours."

Kate found this statement interesting, but Emily thought it was hilarious. "You can write?" she asked the big cat incredulously. "How do you hold a pen?"

"Not with his paws, although he's tried," answered Marak with an exasperated sigh. "Seylin, you've been a cat long enough for now. Change back, and this time stay changed for at least one full day."

Seylin's ears, head, and fluffy tail went down in total dejection. "Change back now?" he yowled pitifully. "But they'll laugh at me."

"Or perhaps your King didn't just give you an order," the goblin remarked.

There was a heartfelt sigh, and then a shimmer, and a tall boy in a black tunic and breeches stood where the cat had crouched. Kate and Emily stared. If they had expected anything, they had expected a goblin or a human, but Seylin was neither one. His neat black eyebrows curved upward where a human's curved down, and his small ears pointed at the tips. His thick black hair curled in luxurious ringlets, his large black eyes were shaded by long, dark lashes, and his pale skin had a fine, silvery texture. Seylin was an extraordinarily handsome youth about thirteen years old. Except for the fact that his striking features wore an unusually glum expression, he could have been an angel in a painting by an Italian master.

"You see, they didn't laugh," observed the goblin King. "Now, go, and if you want to show M your new trick with the colored flames, do it somewhere away from low ceilings so you don't leave a scorch mark." The two turned and went off together, a little bashful at first, but Kate noticed that before they reached the end of the hall-way, they were again deep in conversation.

"I never saw such a beautiful boy," she murmured in complete amazement.

"Don't ever let Seylin hear you say that," Marak said. "He'd never forgive you. He's a throwback, of course, almost pure elf, and in one of our finest high families, too, a goblin-goblin marriage. The parents were devastated. It hasn't been easy for him, as you might well imagine. He tends to avoid the other children, but I've kept him close by, and he's proved exceptional at magic. He's very sensitive about his—well, I suppose you'd balk at the word *abnormality*—his difference, and since I taught him how to change shapes, he's been a cat as much as possible." He chuckled. "He seems to feel that if he's a cat, people will forget that he's not much of a goblin."

Kate pondered this odd speech as they started off again down corridors and stairs. Her head was buzzing with bizarre sights and strange ideas, and she was very tired. It seemed to her that they walked for a long time without speaking, always going down. The windows vanished, and the halls became rougher, more like tunnels than hall-ways. Eventually Marak ushered her into a small cavelike room. It was lit by a lamp hanging high in the rounded ceiling. A table-high ledge stretched across one end, and before it protruded a chair-shaped hunk of stone, the simplest of furnishings left behind when the room was hollowed out.

Kate found the room too dim for her human eyes and stopped right inside the door to adjust. Marak crossed to an inner door and talked in goblin to someone beyond. Kate sat down on the stone seat and studied the ledge in front of her. Four golden circles lay there, along with an oddly fashioned golden drinking goblet that held some sort of dark liquid. She suddenly felt very nervous.

Marak put a shallow bowl of water and a towel in front of her. Then he laid his hands on the door they had come through and spoke aloud. It shuddered and clanked, and Kate jumped. "It's all right," he remarked, seeing her startled face, a hint of his normal amusement glinting in his serious eyes. "It's purely ritual. I've just locked the door with magic. It was important in the old days when a King's Bride might have hundreds of hysterical and highly magical kin storming the doors to rescue her before she could be made the King's Wife. That's a problem we're not likely to face at this ceremony."

He took a small bag from his pocket and threw a pinch of powder into the bowl. Taking her right hand in his left, he pushed both into the water and dried her wet hand on the towel. "Of course, I did wait until you were locked in before removing the Leashing Spell," he admitted with a sigh. "You don't have kin storming the doors, but sometimes I think you don't need them. You do make me nervous, Kate."

Kate looked uncertainly from the locked door to the odd assembly of items on the table. Was she trapped in this little room forever? There being only one chair, Marak sat down on the table, pushing his striped hair back with a big hand and studying her distressed face intently.

"Couldn't the ceremony wait for just a little?" she begged. "I'm so tired; I'm used to sleeping at night. Just another few hours?"

Marak chuckled, his eyes lighting up with admiration as he looked at her. "Kate, what you could do with another few hours, I'd be terrified to see. You'd slip right through my fingers like a ghost. I promise you can sleep right after the wedding, sleep for days if you want to, but the ceremony's critical, and it's always done immediately." Kate hung her head, discouraged.

"In our world, there's nothing more important than the marriage of the King because that's where the new King comes from, and that's how the magic of the race continues. The ceremony tests the bride for certain qualifications, it makes indications about the future, it ensures that she stays underground where she'll be safe, and it protects her against every kind of harm. The King's Wife ceremony is completely practical and, therefore, largely unpleasant," concluded the goblin with a resigned shrug.

Kate considered this information unhappily. Then she brightened.

"But I might fail some test, then?" she pointed out.

"Don't get your hopes up, Kate. You're ideal." He watched her crestfallen expression with a smile. "But it goes beyond tests and protections. The point is that once it's over, you're one of us. Now, that doesn't thrill you, but it does thrill my people. I don't think you can understand what it means to them. Goblins are a close-knit, gregarious society. That's our strength. The King's Wife doesn't become a goblin, of course, but she's tremendously important, so the goblins are fascinated by her. If she waves her hand about in a certain way when she talks, all the goblin women copy her. If she prefers a certain color, everyone wears it. If she has a favorite flower, every goblin who goes outside tries to bring her one, and they adore her if it's at all possible. Everyone adored my mother—my father, most of all." Kate pictured Adele in this same room, years before, and wondered how she had felt.

Marak picked up one of the golden circlets and rolled it in his hands for a moment. "Enough about life beyond the ceremony," he said with a sigh. "We both have to get ready. Kate, the King's Bride is a captured bride, stolen, hysterical, weeping and wailing. That's what usually happens. But you weren't stolen; you came here willingly. You made a promise, and now you're carrying it through. That's very important," he said seriously. "You need to remember that. Don't kick up a fuss. Don't make anyone drag you around. Keep up your dignity. It'll help.

"The entire ceremony presumes a desperate captive woman of great magical powers. During the ceremony, she is shackled both magically and actually. No one speaks to her in a language she understands, and she herself is wordless. She is taken where she needs to go, and she has no control over what happens. Which means that you have the easy part. Everyone else does all the work."

"But I don't have any magical powers!" protested Kate. Marak glanced at her sharply.

"I don't know how you could have," he admitted, "but it makes no difference. The ceremony is always the same. If there's no need for the precautions, we'll never know. If there is need of them, they're always in place." Kate could see the rather brutal logic of this.

"At the end of the ceremony, it no longer matters whether you have tremendous magic or hordes of relations. No power on earth, including my own, can make you back into what you were before. You're the King's Wife from that moment on until one or the other of us dies, and you're underground forever."

Kate stared numbly at the gold circle in his big gray hands. As she watched, he clicked it open into two halves. Reaching down, he closed it again on her wrist. She lifted her hand in the dim light but could see no seam in the metal. An inch-wide golden brace-let followed the contours of her wrist as closely as if it had been designed just for her. Marak was already putting one on her other wrist. Then he knelt down and began unfastening her shoes. Feeling embarrassed, Kate did it herself, and he put the other bracelets on her bare ankles.

"Now, drink this," he ordered, retrieving the goblet and setting it in front of her. He watched her carefully, both amused and a little irritated as her expression turned mutinous.

"What does it do?" she demanded.

"It takes away your words," he said patiently. "Most magic depends on the right words, so this will block you from attempting defensive spells and charms. I know, I know, you can't work spells and charms, but you have to drink it, anyway."

"What if I don't?" Kate asked mulishly.

"Do you see this?" Marak asked. Part of the cup rim was shaped like a metal whistle. "I grab your hair, and I yank your head back, and I wedge this between your teeth. Then I pour the drink down your throat. It's not that hard, really." Kate glared indignantly at his impassive expression.

"Kate," said the goblin, "remember what I told you. You offered to do this. This was all your choice. It'll help you to think about that. It won't make any difference in the outcome of the ceremony, but you'll feel better about it, and you'll keep up your courage."

Kate lifted the goblet and took a small sip. Then she paused. What if I just refuse to swallow? she thought stubbornly.

Marak grinned at her. "It's already worked. It just needs to touch your tongue. You can spit it out if you want to." Glowering desperately, Kate swallowed with an effort. "That's it, then," he said, turning toward the inner door. "You're all set to go to the women now and get ready. Remember, they won't talk to you, and you can't talk to them. And any frantic flailing around you do is sure to be palace gossip for years."

"How perfectly barbaric," Kate sneered. At least, that's what she intended to say. What she actually said was, "Aaah."

"Exactly," said Marak approvingly. "I'm locking this door behind you, so your magic spells won't work, anyway. The only way out is at the other end of the women's chamber, and that's where I'll be waiting when you're ready."

Kate soon concluded bitterly that the ceremony itself couldn't be any more humiliating than the preparation. Goblin women of all shapes and sizes seized her, popped her into a large, soapy tub, and scrubbed her as if she were a dirty cooking pot. Then they pulled her out again, wrapped her in towels, and set her on a stone couch. Two women started combing her wet hair while others rubbed her with oil, puffed her with powder, trimmed her toenails, and polished her fingernails. She felt like a horse being groomed.

Kate drowsily watched the monster women at work on her. Here I am, she thought bitterly, being hustled into marriage just like those poor Sabine women who were dragged away by the Romans. She wondered how many of those Roman men had been old, or ugly, or deformed. It didn't matter because the captive women had to marry them anyway, but she doubted that a single one of them had a husband more ugly than hers.

She thought about the goblin King, with his gray skin, his big, bony head, and those eyes like different-colored coals glowing out of their deep sockets. Her father had taught her that her husband would be her closest companion, her comfort and guide, the guardian of her honor and virtue. A husband and wife belonged to each other body and soul. Husbands kissed their wives, just as Romeo had kissed Juliet. They slept together in the same bed; the stories were very clear about that.

She thought about the poems she had read, about that glorious love shared by man and wife that transformed the poorest people into cherished treasures in each other's eyes. What a mockery of love this was, she thought with a sinking heart. She imagined Marak's wiry arms around her, his awful brown lips kissing hers. When Eve left Paradise, she left with handsome Adam, but Kate was leaving with the snake.

No, that's not fair, she told herself firmly. I promised to be this creature's wife, and I can't be a coward. I'm not really a captive like those Roman brides, and it's not his fault he's ugly. And those arms were around me on the way home. He wrapped me in his cloak so I wouldn't be cold. He didn't feel deformed and hideous; he felt strong, and he was kind. Perhaps, she thought wistfully, perhaps it won't be so awful. I've never been kissed by a handsome man, so I suppose I'll never know the difference. This was my idea. I have to remember that. I saved Em's life, that's the important thing, and now I have to live with the consequences. She recalled her father's favorite lines from Milton: *Nor love thy life, nor hate; but what thou livest, live well.*

Kate became aware of a change in the activity around her and opened her eyes with an effort. Old Agatha stood beside her couch. Picking up a paintbrush and dipping it in black ink, she began to write in small, neat letters straight down Kate's right arm, starting a little above the elbow and ending at the wrist. Kate felt annoyed. She hoped they would wash that writing off because otherwise she was going to look like a cannibal princess at the wedding. Of course, she reflected unhappily, she hadn't seen her dress yet. An arm covered with black ink might be the most stylish thing about her before the goblin women let her go.

Coming to the end of her row of letters, the old dwarf woman picked up a glass bottle and dotted some oil onto Kate's arm. Two of the black ink letters faded and then brightened into gold. Agatha dipped the paintbrush and started on another row. She wrote line after line, first on the right arm and then on the left. Each time, she ended with a dot of some liquid, and each time, one or two of the letters in the line changed to gold. Eventually it dawned on Kate that these were the tests of the King's Bride, and it was obvious from the excited faces around her that she was passing them all.

The women had dried her hair as Agatha worked, and now they were winding it full of ribbons. Kate thought bitterly of Marak's promise to Emily that the goblins would weave ribbons into her hair. Better Em than her. One simple ribbon would have been fine, but they must have ten or fifteen in there by now. The women stood Kate up and brought her undergarments, which she hurriedly put on, worried that they were so short and skimpy. Then two of the women stepped her into a dress. As they hooked up the back, Kate looked down at herself in real concern. Style was not really the issue, and neither was comfort. The simple fact of the matter was that there had better be more clothing than this.

Kate looked around anxiously for more garments, but the women beckoned her to a tall mirror instead. She stared at her reflec-tion in complete dismay. Her hair, twisted and puffed into an elabo-rate swirl, rested high on the back of her head. One long, thin strand of hair hadn't been put up at all, and now a goblin woman tugged it around to fall, loose, down the front of her neck. The dress left her arms and shoulders entirely bare, and her back was bare down to the shoulder blades. She felt deeply shocked at the sight of so much skin.

Even if the dress actually covered her up, it would never have been something she would have chosen. The tight bodice was of gold cloth, and it gleamed in the dim light like polished metal. The skirt was unlike any she had ever seen. It was made of many loose and wispy layers of red silk, as if someone had sewn hundreds of handkerchiefs onto an underlying petticoat without rhyme or reason. Poking out beneath were her shins in their gold bands and her bare feet. I look like a beanpole, she thought disgustedly. And those golden shackles are going to come in handy because if they expect to bring me out in front of a crowd looking like this, they're going to have to use them.

Agatha appeared next to Kate's horrified reflection and beckoned her over to the door. Kate instantly forgot the awful dress in a wave of pure panic. As Agatha pushed the low door open, she tried to reason with herself. How bad can it be? she thought. I don't have to speak lines, and I won't forget what I'm supposed to do next. The King said I have the easy part. She stepped forward bravely.

Ahead of her stretched a low, short tunnel. Two goblin men in golden armor appeared in the doorway. I wonder, she thought sarcastically, if that armor's there to protect them from my powerful magic. After all, goblins don't believe in taking chances. Each carried a short chain of thick gold links. They stopped on either side of her, touched the chains to her golden bracelets, and there she was, effortlessly shackled. But they didn't haul her off. Instead, they hesitated. Kate remembered what Marak had said: "Don't make anyone drag you around." She squared her bare shoulders, lifted her chin, and walked down the tunnel, the armored goblins keeping pace on either side.

At the end of the tunnel, she stopped inadvertently, her eyes trying to make sense of the dim cavern beyond. These creatures just don't use enough light, she thought. Turning her head to the left, she could see through the gloom that a huge crowd of goblins was gathered above her in some sort of rough amphitheater. The stage area was floored with black stone, and she could see two stone tables arranged on it, each lit by its own set of torches.

The goblin King was standing sideways to the crowd, facing her, about twenty feet away. He could have been properly dressed,

Kate thought resentfully, but no, he had to look barbaric, too. His striped hair was wild, as usual, and he wore a loose black shirt untucked over baggy black trousers, the ends of which were stuffed into short boots. Kate decided that he looked like a peasant in an old tale. He was wearing the cape that he had worn at court, and the gold letters on it shimmered as they caught the torchlight. At a gentle tug from one of the guards, she stepped out from the shadow of the tunnel, and a great shout went up from the assembled goblins. So it's going to be like that, she thought. There'll be no pretty music at my wedding.

On the black floor of the cavern in front of her were four large, square sand paintings, a goblin letter against a different-colored background of sand. They were rather pretty, and she hated to step on them, but the guards left her no choice. As she walked across them, the letters shifted and writhed alarmingly under her bare feet. Stopping in front of the goblin King, she glanced back to find that the letters had already blown away.

The crowd roared with approval at whatever had happened, and Marak walked toward the first table. Her guards started off after him, Kate between them. She couldn't help looking around for something she could recognize—a vicar, flowers, church steps. I don't even have a bouquet, she noted gloomily. I'll have to press a shackle in my diary.

The first stone table was ringed by torches in stands. It was long and narrow, and it was just tall enough to be convenient to someone standing by it. The table held a variety of items, but the most star-tling was a set of three small golden knives. These captured Kate's complete attention. Kate's guards stopped in front of the table, and Marak walked around to face her across it. The guards fitted her wrist bracelets into two metal brackets, then detached the chains and stepped back, leaving her anchored, palms up, to the table with the knives.

Kate could hear the crowd shifting and murmuring. She couldn't resist a pleading glance at Marak even though she knew he wasn't supposed to speak to her, but the goblin King didn't make any reassuring gestures. First he took a small paintbrush and wrote some symbol on her forehead in gold paint. The searing pain of the acidic paint took her by surprise. Then he uncurled her hands and stretched them out carefully so that the palms were taut, tracing with his thumbs the lines across her hands. When he turned away, Kate found that she was unable to move her hands at all. Marak picked up two knives from the table, unmatched eyes stern with concentration as he studied his marks. Kate felt that he had never looked so inhu-man before, so completely removed from the world she understood. I will not believe that this is really happening, she thought desperately, and she screwed her eyes shut as he raised the knives.

It was over with a swiftness that left her time for nothing louder than a gasp. She opened her eyes to see two long red slashes stretch-ing from the bends of her wrists down to the center of each palm. Marak quickly dropped the knives and pulled her hands free from the brackets, holding them so that the blood spattered into an empty bowl. Kate gave another gasp as the stinging pain of the wounds reached her. What a hideous, heathen, barbaric thing to do! Satis-fied, apparently, with the amount of blood he had collected, Marak next plunged her hands into a bowl of water. It wasn't water. Kate's vision went black as the wounds seared like fire, but when he lifted her hands out, the bleeding had stopped. He wrapped a cloth around each hand and put them back into the brackets again. She wasn't entirely sorry to have some sort of stable support because she was shaking all over.

As Kate's vision cleared, she saw with horror that the goblin King was reaching for the last knife, but this time he bared his own pale arm, wrist up, and held it over the bloody bowl. She felt a dis-tinct satisfaction as he made his cut, but then she had a further shock.

The goblin's blood was a dark, clear brown. Kate watched it drip into the bowl, brown pool on red pool, feeling a little sick.

The goblin King reached for a small plate of powder and threw some into the bowl. Kate saw the blood inside blend and swirl. A thick red vapor began to fill the bowl, climbing over the sides and rolling across the table. She pulled back in disgust. Marak stepped closer to the bowl, watching intently. A silvery mist was forming over the top of the red vapor. It sparkled in the torchlight as it rose into a swirling cloud several feet high. Kate thought in surprise that it was pretty. Marak looked completely stunned, and the huge crowd of goblins erupted into bedlam. Startled and anxious, Kate glanced at Marak for guidance and found him staring as if he were seeing her for the first time.

As the strange cloud faded away, Kate saw that the revolting blood was gone from the bowl. In its place sparkled a silvery pink cream as thick as cake frosting. Marak dipped his finger into the glit‐ tering cream and rubbed it along the slashes on Kate's hands. The pain faded out as he did so, and the puckered edges of the wounds flattened, but an iridescent silvery pink line stayed in each palm. As the crowd hushed, he studied the lines. Turning to the throng, he called out something in goblin, whereupon they cheered and stomped again.

Kate's guards fastened their chains to her and set off for the next table. By it lay a cushion between two brackets on tall rods. Marak helped her to kneel on the cushion and adjusted the brackets beside her. These came up and cradled her elbows, locking over the bend in the arm. Then the goblin crossed to the table a few feet away. It also held a variety of small instruments. These items didn't worry Kate, although perhaps they should have. She was staring instead at the largest thing on the table, a golden sword about five feet long. It was elaborately engraved, but she could make out nothing except faint scratches in the gold. The hilt was a simple continuation of the metal of the blade; it had no guard to give it a sword's familiar crosslike shape. Kate stared at it, deeply frightened. Maybe this had all been some horrible ruse. Maybe the goblin King had intended all along to kill her in some hideous sacrifice.

Leaning down, Marak kindled a magical flame in the middle of a large golden plate. Then he came toward her with small scissors and a tiny bowl. He pulled one of her hands out straight and cut off several fingernails into the bowl, then added several of his own and fed them all to the fire. He sheared off the ridiculous lock of hair that the women had left loose on Kate's neck, then one of his own pale horse tail locks, and burned them as well.

Marak picked up a large needle and a small golden plate. Kate recognized danger. She clenched her fists so tightly that he had to set the plate down and use both hands to free a finger and jab the needle into it. He forced several drops of blood onto the plate. On one knee by the table, he next stabbed his own finger. Kate watched in pan-icked revulsion. She didn't know how much more bloodshed she could take.

Very intent now, the goblin King bent close to the little fire, hold-ing the plate upside down over the flames so that they could lick off the drops of blood. The fire vanished, leaving a small mound of sil-ver ash behind. Carefully and deliberately, he took these ashes on his finger and rubbed them all over the blade of the long sword. The entire crowd was still now. Kate held her breath.

From the sword came a musical tone, as if it had been struck against the table. Marak picked up the weapon and walked toward her, his expression distant and impassive. He's going to kill me, Kate thought desperately. The goblin King seized the hilt in both hands and whirled the sword over his head. Then he brought it down upon her in a whistling arc.

Eyes tightly shut, Kate felt the cold metal touch her hair, slide down her back and loop around her shoulder. She waited in breath-less suspense for whatever people feel when their heads are split open. But something wasn't right. She opened her eyes cautiously. A long golden snake glided around her neck and reared up in front of her face. Swaying back and forth, it considered her terrified features carefully, a slender golden tongue flicking from its long, curving jaws. Kate couldn't move a muscle. She couldn't even blink. The snake turned away from her dismissively and looped its length three times around her upper right arm, tail almost by her elbow, before arranging the rest of itself about her neck in a loose spiral. Petrified at no longer being able to see her enemy, Kate bent her head slowly and peered down at her arm. As she watched, the tight coils collapsed and became flat with her skin, just as if an artist had painted a golden snake on her.

Kate screamed, twisting in her brackets to try to reach the flat-tened snake. But no one could hear her. The goblins were screaming themselves, chanting, cheering, and yowling at the top of their lungs. The King's Wife ceremony was over.

Chapter
Ten

There was a confusion of intense noise and movement. Kate could hear her own voice screaming and see Marak's face before hers. Her scream died down to a whimper as she looked around for the torches, the table, the crowd. She was sitting on a couch in a small room, and Marak was by her, clamping her hands in a strong grip. She caught sight of the shining gold coils on her bare arm and began to struggle again, but when she called out for help, all that emerged was a long wail.

"Drink this," said Marak, and a cup rim was in her open mouth. She choked, and her wail resolved itself into words.

"Get it off! Get it off! It's inside my skin!" she cried. Marak held her wrists with one hand as he put the cup down.

"Kate, for pity's sake," he said matter-of-factly, "it's not in your skin, and neither of us can possibly get it off. It isn't even a snake. It's a powerful magic charm that protects you. Right now it's in a resting form, and you can only see it. You can't feel it at all, so don't rip yourself up trying to scratch it off."

Kate craned her neck to see as much of the flat snake as possible, and she stopped trying to struggle. "But I want it off," she insisted desperately.

"Well, you'll just have to put up with it, because it's there until one of us dies, and I'm not prepared to resort to that option just for a whim. That's the King's Wife Charm, the most powerful piece of magic we goblins have. It comes from the days of the First Fathers, from the very first King. You're better protected by that charm than I am by my magic. If anything were to attack you, it would give a paralyzing bite far faster than a real snake could, and the creature would stay paralyzed until I delivered judgment on whether it should live or die. It safeguards you from accident and keeps you from doing anything dangerous to yourself. If it has to, it will bite you, too, and then come report to the King that you've done something foolish."

Marak released her hands, watching her closely. Kate rubbed her fingers experimentally over the coils on her arm, but she couldn't tell that anything was there.

"I can't believe that you've done this," she said furiously. "I've never been through anything so barbaric in my life. And you people call that farce a wedding!"

"I told you the ceremony was unpleasant," said the goblin with a shrug. "Unpleasant, but very, very important. Kate, did you know that you're an elf?"

Kate stared blankly at him. "A what?" she demanded.

"No, you didn't," he affirmed. "I thought not. It must have been that adopted girl who played with my mother, since my mother was entirely human, and after that, the family moved away from the elf lands. You're an elf-human cross, but you're quite powerfully elf, much more so than your sister. I couldn't be more pleased. With their innate magic, elves make the best King's Wives. Our son will be a stronger King because of it. We thought that all the elves were dead, and the scholars suspected that the goblins wouldn't survive it."

Kate felt very offended. "I am not an elf," she insisted. "I'm an Englishwoman!"

The goblin King chuckled, surveying her fondly. "Then perhaps you can tell me what in your English heritage taught you to watch out for goblins," he suggested. "You hadn't even heard of them, but you knew not to let me touch you, much less put you on a horse. And what about your breaking out of my sleep spells? Do you have any idea how frustrating that was for me? That's why you ran to the truce circle, too, and why you fought off the Persuasion Spell as well as you did. You even look like an elf, come to think of it. I had enough hints; I should have realized it. All my training told me you were working magic on the ride home."

"You can't be sure of that," Kate said severely. "You're just guessing."

"Of course I'm sure," he replied. "I tested your blood against mine. That test shows all the races shared by the King and Wife. You remember the red cloud?" She nodded. "Our shared human blood. And the larger silver cloud?" She nodded again. "Our shared elf blood. Much stronger than the human blood, if you remember. I imagine that adopted girl was actually half human, and that's how she wound up an orphan. The birth would have killed her elf mother, and her human father likely didn't know what to do with her. We'll have to be careful with you, too," he mused. "Childbirth will be quite a problem. Elf women don't get through it easily."

Kate didn't have any idea how to answer him, but she wasn't swayed in her opinion. It was bad enough marrying a mythological beast. She wasn't about to become one herself. "I am *not* an elf," she stated again.

Marak laughed. "You don't really believe in elves, do you? And you don't believe in my nice magic, either. You think I did all that complicated work out there just to show you how barbaric I am. That reminds me," he added, "I wanted to take another look at your palms." He lifted her hands in the dim light, studying the silvery lines.

Kate was overcome with righteous indignation. "How could you do such a thing!" she demanded with a shudder.

"It isn't easy, two knives at once," the goblin King admitted absently. "But fortunately, the magic guides the blades." She glared at him, but he remained oblivious, probably because he wanted to. He turned her palms to and fro, looking closely at them. "You see, mine has a skip in it," he murmured. He glanced up to meet another blank look.

"The lines," he explained patiently, "indicate something of the future lives of King and Wife. Here's yours," he said, showing her the left hand. "A nice long life. And here's mine," he added, holding up her right hand. "Another nice long line, but right here toward the top, there's a skip. I wonder what it means," he mused, frowning at it. "I think it must mean some long illness or absence. That's unusual. Goblins don't generally fall ill, and I'm not likely to leave."

"Maybe the knife just slipped," Kate suggested, and received an indignant glare in her turn. Embarrassed, she studied her maimed hands. "I thought you said you wouldn't hurt me," she remembered resentfully. "You cut me open, you stabbed me, you burned me—"

"I didn't burn you," he contradicted in surprise.

"You did! That paint," she declared, and she pointed to her fore-head. "It still hurts."

Puzzled, Marak took her face between his hands and studied the golden symbol. He pulled one of the wispy pieces from her skirt, dipped it into a goblet of water, and wiped the paint off.

"Ouch!" cried Kate. "You're hurting me!"

"No, you're hurting yourself," he murmured. "A bright red burn in the shape of the King's Wife symbol. You're fighting the Door Spell. This is the spell that tells my iron doors not to let you out. It's unbreakable," he added sympathetically, laying his six-fingered hand on the letter, his fingers icy against the burning pain. "You might as well come to terms with it, Kate. You're locked in."

Kate closed her eyes under the soothing magical touch and struggled to hold back her tears. She couldn't be locked in here where the moon and stars never shone and where monsters took knives to perfectly civilized young women. "I'm not fighting anything," she muttered. "Humans can't work magic."

"They can't, but you are," answered Marak, studying the letter again. "You're devoting a lot of magic to this fight, probably all the magic you have. To think that I laughed when you said you wouldn't come to my kingdom. It's no joke to an elf to go underground. You were tired and upset enough to begin with, and now you're caught up in a useless battle against an unbreakable spell. You need rest, Kate. I promised that you could sleep for days after the ceremony, and you probably should. Would you like to sleep here or in our bedroom? The King's Wife usually spends her first night in this room."

Kate looked around the little room, shivering. Her first night locked away from the stars. Her first night with a goblin for a husband. The idea of a first night, with many nights to follow it, sounded so horribly permanent. She pressed her hand to her forehead as the burning letter darkened again. "I'm not sleepy," she said firmly, standing up and roaming the small space unhappily.

Marak watched her in exasperated amusement. "I should have given you the Stamp of Truth," he pointed out. "Are you just going to wander my palace like a ghost until you fall down unconscious?" The anxious look in her eyes as she turned his way answered his question. "All right then," he sighed. "Come with me. Since you're not sleepy, I'll take you to see something my mother always liked to see."

This time they walked up staircase after staircase. Kate was desperately tired. I promised to do this, she reminded herself sternly; I'm married, and I live here now. But she just couldn't bring herself to face the thought.

They came up a wide staircase, the steps gleaming like gigantic gold bricks. They struck Kate as rather gaudy. The wide hallway that opened out at the top had a gold floor to match them, and the walls were composed of small, precise geometrical inlays of stone that repeated continually up their surfaces. They, too, were rather gaudy, like something in the palace of an Oriental despot. Great square windows lined one side of the hallway, but only one broad set of doors faced them. Kate could see from her vantage at the top of the stairs that guards stood on either side of the doors.

"This is our floor," said the goblin King, "the royal rooms. Would you like to see them?" he asked, evaluating her thoughtfully. Kate hastily shook her head, thinking with a homesick rush of her little wooden-floored room at the Lodge, her shoes still in a row under the bed. "No, I didn't think you would," he laughed, "since you're not sleepy." At the word, Kate felt such a wave of exhaustion come over her that she thought she would drop onto the floor. "I brought you up here to see something else, anyway," he added more kindly. "Through here."

Marak turned toward the window to their right and led her out onto a shallow balcony. Kate felt dizzy at the view. They were high above the broad, bowl-shaped valley. Tiny lights twinkled across it, seemingly for miles. Above the valley was a velvety blackness. No, not a blackness, a dark purple. Kate had a sense of lofty space as she stared up into the purple heights.

Marak waved her to a couch between two of the windows. Then he stepped away for a moment, and the light from the windows went out. Kate leaned back against the couch, and Marak sat down beside her.

"How can a cave this big fit under the Hill?" she asked curiously, turning toward him. She couldn't really see him in the gloom.

"It doesn't," he answered, looking down at the white face and heavy-lidded blue eyes, which he could see perfectly. "You're looking up through the lake. I told you the first time we met that it was hollow."

Kate stared up at it, aghast. Then she looked down at the twinkling lights in the valley. They looked so pleasant and cozy, blinking away under vast tons of suspended water.

"But what holds the water up?" she gasped.

"Magic, of course. Do you know anything else that could do it? This isn't our first home, but it's an ancient one. The elves came to this region millennia ago, and we goblins followed the elves. My palace looks like a building, but it's more of a subtracting. Originally it was a solid wall of rock between the two parts of my kingdom. Above and behind us, the wall continues, becoming the shore of the lake at the foot of the Hill. Farther up in that wall is the window that forms my water mirror. The same force that keeps the water from pouring into that cavern keeps all the rest of the water from pouring down onto the valley."

Kate gazed up at the water sky. It seemed to her that it was not so dark a purple as before. She thought sleepily about the strange world she belonged to now. Palaces, hollow lakes, elves and goblins. The twinkling lights spun and blurred in her drowsy vision. Marak folded his arms and patiently waited for her to fall asleep. He could have enchanted her in an instant, but he scorned the thought of inflicting unnecessary magic on her now that she was his wife.

"Where did the elves come from?" she asked softly.

"From the First Fathers, like the goblins," Marak replied. "The First Fathers had no bodies and no young, but they wanted to make a race of their own. They probably intended to found one race, but they couldn't agree. The First Fathers of the elves wanted to take only what was beautiful to make their children, but the First Fathers of the goblins wanted strength. Our Fathers thought that if a creature had a powerful eye or a claw, then it should be used, but the Fathers of the elves couldn't endure such irregularity. The elves must be beautiful," he remarked, studying the sleepy face beside him, "even if they can't defend themselves."

"What's that?" Kate murmured. The purple darkness above her had lightened to violet. Now a dark silver circle began to shimmer in the sky. Kate sat up to look at it. It seemed to wobble and shake about, high above her. As she watched, it brightened to a luminous opacity.

"It's the sunrise from my kingdom," Marak told her. "My mother liked to watch it, so I thought you might enjoy it, too."

The violet became cobalt. Gradually, the silver circle faded, and the color changed and became more transparent. It formed a sky she never could have imagined, a sky of the darkest, clearest blue, and everything below it was bathed in a shifting twilight. She looked down at her lap. Under the light, her red skirt was dark purple, and her hands, a bluish gray. They seemed to be detached from her, as if they belonged to someone else.

Kate thought longingly of that sunrise on the shore of the lake, of the pink and gold clouds and the birds singing. The same sun, the same lake, but now she was underneath the water. Her heart squeezed painfully in her chest. I promised to do this, she thought, closing her eyes. I live here now. Her head rolled back on the couch as Marak watched her closely.

"When I became King," he said quietly, "the last known elf had already been dead for fifty years. Now I have several strong elf crosses in my kingdom. I wonder if the elvish race is reviving."

Kate didn't hear him. She was fast asleep, her young face still worried and anxious. Marak studied her for a long minute, touching the angry burn on her forehead. Then he picked her up carefully and took her in to bed.

The next evening, Kate went out in public for the first time since the ceremony. Sitting by the King in the banquet hall, she surreptitiously watched all the goblins openly watching her. Their bizarre shapes and sizes took away what little appetite she had. Emily sat beside her, terribly impressed with her sister's new appearance. Kate was wearing a loose gown of blue silk that pleased her much more than the awful wedding dress, but she felt unhappily that it did no good to try to look nice. Everyone just stared at the coils of golden snake visible above the neckline. All the unwanted scrutiny made Kate nervous.

Marak warned Emily not to make any threatening moves toward her sister. "Otherwise, the snake will paralyze you, and then I'll have to deliver judgment on whether you live or die," he teased. Emily thought that she would love to have such a snake. She had hoped for her own, but Marak told her that only Kate got one.

Kate watched the goblin King pile up food on her plate. Some of it was vaguely recognizable, like the flat bread. Some of it looked very unfamiliar, like the skewered chunks of meat.

"Where are the forks?" she asked, looking around.

"Forks are absurd," he scoffed. "They insult your food. They make it think you're killing it twice."

"But I can't eat without a fork!" Kate exclaimed, distressed.

"Really!" Marak laughed. "I'll bet that you can. I'd be very surprised if you gave up eating at such a young age." He ate heartily and surprisingly neatly with his hands, using the bread as an edible utensil. Kate nibbled at the bread and pushed things around experimentally with it. Everything tasted unusual, and most of the food had a rather strong flavor.

"What kind of meat is this?" she asked cautiously. Marak grinned, understanding her concern.

"Goblins eat sheep for the most part," he told her, "and we never eat a female animal. In part because our own females so often can't have children, the beast goblins cross out to all kinds of different species. We view any female as a mother, a sacred life."

"That reminds me," interrupted Emily. "When are you going to have your baby, Kate? Soon?" Her sister turned bright pink, embarrassed to discuss such a topic in public. Marak raised an amused eyebrow at his young wife's distress.

"It could be soon," he answered for her, "but that's not very likely. It's not so easy for goblins to have children. Married couples spend a lot of time trying and hoping, and eventually things work out. That's the way it is for the Kings, too. My parents were married for ten years before I was born, and I've read of fifteen or even twenty years of marriage before the Heir is born."

"Twenty years!" said Emily in horror. "I can't wait that long."

Marak picked up Kate's right hand and rubbed his thumb over the skip in the knife wound. "Neither can I," he said thoughtfully.

Marak brought up the subject again when he and Kate were alone. She was sitting on the tall stool in his workroom, watching him make salve. "Humans have the easy life," he told her, grinding herbs. "Many humans can have a child a year. But goblins and elves don't reproduce nearly that easily, and the King has the hardest time of all. In order to pass his magic on to his son, he has to find a wife from outside his own race, and it's not enough just to marry her. He has to become interested in her and look for traits in her to admire. The way the King thinks about his wife affects the way the Heir is formed, so if he has a strong wife and he cares about her, his son will be a better King. It's the goal of every King to have a son greater than he is. Often the marriages don't work out that well, but that's the idea."

Kate thought about this while he fetched and measured ingredients. It struck her as rather one-sided. "What about the way the wife thinks?" she demanded indignantly. "Don't I contribute something to all this?"

"Of course," answered Marak, much to her surprise. "The best Kings are the sons of wives who care about their new people. There are traits about the son that will surprise the father, but they're things the mother appreciated—about herself, her husband, or goblins in general. And the better the wife settles in, the sooner the Heir is born, so you do have a big part in the process."

"Did your mother settle in well?" asked Kate.

"Oh, yes." He laughed. "Not that she wasn't homesick at first, like you, but soon she was marching all over the kingdom, looking for adventure. She turned the place upside down. She talked the bird goblins into trying to take her up over the valley in baskets and persuaded the tall goblins, the ones who got you lost, to carry her for rides. More goblins were bitten for endangering the King's Wife in my mother's first ten years than in the whole previous century. Half the time my father didn't know where she was. She settled in, but she didn't settle down."

Kate felt instinctively that she was unlikely to be this sort of King's Wife. "If the things I appreciate show up in my son," she asked, "why would I cry when I see him?"

"Because your husband is a goblin," explained Marak, stirring the salve, "and your son will be a goblin, too. In spite of the constant crossing out, the King is the most goblin of his entire race. And goblin means asymmetrical—you'd say, deformed—and full of unusual animal traits. The Kings are known by their strong traits: Marak Bearpelt, Marak Batwing, Marak Birdclaw. The beast goblins bring the traits into the goblin race as they cross out to different animal species. Once a trait comes in, it can show up anywhere. That's how a goblin from the high families, who never marry animals, can have the fangs of a leopard or the wings of a bird. And there are even traits that exist in no species alive, just from all the odd magic at work.

"Because of all the possibilities, there's no way to predict what the magic will do. After all, it's not a conscious process. Something you admire may be exactly what causes your son to have what you would call a terrible deformity. My father loved my mother's eyes, and my mother loved my father's eyes." Marak grinned at her, his unmatched eyes sparkling. "So I have one of each."

Three months passed. Kate struggled to come to terms with her new life. She had agreed to her marriage, but she hadn't realized just how long life could be. She had dealt bravely with loss before, but the loss of her entire world was beyond anything she had imagined.

The goblin King was very aware of her misery; indeed, he had expected it, and he did what he could to try to help her. When she woke up screaming from horrible nightmares, he took the nightmares away, and when she lay awake, restless and anxious, he sent her to sleep with magic. When she cried, he held her patiently, which was the best thing that a great magician could do for a crying wife. Kate found to her relief that she had been right: being kissed by an ugly goblin was not really so bad; in fact, it was one of the few things about her new life that she began to enjoy. The other was sleeping. She would have slept all the time if she could have. The nights seemed very short, but the days were terribly long.

Kate woke out of a dream about Hallow Hill one morning and couldn't recall where she was. "Good morning," said Marak, and her view resolved itself into the stone ceiling of their bedroom. Disappointment overwhelmed her, and she closed her eyes tightly. A lump rose in her throat.

"Or maybe not a good morning." He reached out for her. She buried her face in his arms, hiding from another long day under the earth. "Come on, time to get up," said her husband. "I have court this morning."

Kate shook her head, her arms around his neck as he started to turn away. "You said the King's Wife is more important," she whispered.

Marak studied her pale, sad face. "Much more important," he said, and he bent to kiss her. "All right. We don't have to get up just yet."

Later that morning he came into her dressing room, ready for court, and found her still sitting before her mirror in her robe. In her old life, she had never wasted time getting ready. Now there didn't seem to be any point in hurrying. He took the brush from her and began working on her hair. Kate watched him in the mirror.

"I should put my hair up," she announced. "That's what married women do."

"Put up your hair!" exclaimed Marak. "Why not just cut it off! That hair," he added pensively, "was the first thing I noticed about you when I saw you walking away from the truce circle."

Kate stiffened, remembering those horrible nights when she had known someone was watching her. In fact, Marak had often been standing right beside her in the shadows, amused at her pathetic attempts to see in the dark.

"That's just your elf blood talking," she said spitefully, "noticing a pretty thing like hair! A goblin King should have been looking for strong traits in a wife."

"Oh, your hair is very strong," he laughed. "I think it's magical. I'm sure when our son is born, he'll have your hair." And he began brushing again, perfectly serene. Kate scowled into the mirror.

"How are people supposed to know I'm married if I wear my hair down like a girl?" she asked indignantly.

"By looking at this?" he suggested, pointing at the snake around her neck. Misery flooded Kate as she thought about the snake and all it represented. But I did this for Emily, she reminded herself, and she loves living with the goblin children. Maybe our guardian would have killed her by now.

Emily was a page, one of about a hundred likely children from the high families. They lived on the pages' floor, had lessons from a variety of masters, and took turns serving at court. In spite of her elf blood, she was proving hopeless at magic. As the two nongoblin children among the pages, she and Seylin were inseparable. Emily admired Seylin tremendously, and he had never before been admired. He still divided his time pretty evenly between being a cat and being a boy, in part because Emily was more impressed by his exploits when he performed them as a cat.

A little later, Kate sat in the banquet hall, ignoring her breakfast. I'm surrounded by monsters, she thought bleakly. Monsters everywhere.

"Kate," said the goblin King, "do you know why today's harder than yesterday?"

"What do you mean?" she asked listlessly.

"You know perfectly well what I mean," he replied, unperturbed. "The last couple of weeks haven't been so bad. Today's very bad, and I'm wondering if you know why."

Kate's homesickness welled up inside her until it hurt like a physical pain. "Em and I had done chores all day," she whispered, "lessons, needlepoint, housecleaning. And we were finally finished. We were going up to the tree circle to watch the stars come out. We had just walked to the door, and that's when I woke up."

The King drank his tea with a thoughtful expression. "You haven't had nightmares in a few weeks," he mused, "but it would probably be a good idea to take away your dreams again. They aren't helping."

"No, it's all right," said Kate, feeling ashamed of her childishness. "I just got up on the wrong side of the bed."

Marak laughed. "Sides of bed aren't your problem, Kate. Poor little elf. It's sad, really. The very things that make you a perfect King's Wife make it harder for you to be happy."

"I'm not an elf," said Kate softly.

"When you tell me what you miss," Marak observed, "you always tell me elf things: stars, flowers, walks in the forest. My mother was a human, and the things she missed were human things: her father, her horse, Christmas dinner with the family."

"Did she tell you that?" asked Kate, interested in something at last. Marak noticed it and put down his teacup.

"No," he answered. "I read Father's notes about her after he died."

"Why would your father write about your mother?" Kate wanted to know.

"All the Kings do. They keep their wives' histories in the King's Wife Chronicles. I think it's forty-seven volumes now." Kate was intrigued. He studied her thoughtfully. "Would you like to see them?" he proposed, and she nodded. "Then do me a favor. Come with me to court this morning, and I'll read you some entries this afternoon."

Kate looked away. She knew he only wanted to distract her. He usually found some excuse for keeping her nearby on very bad days. Part of her was grateful for this, but another part was resentful. She didn't really want to feel better. But she knew it was the best thing, and besides, she was curious about the chronicles.

"All right," she said with a shrug.

She went to court with him and sat on his throne, which he never used. The crowd of sumptuously dressed goblins cheered her entrance, as they always did, and that perked her up a little. This morning Marak was working with the dwarves on building plans. Dwarves liked to build constantly in addition to their mining, and one of the hardest tasks of any goblin King was finding new projects for them without wrecking the beauty that previous generations had produced. Marak had them building a series of terraces and balcony gardens up the almost sheer sides of the lake valley in order to increase the goblins' arable land. This offended the dwarves' sense of aesthetics. They did it, but they insisted that all the ramps and stairs connecting the balconies be decorated with elaborate traceries of wrought iron.

Court proceedings took place in goblin, but Marak stopped what he was doing every now and then to tell Kate what was going on. She looked at the work drawings with him and used her small stock of goblin speech on the dwarves standing nearby. Dwarves were terribly dignified, and Kate's gentle manner had already won them over. Rings and bracelets covered her small hands, and they were forever bringing her more. Some of the jewelry was magical. Her favorite bracelet was a triple rope of diamonds that sparkled with a clear light whenever she was in the dark. But she found it tiresome to wear so much jewelry. She had never had a taste for it.

That afternoon they went to Marak's library. Kate already knew it well. Here were the records from all the previous reigns since the founding of the kingdom under the Hill. Marak showed her the King's Wife Chronicles. Fascinated, she paged through the old leatherbound volumes full of different handwriting styles as one King after another took up the tale. She couldn't read them because they were in goblin, but Marak read a few entries to her. Then he worked on some chronicling of his own as she continued to look through the old books. While scholars did a certain amount of the record keeping, the Kings recorded much of their reigns themselves.

Kate became interested in one particular story that she found. The handwriting was easy to read, and she found several script characters that she knew, including the King's Wife Charm, repeated quite frequently. So far, the charm had been nothing but a painted snake to her, and she wondered what it could have done.

"Marak," she said, coming over to him, "tell me about this one." The goblin King glanced up from his own page to study the story for a minute. Then he looked at her with a shrewd smile and shook his head.

"Let's read it tomorrow," he proposed cheerfully.

Kate's bad mood instantly returned. "You're keeping something from me," she accused.

"I certainly am," he agreed. "That story. Today's not the day for it."

Kate sat down across from him. "You're treating me like a child," she protested. "I went with you to court, and you promised to read these in return. I hate being read to like a child, and now you're hiding some secret as if I really am one. This is a story about a King's Wife, and I'm a King's Wife. I ought to know what it says."

The goblin King studied her for a minute. "All right," he said calmly, putting aside his own work, "but you're not happy about being a King's Wife right now, and this story isn't going to help. This is about the elf wife of a King who was four feet tall and dark green. She lived for only three years, and she tried to kill herself six different ways. The charm always saved her. One time she threw herself off our balcony into the lake valley, and the snake wound itself around a hook in the palace wall as they fell by."

Kate stared at him in horror. That poor woman, trapped just like she was. "Did she finally succeed?" she whispered.

Marak scanned the pages. "No," he said. "She died when the Heir was born. There were complications. He weighed twenty pounds."

Kate shivered, the hair rising on the back of her neck. Those hideous, deformed babies. Marak continued to read. "This is nice," he added. "He's written a tribute to her determination and resource-fulness."

Kate jumped to her feet. "You people are just ghastly!" she cried. The goblin King shook his striped hair out of his face and looked up at her with a smile.

"Which ones of us?" he asked.

"All of you! You wife stealers!"

"I didn't steal you," replied Marak complacently.

"But you're just like that other King!"

Marak laughed as he shut the book. "No," he retorted. "I'm not green."

Kate was beside herself. "You know what I mean!" she shouted. "You're one of them! The descendant of all those wife-stealing Kings!"

He thought about that as she marched from the room. "I'm the descendant of all those wives, too," he mused, but Kate had already slammed the door.

She roamed the stone gardens alone that evening, unable to calm down. When she went looking for her sister, she found that Emily had left with Seylin. Mindful of their elf blood, Marak let them go outside at night, provided they stayed leashed together. He trusted Seylin to come home, but he wasn't so sure about Emily. The dis-traught Kate took her sister's absence as a personal insult. How dare she come and go while Kate was trapped down here! Feeling betrayed, she headed for the front door.

"Hello, King's Wife," boomed the door politely but a little unhappily. It knew what these visits meant.

"Hello, door," said Kate decisively. "Please open up and let me through."

"But you're the King's Wife," protested the door.

"Yes, I know that," Kate said. "Please open up."

"But you have the symbol on you," the door added.

"I know that, too." Kate could feel it. The symbol was starting to smart.

"I can't open for the King's Wife," explained the door ponderously.

"Not even if I was on the outside?" Kate asked in sudden inspiration.

"But you're not," the door cautiously answered.

"But I could be," Kate insisted.

"How?" asked the door. And this Kate couldn't answer. She put her hand to her forehead as the letter began to throb.

"Let's say, just for the sake of argument, that I was on the outside," she suggested.

"What does that mean?" the door wanted to know.

"It means that I say something, and then we argue about it," explained Kate. "Assuming I'm on the outside, would you open then?"

"But you're not," said the door triumphantly.

"But I'm saying it for the sake of argument!" shouted the frustrated Kate.

"I'm arguing," said the door.

Marak came up then and put his arms around his harried wife, pulling her hand away from her forehead and replacing it with his own. Under his soothing magical touch, the pain slowly began to ebb.

"Do you know what's wrong, Kate?" he asked, holding her. "The same thing that was wrong last month. There's a full moon rising outside, and it's dancing night for the elves. You've known it all day, and it's making you miserable."

Kate started to protest that she wasn't an elf, but the longing for that full moon overwhelmed her. She thought of it rising above the forest, riding up the vast sky, silvering everything it touched with its beautiful light. The goblin King felt her droop in his arms, exhausted and discouraged.

"Poor little elf, locked up underground," he said kindly. "Come on, let's go to bed."

＜∼

Kate lay in the darkness, trying not to cry. He's right, she thought unhappily. He didn't steal me. "Marak?" she said softly, turning toward him. He laid his cheek against her hair.

"What is it?" he asked quietly.

"Do you write about me?" she asked. He nodded. "What kinds of things do you write?"

"The same sorts of things as the other Kings," he said. "What you love about your new life, what you hate."

"What do I love?" she wondered.

"It hasn't been very long," he answered, "but I think you love coming with me to my workroom."

Kate thought about that. As the realm's greatest magician, the goblin King worked magic all the time, whether he was healing illness, supporting building projects, or making sure the correct weather occurred. Sitting on her high stool, Kate watched him preparing and mixing things, and he showed her odd bits of magic as he studied and practiced. She enjoyed the magic; it was one of the things she was starting to appreciate about her unusual husband. The workroom was like a refuge to her. It was almost the only place in the entire kingdom where no one was watching her.

"I do love the workroom," she said softly. "What do I hate about my new life?"

"Being locked in," he answered. "Being stared at, being teased."

"If you know I hate being teased," she asked, "why do you always do it?"

"Because that's one of the things about your new life that *I* love," he chuckled. That made her smile. "And I write about the mile-stones that the Kings look for their wives to pass. The first time you spoke to me—that was when you met me. The first time you called me by name—that was the day after you came here. The first time you smiled at me—that was a week after you came here, but the first time you smiled because you were really glad to see me—that was only a month ago. The first time you were happy when you woke up in the morning, full of plans you wanted to accomplish . . ." He fell silent.

"When was that?" Kate wanted to know.

"That one hasn't happened yet," he admitted. "Maybe tomorrow."

Kate shifted in his arms and laid her head against his chest. "Maybe so," she murmured, closing her eyes.

PART III

Darkness

Chapter
Eleven

One day, a year and a half after her marriage, Kate was sitting with the older pages and hearing their English lesson. Marak had asked her early on to help the pages improve their English because the most human-looking goblins, posing as gypsies, made frequent trading journeys outside the kingdom to sell watches and jewelry. This allowed them to buy silks, laces, and other luxury items, including the excellent tea that Marak enjoyed.

Kate's father, overseeing her education, had instilled in her a deep love of literature. Since the older pages already had an excellent grasp of English, she had decided to have them read some of that literature with her. Today one after another was reading out loud from Shakespeare's *Romeo and Juliet,* their grotesque faces solemn over the plight of the star-crossed lovers.

She looked up to see a member of the King's Guard at the door, and she dismissed the pages. The guard's round eyes were large with concern, and he was clacking his beak in agitation. "Hulk is missing," he told her, "and the King needs your help at the water mirror."

Kate considered his news as they hurried along. The feathered ape was so large that she couldn't imagine anything harming him. Surely it wouldn't turn out to be serious. She entered the big cavern to find Marak, his lieutenants, and a number of the Guard already there.

"I need to find Hulk with the water mirror, Kate," the King said, "but it's too bright for me to see now that the sun is up. We need you to look with your daylight eyes and tell us something about where he is." Then he turned to the lapping sheet of water and held out his hand. The room blazed with light, and the goblins shielded their eyes. Kate squinted at the unaccustomed brightness, her own eyes now more used to the twilight than the sun, but she could see more than they could.

"It looks like it might be a closed wagon or carriage," she said finally. "I think those are horses at the front. It's moving, and the land around it is flat. I think there's water by the road. A big river, maybe. Not a lake. It's very blurry." She looked away as the mirror went dark again, her eyes watering.

"It's blurry because it's far away," said Marak. "It's well past the edges of my land. When I looked for Hulk earlier, I couldn't see him at all because something was blocking or hiding him. Someone has kidnapped him, probably with a trap because Hulk's too big to take by force. I suspect that magic was used to hide him, and the trap that caught him must have had some magic built into it as well. And now he's being moved in daylight when we can't counterattack. Who has him and why? Has anyone new been on the land?"

"No one has been in the Hill area," said Sayada, who with Thaydar was one of the two lieutenants. Sayada, although man shaped, had hands that looked like bird talons. He had no nose at all, just two holes in his face. "No one has come or gone from the estate grounds in the last several days. It may be that the intruder stayed in the Hollow Lake village. We don't monitor the traffic past the three roads there. Hulk was patrolling the lakefront last night, so he would have been close to the village."

The goblin King thought for a moment. "Bulk," he said, turn-ing to Hulk's brother, "do you think you could fly in the bright light?" The ape, yellow eyes anxious, nodded quickly. Both apes could change to a bird form that could stand the daylight. Seylin was another who could venture outside at any time, his cat eyes suited to either daylight or darkness. "Good," said Marak decisively. Turning to Kate, he asked, "Are you sure there were no hills? That the land was flat?"

"I think so," she answered hesitantly, "but I couldn't see very far. There may have been hills farther away."

"Probably the Liverpool road," suggested Thaydar when Marak shot him an inquiring glance. "But if that's the case, they've been traveling for hours and making good time."

"I was afraid of that," said Marak grimly. "My guess is that they started moving Hulk well before his watch was over. By the time we noticed him missing, he was probably at the edge of our land. Bulk, I can put you on the outskirts of the Hollow Lake village. Follow the Liverpool road as fast as you can to see if you can catch them. If you do catch up, stay with them as a bird. If you don't come back at twilight, we'll follow you. I should be able to track you as we move. Hulk will probably be hidden again after sunset, just as he was on our land. That's difficult magic," he added absently, eyes distant for a moment.

Bulk shimmered as he turned into a large, ugly bird, and Marak stepped to the water mirror.

"Kate, I need your help again," he said, taking her hand. "You'll have to tell me what I'm doing."

The mirror blazed, and Kate squinted into it. "It's the crossroads by the inn," she reported, and then, as it shifted, "we're following the lakeshore road away from the Hill. We've passed all the houses. Now the road is leaving the shore. There's a large oak tree on the right side."

"That's it," said Marak, one hand shielding his eyes. "Bulk, if you can't find them by the time the sun starts westering, come back so you can report at twilight." With a clack of his beak, Bulk took off into the mirror. Kate watched him soar into the sky over the road.

The mirror went dark again, and the goblins turned back to their King. He had done all he could for the moment. Now he pondered his next move, running his fingers through his striped hair as he turned the details over in his mind.

"I need Thaydar and Brindle to go to the inn tonight and find out who's been through. Thaydar, see if you can get Harry Bounce to drink with you back in the stables. He knows all the gossip. And if Hulk was caught in a trap, I would suspect that several were placed and that the enemy may have left the others behind. It would help tremendously if I could see one, and they're a constant danger till they're found. Turn out all the Guard to hunt for traps in a wide sweep of the lakeshore from the village around to the Hill.

"Sayada, we'll need a fast and magical force ready if Bulk doesn't return at twilight. I think it had better be you, me, Katoo, and Dibah. Two horses for each goblin, and light packs. I leave their contents up to you. Plan for a pursuit of four days. Thaydar, if you learn something interesting, follow us. We'll stay with the road, pitch tents at sunrise, and leave markers if we take a turning. Bring the trap with you if you find one.

"All of you spend today sleeping," he concluded, "and if you can't sleep, send word to me. I need you ready for tonight. Thaydar, on your way to your rooms, tell the pages to gather the Scholars in the library."

The sober goblins filed out. Marak continued to stand by the water mirror for another moment. "Do you know, Kate," he said thoughtfully, "the Guard should never come in so close to dawn. We don't even find out someone's missing until the sun's about to rise. It gives us no time to react. We should be doing cross-checks of the guards at regular intervals throughout the night, and they should come in at least an hour earlier. I don't know why I didn't think of it before."

"Has a guard ever been missing before?" asked Kate as they walked toward the library.

"No," said Marak, "that's just it. No member of the King's Guard has been attacked in my reign. We've gotten sloppy now that the elves are gone. Well," he amended, glancing at her, "almost gone." He gave a wry smile. "I think the guards felt they were mainly out on bouquet detail."

The Scholars began filling the library. There were eight goblins, five female and three male. Several of them were very old, but not all were, and none of them showed their years. Goblins didn't usually age. They simply grew up.

"Aside from skirmishes with elves," Marak asked the assembled Scholars, "has a member of the King's Guard ever been kidnapped before?"

There was silence while they considered this.

One Scholar had long fangs, like Thaydar, and was clicking them with a fingernail while he thought. "About two hundred years ago," he said, "a goblin guard changed to wolf form was caged for a local hunt. Does that help?"

"Not really," answered Marak. "We have a member of the Guard kidnapped in his regular goblin form by an enemy who has used magic to hide him and probably used magic to help trap him. Now the enemy is moving him rapidly away from our land in the daylight and across fields. I want to know if anything like it has ever happened before."

"During the day and across fields," one commented thoughtfully. "That rules out any elves we may not know of," and she glanced in Kate's direction. Kate frowned. She didn't like being thought of as an elf.

"Yes, it's not elves," said Marak patiently. The Scholars always rethought things that he had already told them, but he tried not to let it annoy him. He knew they worked better when they didn't feel rushed.

"In my time there were a number of kidnappings," said a very small goblin, almost a gnome. "But none involved magic."

"There was something like it in my time," said another. "That was in the reign of Marak Horsetooth. A sorcerer from Rome who had studied texts from Egypt kidnapped a goblin using magic. The King freed him and turned the sorcerer into a toad. Then he stepped on him."

Kate winced. She had never cared for goblin revenge. She didn't really understand it.

"I'd like to see that text," said Marak. There was another moment of silence.

"I believe I remember something useful," said a quiet goblin. Her skin was a light silver-gray, and she had white hair. Kate liked her because she always spoke so gently. Marak could have told Kate that she was just identifying with another strong elf cross.

"In the old country," continued the elvish goblin, "there were pagan priests who used magic to hunt goblins. That was one factor, along with the elf migration, that led to our leaving the land."

"Hunting," mused Marak. "How? And why?"

"I believe with traps," she answered. "They used the goblin blood to work magic, to lure the demons and buy favors. I'll show you the texts as soon as I find them."

"Blood," echoed Marak pensively. Deeply distressed, Kate thought of Hulk. He always looked so sad and patient, and he never spoke. He had brought her water lilies just last week. Perhaps he had stepped into a trap trying to reach one for her.

"Kate, I need you to help me with ingredients," the goblin King said as they left the library. In the workroom, he walked to his spell books and ran a finger across their spines.

"If Bulk doesn't come back, I have to take whatever I'll need with me. I think I'm facing a human adversary, but that also means a demon adversary, according to my training. The human thinks he controls the demon and has him as a servant. Really, the demon has made promises to the human in exchange for certain payments, and he collects the human's soul upon death.

"My problem is how to fight the two of them," declared Marak. "The demon is quite beyond my abilities. Demons are very power-ful, and they love destruction and pain. They would enjoy making a goblin suffer. But this one wants his sorcerer's soul. If the man dies soon enough, the demon will be satisfied, so I need spells that kill, and kill quickly."

Marak brought several books over to the writing desk and made a list of the desired spells. Kate could read goblin pretty well now, but she didn't look at the list. She didn't want to know what the spells would do.

All that day Kate found, measured, and pounded ingredients. Meanwhile, Marak copied and learned the spells. Late in the after-noon, he mixed the ingredients she had prepared into the potions he needed. Then he finally lay down to rest up for the night ahead. But Bulk came back at sundown. He had flown for so many hours, Marak had to treat his arms with salve, but he hadn't found the wagon that held his brother.

Kate woke the next morning to find Marak already up. The Guard had returned with a trap, and the Scholars were examin-ing it. To Kate, it looked like an ordinary wolf trap with symbols on it, but Marak was very grim. He refused to touch it with his bare hands.

"The writing is Egyptian," he told her. "You'd think we're far enough from the old lands to be safe from their spells, but more and more humans are traveling back and forth these days."

Thaydar reported that a man had come from Liverpool to do some hunting, bringing a closed wagon and two drivers with him. Harry Bounce said the drivers didn't know much about their employer, but he had hired them to drive him in shifts without resting along the way, renting fresh teams of horses to avoid slowing down. He had left very early the previous morning, and everyone agreed that he had been terribly peculiar, but they were sorry he was gone because he had spent a great deal of money. "Liverpool," sighed Marak. "Such a grimy place. It's enough to put you right off humans."

At twilight, the small band of goblins prepared once more to embark, and Kate was with them in the stable room to see them off. Marak gave Thaydar a long list of instructions. Kate realized, listening, that it was a risky thing for a magical kingdom to have its greatest magician leave. Now the group was standing idle and waiting impatiently for Sayada. He had not arrived with the others, and they had sent Seylin after him. They were wasting time, and Kate could see that Marak was becoming angry. His hands were clasped behind his back, something he often did when he wanted to be sure not to work rash magic.

Seylin came racing into the stable in cat form. His black fur was standing out, and his tail was puffed. "Sayada is sick!" he shrieked. "He's asleep!"

"Asleep?" echoed Marak, staring. "Asleep where?"

"I found him in his rooms," squeaked the cat, "and he was lying in the middle of the floor, sleeping. I couldn't wake him up." Marak didn't comment. He was still staring into space, thinking hard.

"But that makes no sense," growled Katoo. "He knew we were waiting for him."

"The sorcerer is home," murmured Marak. "Poor Hulk. I can't leave now, and I don't think I'd be in time anyway."

Sayada didn't seem asleep, thought Kate unhappily when she saw him. He seemed dead. He was barely breathing, and he didn't move at all. Marak examined him carefully.

"He isn't asleep," he said quietly. "He's been called away. His spirit is enslaved, and his body's been left behind to take care of itself. Seylin, run downstairs and have the Guard called in. Tell them no one is to go outside."

Back in his workroom, Marak leafed quickly through book after book, gritting his sharp teeth impatiently.

"Are you looking for a way to break the spell?" Kate asked.

"No!" he told her with a short, bitter laugh. "I can't break that spell, not without breaking Sayada, too. I'm looking for a way to keep him alive." When Kate left him to go to sleep, he was still looking, but he woke her in the morning and held out a book triumphantly.

"I've found it!" he said. "We have something to feed them. We can keep them alive."

"Them?" she echoed, sitting up.

"Them," said Marak. "The count is up to twelve."

All day the count rose, and they put the sleepers on pallets in the banquet hall. Thaydar and Bulk both slept there now, along with most of the Guard, and Marak could do nothing to stop it. He spent a hectic morning shifting assignments as people fell asleep and teaching the cooks how to prepare the special concoction that would keep the sleepers alive. By the afternoon, the count was up to fifty.

"Sooner or later, the sorcerer will have to stop calling goblins away," Marak told Kate. They stood in the banquet hall, looking at the sleepers, goblins hurrying to and fro ministering to the quiet forms. "When that happens, he may come back for another goblin to use, and we can catch him. But if he doesn't, we can go after him once we're sure he's not going to enchant someone on the road."

"Why will the sorcerer have to stop calling goblins?" Kate asked.

"Because he'll run out of blood," Marak said harshly. "He's using Hulk's blood to call our blood and bind these goblins into slavery. And he's taking my best!" he snarled in a rage. "The highest families, the most magical, the most goblin!" He glared out over the silent crowd in an agony of frustration, his horse tail hair beginning to blow about his face in a wind of its own. Kate put her hand into his, and the wind gradually died down. He stood looking at his enchanted subjects and idly running his thumb up and down the King's Line scar on her palm. Suddenly he squeezed her hand so tightly that she cried out in pain.

"The skip, Kate!" he shouted. "The skip!"

He whirled on the ministering goblins, barking out orders faster than Kate could decipher them. Goblins began scattering in all directions, running. Agatha showed up in a minute, and Seylin a moment later. Marak beckoned them to his side.

"I expect to be one of the sleepers soon," he said. "I hope I'm wrong, but if I sleep, you know what will happen. The lights will go out and the weather will change. Our kingdom will be destroyed. Seylin, you're the most magical one left, and I know he won't enslave you"—he hesitated—"because you're not goblin enough." The boy flinched as if he'd been struck. "Seylin, I need you to work the Kingdom Spells while I'm away. Dayan will bring you the book, and she can help you with the schedule. Don't keep the lamps lit during the night anymore, and don't try to light the valley. Don't try to work the Rain Spell every three days, either. Every six days will be fine. Gauge yourself, Seylin. Don't wear yourself out. I don't know how long you'll have to do this, but I know that I can count on you." Kate looked at the young elf. Seylin had grown taller this year. His face, pale at first from the insult, went still paler at the commands.

Marak turned to his former nurse. "He won't call you, either, old dwarf," he said affectionately. Her black eyes twinkled up at him.

"Keep us alive, Agatha. You're in charge of the doors. Don't let anyone out till the call stops, and organize the Guard as best you can out of whoever is left.

"Kate, come with me," he said urgently, taking her hand and pulling her along with him. "I'm going to let you out." She had to trot to keep up with his rapid strides as he hurried down the hallways.

"Out?" she wondered. "What do you mean, out? Why?"

"Because you'll be trapped down here when the lamps go out because Seylin can't keep them lit anymore, and the winds howl through, and the crops all die, and everybody leaves. You'll be trapped feeding potions to a sleeping husband. A long life!" He gave a bitter laugh. "A long life in the dark."

Kate felt a stab of fear and an even more painful stab of hope. Out! Was it even possible?

"But how can you?" she whispered.

"There's a spell for it," he said grimly. "Only the King can work it. He has to be able to take his wife with him if there's a disaster."

Kate felt dizzy. "But the King's Wife—"

"Is supposed to have a King!" he snarled. "A husband and a son. Not a living corpse, and that's what I'll be, and I'll be one for a long time. Do you think I want you chained down here just to watch at my bedside? Do you think I brought you underground for this?!"

"But I want to stay with you," she faltered, and when she said it, she knew it was the truth. Marak knew it, too. He stopped walking, stunned.

"It's all right, Kate," he said quietly, squeezing her hand. "I won't even be here."

Once in the workroom, he went into a frenzy, scrabbling through books and tossing them to the floor. "Here it is!" he cried at last. "Kate, quick, help me. I need some kind of liquid—the red bottle over there will do." She fetched it. "And my paintbrushes are in the little bottom drawer on the right." She retrieved a paintbrush. "Now we need the erasing part. Bring me the powdered lead."

"I can't reach it," said Kate, looking up at the shelf. "Can you get it for me?" And then, when there was no step to her side, "Marak, can you get it?"

The goblin King pitched forward on his face over the spell book. Kate caught him as he collapsed onto the floor. His eyes were still open, but they were glassy. She tried to jump up to get help, but his hand gripped hers, and his gaze found her face.

"Don't go," he whispered, staring at her. "If you go, I go." She stared back, stricken. "I have to fight him," he muttered. "For my wife and son."

"We don't have a son," whispered Kate.

"We would have." He smirked. "A great one." He started to relax, and his hand loosened its grip. Then he struggled back. "What a son," he whispered. She wasn't sure he could see her anymore.

"Kate!" he hissed. "Kate!"

"What is it?" she asked, bending close. He stared about, looking for her, and slowly focused on her again.

"No King ever had such a wife," he whispered. He began to go limp. "My wife and son," he murmured. "My wife and son." His eyes closed. Kate waited a long moment, then two, then three, but he didn't move. Marak had joined the sleepers.

Kate laid him down carefully and climbed to her feet, shaking all over. As she turned to get help, she saw the book still open to the spell that would have freed her. Only the King could work it, and the King was gone. She looked down at the scars in her hands.

A long life, they told her. A long life alone in the dark.

Chapter
Twelve

Kate sat by Marak's pallet in the banquet hall, oblivious to everything around her. She didn't cry, and she didn't move. She stared at
the inhuman monster who had teased her, worked magic on her, and
dragged her down into this place for the sake of an entire race of
monsters. Well, she thought grimly, looking at the slight frown on
his still face, he wouldn't ever laugh at her again. And if he didn't,
Kate didn't think she would be able to bear it.

She saw clearly what he had refused to tell the others, that he
didn't think the goblins could save themselves without him. The sorcerer would come back, and he would enslave the rest. Seylin would
be occupied with the Kingdom Spells, and no one else had the
magic to stand against the sorcerer. One by one the goblins would
fall asleep until there was no one left but her and the dwarves. Marak
would eventually die, and the goblins' magic would be lost forever.

Kate had never really wanted that son he had longed for. She
hadn't wanted to cry over a goblin baby and its awful deformities.
But now she would be thrilled to know she was going to have a
hideous goblin baby. He would be the hope of his people, and he
would be Marak's son and hers. She smiled in bitter amazement at
her own stupidity. How had she ever thought she could cry at the
sight of Marak's son?

Night came, and the lights flickered out. Kate's dwarf-made
diamond bracelet flared to brightness. In its magical light, Marak

looked as if he were already dead. Kate couldn't stand it any longer. We don't have a King or an Heir to save us, she concluded firmly, but I'm not going to spend the rest of my life down here feeding potions to a sleeping husband. If he can fight for his wife and son, then I can fight for my husband. That sorcerer's outside in the world I know. I'm not afraid of monsters, I'm not afraid of magic, and I'm certainly not afraid of him.

She got up and went to find Agatha.

"Kate," called a voice behind her, and she turned to see Emily with a lantern in her hand and a goblin baby in each arm.

"Em, what are you doing here?" Kate asked.

"The pages volunteered to watch the children whose parents are asleep," said Emily. "I have six babies up in my room right now. But Mongrel and Lash wanted to kiss their mommies and daddies good night, didn't they?" she baby-talked to the little goblins. "Actually Mongrel gave his mother more of a lick," she confided. The fuzzy, floppy-eared goblin looked up at Emily with his big brown eyes and gave her a swipe on the cheek. "That's my boy." She smiled down at him. "Aren't they the cutest things?"

"Yes," murmured Kate, ruffling Lash's feathers. "Em," she said, hesitating, "I don't know—nothing may happen, but I may—"

"You're going to go bring them back, aren't you?" said Emily.

"How did you know?" gasped Kate.

"I already told all the pages you would," she said. "You've never been afraid of anything. Besides, you already know your way around Liverpool; you were there once for three days."

"But, Em!" spluttered Kate. "It's hardly that simple!"

"I never said it was," replied Emily carelessly, "but I know you can do it. Good luck." She kissed Kate on the cheek, and Mongrel stretched up to give her a damp swipe on the chin. "Bring me back a box of that almond brittle like you did last time. Now, let's go find

Lash's mommy." And Emily walked off, leaving Kate to stare after her in stunned disbelief.

Agatha was bustling about the darkened banquet hall with a pot of Marak's concoction in one hand and a lantern in the other. Her wrinkled old face was wet with tears.

"Agatha," Kate said urgently, "I have to talk to you." The dwarf woman motioned her to sit down on a pallet.

"Old Mandrake won't mind," she sighed.

"I must go after the sorcerer," Kate explained. "No one else can. I know that world, it's my world, and I can travel in the daylight. I'm well protected, too. Marak said once that I was better protected by my charm than he was by his magic."

Agatha stirred the concoction for a minute while she considered this plan. "You're right, my lady," she said. "You're the best one to go. You've a powerful lot of magic in you, as I should know better than most. You used it on me once to get away, and oh! was Marak mad at me!"

Kate remembered the meeting in the forest when the old dwarf had glued her feet to the ground. "I didn't use magic at all," she protested. "You just gave us a sporting chance."

"Be sporting to the King's Bride!" Agatha chuckled. "You know better than that. There's nothing sporting about it, dear, nothing at all. No, you worked a fine persuasion spell on me, and being mostly dwarf, I fell for it right away." She sighed again. "The King always used to do it, too, when he wanted to get out of his lessons. No, you're right, you must go, dear. What a day it will be when the elves save the goblins after all!"

"But I can't get past the door," Kate pointed out. Agatha turned to look at her, black eyes thoughtful.

"You'll have to talk to the snake," she decided.

"What snake?"

"That one, dear," said Agatha, pointing to the golden coils above her neckline.

"Oh!" said Kate, dumbfounded. "It can talk?"

"Yes, but not many know it. It only talks to the King ceremonially, but sometimes a King's Wife comes along that it'll talk to. I don't even know if the Kings know."

"Marak never mentioned it," murmured Kate, "but then, he only brought it up to tease me because he knew how much I hated it. How do you know, Agatha?"

To her surprise, the little woman began to chuckle. She rocked back and forth in quiet mirth. "Oh, because of the King's mother, Adele. She got in more trouble! If you told her she should try flying, she'd have jumped out a window just to see. She wore that poor thing out. And they talked. I used to hear them sometimes when I was looking after the baby. It's terribly old, that snake, and it's seen everything. If anyone can get you out and save the King, it'll be the snake."

"But how do I talk to it?" asked Kate, nonplussed. "It's been nothing but paint for the last year and a half."

"I don't know," said Agatha slowly. "The only time I know it wakes up is when you're in real, right-now danger. If you do something dangerous, that'll wake it up."

"But then it'll bite me," Kate pointed out in alarm.

Agatha sighed. She picked up her spoon and stirred the pot again. "I don't know, dear," she admitted finally. "It's your snake."

Kate thought about this. "All right," she said gloomily. "I'm off to stab myself. If it bites me, you can put me down here next to Marak and feed us both that nasty concoction until the King wakes up and renders judgment. Which he may never do, but I don't think I have much of a choice."

"Good luck, my pretty lady," said Agatha, patting her on the hand, and she went back to her work as Kate stalked out of the hall.

A few minutes later, Kate sat at her dressing table, staring at herself by the light of her bracelet. She had taken a small knife out of Marak's workroom, and she looked at it nervously. How much danger was enough? What if the snake bit her? Would she sleep, too, or would she still be awake even though she was paralyzed? Kate shuddered. Best get on with it before I lose my nerve, she thought. She lifted the knife and moved it slowly toward her chest.

Kate heard a metallic zing, and the head of the golden snake reared up before her face. She dropped the knife, staring into those golden eyes.

"Don't bite me, don't bite me!" she begged.

The snake studied her face, weaving back and forth. It flicked its golden tongue out as it gazed regally at her.

"What are you doing, King's Wife?" it hissed softly. "I have guarded one hundred and sixty-seven King's Wives before you. You are the one hundred and sixty-eighth. Fifty-four King's Wives have tried to kill themselves. You are the fifty-fifth."

"I wasn't trying to kill myself," gasped Kate. "I'm in danger."

"You put yourself in danger," hissed the snake. "You had a knife. Twenty-eight King's Wives have tried to kill themselves with knives. One, with a two-headed battle-ax."

"Ugh." Kate grimaced. "I wasn't going to do anything with the knife. I just wanted to talk to you."

The snake twined down Kate's left arm and turned from her wrist to get a better look at her. "If you wanted to talk to me," it hissed, "why didn't you just do it?"

"Well," began Kate, and then realized that she had no answer. The snake studied her.

"I have guarded one hundred and sixty-eight King's Wives," it hissed. "Sixty-four of them were unintelligent. Two of them were so stupid they didn't know their own names."

"I see," said Kate a little coldly. "But wait! I need your help. The King has been enchanted by a sorcerer. I know where the sorcerer is, and I need to go find him, but I can't get out the door."

The snake studied her for another long moment, weaving slightly. "I must see the King," it hissed. "Only eight King's Wives have left the kingdom. Four of those were on the migration. For two more, the Kings erased the Door Spell. Your King," it said softly, "has not done that."

"He ran out of time," Kate answered unhappily. She walked back to the banquet hall, explaining the last few days' events on the way. She stopped at Marak's pallet, her heart sinking at the sight of his motionless form.

The snake uncoiled almost all the way in order to glide back and forth across the King, keeping only the smallest loop about Kate's wrist. At last it returned, twining quickly up her arm and rearing its head above her shoulder.

"The King is not here," it hissed very quietly. "He is far away. Too far for me to find."

"I know where he is," said Kate decisively. "I need to go free him. Unless he comes back, there won't be another King. Or," she added wickedly, "a one-hundred-and-sixty-ninth King's Wife."

The golden snake looped itself about her neck and slowly traveled down the other arm. Kate didn't exactly care for the feeling.

"Even if there is another King," it hissed, "he will not be King for long. The sorcerer will enslave him, too, and there will be no more King's Wives. I think you must take me to this sorcerer. He is a danger to my Wives."

"Can you make the door open?" asked Kate.

"No," it whispered, "I would not make the door open to let out the King's Wife. It would break. There would be no door, and there is no Guard. We will leave by the water mirror."

"Really?" asked Kate excitedly. "Can you make it work?"

"No," hissed the snake. "You can."

Kate stared. "Of course I can't!" she said indignantly. "I can't do that kind of thing."

"You're an elf woman," said the snake, buzzing slightly. "Ninety-nine of the King's Wives have been elves. You can certainly operate the water mirror."

"Even if I have elf magic," Kate protested, "the King says it's locked fighting the Door Spell."

The golden snake twirled gracefully, studying the red burn on her forehead.

"Why do you need to fight the door?" it asked softly.

"Because I never wanted to be here," explained Kate. "I wanted to leave."

"We are leaving," hissed the snake, "but not by the door."

"Oh," breathed Kate in discovery. The snake surveyed her with its slitted eyes.

"Sixty-four of the King's Wives have not been very bright," it whispered. "The last one was a blithering idiot."

"Yes, I think you told me that already," said Kate, tight-lipped. She squeezed Marak's cold hand good-bye and headed to the water mirror.

The snake explained that Kate must think of a place on goblin land and spread the scene on the water like a blanket. She tried and tried, but nothing happened. A couple of times, the water changed color, but that was all.

"Twelve of the King's Wives have had trouble with their magic," said the snake softly. "One of them set her own hair on fire trying to light her tiara with a sparkle charm."

"Good for her," snapped Kate. She was getting tired and very frustrated. But she noticed that in spite of her frustration, her burn didn't hurt her at all.

"Do you know the land above ground well?" hissed the snake. "You must be able to see it exactly as it is."

"I didn't live there very long," she admitted. "Maybe I just can't picture it clearly. Wait!" she said. "I know what I can picture." She went to the workroom to study the star charts, comparing the charts to the stars' positions in her mind. Then she hurried back to the mirror. Hand outstretched and eyes closed, she pictured the stars above goblin land, and when she opened her eyes, there they were, rippling in the lapping water. She could see the half-moon and the great jewels of the planets. With a happy cry, she sprang at the mirror to escape the underground, ignoring the snake's warning buzz. She felt the cool bubble of the water surface stretch against her and then break.

Something was horribly wrong. No ground was under her feet. She was ice-cold and she could barely move. She opened her stinging eyes, and there were the stars, still rippling and shining. Bubbles poured out of her mouth. They rose toward the stars, and Kate struggled with all her might to follow them.

In another instant, she broke the surface of Hollow Lake, splashing and gasping. She just had time to glimpse the village lights not far away before she went back under. She bobbed back up to the surface, thrashing frantically.

"Hold your breath!" buzzed a voice in her ear. Kate gasped in a great breath and held it. This time, when she went under, she didn't go down very far. "Now go limp," directed the buzzing, "and look at the stars." Kate rolled onto her back in the water, staring at the stars, and a rope around her neck began to tug her along. It was the snake, swimming furiously, throwing itself back and forth across the water and filling it with bubbles.

Kate stared up at the night sky, unaware of her danger or of the supremely annoyed snake who was saving her from it. She couldn't look at the stars enough. After a minute, she had to let out her breath, but this time she didn't panic, and she was ready to take in another breath when she bobbed back up.

After several more breaths, the snake buzzed ungraciously, "You aren't in danger anymore, King's Wife. You can walk now." It drooped about her neck as she splashed around, feeling for her footing. "I have guarded one hundred and sixty-eight King's Wives," it buzzed like an enraged bee. "I have saved ten of them from drowning. I saved one Wife from a bucket. I saved another from the Flood. But I never saved a single one from walking into the middle of a lake before. You are the very first. When you operate the water mirror and use stars to guide you, please be sure you are seeing them as they look from dry land and not as they look under ten feet of water."

Kate, wet and chilled, scrambled up the crumbly shoreline, her dress front and shoes covered with sandy silt. She shivered in the cold wind blowing over the lake, but she had never been so happy before. The entire vast sky was above her. Moonlight flooded her, inside and out. She thought she could probably fly.

"You are in danger, King's Wife!" buzzed the infuriated snake. "In danger of catching pneumonia." But Kate ignored her unusual companion as she squelched toward the village.

She slept the remainder of that night in an old woman's cottage. Those wise eyes took one look at her lavish jewelry, her elvish beauty, and her painted golden snake, and they drew their own conclusions. Kate decided unhappily that there would be a folktale about her soon.

In the morning, the woman left the cottage to hail the post coach for her. When she was gone, Kate called out, "Snake?" in a low voice. There was a rattling zing as the golden object uncoiled once more.

"Not a snake! Not a snake!" it buzzed in some disgust. "I was a sword before I was anything, and now I'm a magical charm."

"But you look like a snake," protested Kate. "We humans judge on appearance."

"Forty-eight of the King's Wives have been humans," it replied. "Nothing they do would surprise me."

"Well, what should I call you, then?" asked Kate sensibly. "Do you have a name?"

"I am the King's Wife Charm," it hissed royally. "That is my name and my function."

"That's a little hard to say, all at once," said Kate. "I'll just call you Charm." She looked at the snake a little doubtfully as she said this. It was a great many things, but it was not charming. "I'm traveling in the human world today. I don't want them to stare at you and ask questions. Can't you be a little less conspicuous?"

The snake weaved back and forth before her face. She hated this; it made her dizzy. "One hundred and twenty-seven King's Wives have been embarrassed to be seen with a snake around their necks," it buzzed, but it whisked out of sight down her sleeve.

Kate hurried to the coach as it stopped by the cottage. "No bags, miss?" asked the freckled coachman, helping her in. Kate sat down on the hard leather seat and looked around. A large, fleshy woman and a rather beefy man sat across from her in the coach. The man was reading a paper and barely glanced over, but the woman was eyeing her with interest. Under her gaze, Kate colored up. What a sight she must be! The yellow silk gown, lovely yesterday, was crumpled and stained with mud. Accustomed to the underground, she hadn't realized that it was early winter and had brought no wrap, so the old woman had persuaded her to accept a patched black coat. To top it off, the amount of jewelry she wore was by English standards truly shocking. Kate sighed. She shouldn't have scolded the snake. It couldn't have made her look more bizarre than she did already.

"You poor, poor girl!" exclaimed the woman in a loud, penetrating voice. "What on earth happened to you?"

Kate blushed more deeply as she considered her answer. Having lived so long with the goblins, she hated to lie. "I had an accident while traveling," she said at last. "I almost drowned. I don't have any other clothes to change into."

"Oh, my poor dear," boomed the woman. Kate suspected that the horses could hear her. "You'll catch your death of pneumonia! How far are you traveling, you poor thing?"

"I'm going to Liverpool," replied Kate, glad of a simple answer.

"That's wonderful!" declared the woman. "We are, too! What's your name?"

"My—my name?" stammered Kate. "I'm Kate, I mean Catherine Wins—or Miss Wins—well, Mrs. Marak, I suppose. But please," she added, mortified, "you may call me Kate."

"My dear, you're not well!" exclaimed the woman. "The shock! We must put you up at an inn the next time we change horses."

"No," said Kate hurriedly. "My husband is ill, and I have to get to Liverpool right away."

"Hurrying to his bedside, no doubt," stated the woman. "Married so young! Whatever were you thinking! Do tell me all about him."

Kate stared at her in horror. Tell her all about a goblin? "I— well—um," she stammered hopelessly. The woman watched her, fascinated.

"Tell me how you met," she insisted stridently. Kate took a breath and thought this over.

"My sister and I were lost in a storm," she said, "and he led us back to our house."

"How romantic!" cried the woman. "And you lost your heart to him right away!"

"Not right away," averred Kate, remembering his sarcastic comments as she slogged home in the dark beside his horse.

"Oh, come! He swept you off your feet, I suppose!" exclaimed the woman.

"Well, he tried," admitted Kate with a helpless giggle.

"Young and handsome, no doubt!" Kate thought about this.

"He's not young," she said, "but he doesn't look that old." Handsome? Marak? Best not to say anything.

"And where do you live?" demanded the woman. Kate's head was beginning to throb.

"Where do we live?" she gasped. Under Hill, under lake, locked behind magical doors. "Not—not far from where the horses stopped." Too late, Kate realized that the woman couldn't possibly believe her. If she lived so close, she could have gone home to change clothes.

"You poor, poor thing," the woman commented emphatically.

Wonderful, thought Kate. Now she thinks I'm crazy.

When she staggered out of the carriage that evening, Kate felt sure she knew every moment of the woman's life from birth. She had an intimate acquaintance with the furnishings in her home, the local shopkeepers' best bargains, and the grandchildren's childhood diseases. Kate's head pounded, and she longed to be home among the goblins. They would never have dared to pummel the King's Wife with so much boring talk.

"Charm!" she called, standing in a corner of the inn yard. The snake uncoiled from her arm with a little zing.

"Thirty-six of the King's Wives have been fat," it commented quietly. "Twenty-four have been loud. Eight have been fat and loud," it added in a soft whisper.

"I couldn't be more sorry," said Kate with a shudder. "Charm, should I stay here tonight and travel tomorrow? It will take three days to reach Liverpool if I stop at night."

"You should not be outside the kingdom," whispered the snake. After her awful day, Kate heartily agreed. "Travel at night. Then you will be home sooner."

"That's a good idea," murmured Kate. "Charm, has this ever happened before?"

"Yes," hissed the snake softly. "Two other King's Wives have been outside without the King's permission. One no longer had a King. He was dead, and she was awaiting the birth of the Heir. The other was in danger when the Kingdom Spells gave way and her King was far from home. And one King's Wife traveled by closed wagon with a loud, fat woman during the migration. But it is true," it whispered, "that you are the first King's Wife to travel by closed wagon with a loud, fat woman and without the King's permission."

"No, that's not what I meant," said Kate impatiently. "I mean, has the King ever been held prisoner under an enchantment before?"

The snake had no shoulders, but it managed to convey a shrug. "Why would I remember that?" it buzzed. "Do I guard Kings? I do not worry about the minor details of Kings' lives. I only remember what is important."

Supplied with an explanation and several gold pieces, the innkeeper found Kate a coachman who would drive her straight through to Liverpool, hiring horses for her along the way. As the innkeeper's wife packed her a supper to eat in the carriage, the coachman intro-duced himself. Bingham was tall and handsome, with brown hair and large brown eyes.

"No bags?" he asked in astonishment, and she repeated her explanation about the near drowning. "Then I'll ask the innkeeper to give you a blanket or two. You'll be cold in the carriage, miss.

And since we're driving straight through, you'll need a pillow. Don't worry, miss, I'll take care of everything."

"How thoughtful!" exclaimed Kate, looking admiringly into those dark eyes. There was nothing like the human race after all. "But what about you? You'll be so tired. They tell me the trip will take until late tomorrow night."

"Oh, never mind me, miss," said Bingham. "I do this all the time. Besides," he added, gazing at her warmly, "I think it will be a rewarding experience."

Bingham was as good as his word. Armed with more gold pieces, he made sure she lacked for nothing on the way. The views became steadily uglier as they approached their destination, and the winter twilight fell long before they reached Liverpool. Kate had not enjoyed the port city when she had seen it with her father. This time she found herself even more disheartened at the close streets, the choking smoke hanging in the air, and the pressing crowds of ragged people. Hordes of beggar children chased the carriage until Bingham used his long whip to drive them away. Kate's father had explained to her about the poor people who poured into the city, hoping to find work on the docks or in the huge textile mills. Nine-year-olds might work twelve hours a day at the weaving machines, losing fingers or even their lives to the machinery when their fatigue made them careless.

Tired and depressed, Kate began to long for the end of the journey. Soon they would be at the inn. The carriage stopped, and Kate peered out the little window in the door. They were in a dark, narrow alley lined by ugly brick buildings with unusually large doors. They looked like the warehouses that she and her father had driven through near the harbor docks. Trash glistened in the puddles on the rough cobbled street. Bingham, his handsome face tired and grave, opened the door and helped her out.

"Where's the inn? I don't see a single soul," Kate remarked. Bingham didn't respond. As she turned around, she saw him step toward her, a long knife shining in his hand. The horrified Kate felt a rustling zing, and Bingham stopped, shuddered, and fell over backward. He lay motionless, his big brown eyes still watching her as the knife slid from his grasp. The golden snake wove above his body, metallic fangs glistening.

"I have just bitten a man," announced Charm with arrogant contentment. "There he lies, awaiting the King's Judgment." Kate stared at the treacherous young man in astonishment. She had never thought villains could be quite so handsome and considerate. But she remembered the look in his eyes when he saw the gold pieces and her many costly rings and bracelets. She didn't need to ask why he had done it.

Kate was struck by a sudden thought. "Charm," she said, "the King told me once that if you had to bite me, you would go find him to report that I had been foolish."

"That is quite right," whispered the snake. "I do not leave the King's Wife unless I must, but if she is where she will not quickly be found, my bite endangers her. Then I myself seek the King for her. I have had to leave eighty-seven King's Wives alone. It is never good. They are not safe without me."

"Then does your magic tell you where the King is?" asked Kate.

"Yes, if he is close enough."

"Charm, we are in the city of the sorcerer," said Kate, "and the King will be with him. Is he close enough for you to find?"

The golden snake twirled slowly up one of Kate's arms and down the other. Then it wound itself around and around her neck, climbing into her hair. Finally it dropped back to her shoulder, hissing like a boiling teakettle.

"Yes," it announced grandly. "I have found the King. He is very near."

Kate left the paralyzed coachman lying in the alley by his carriage, his dark eyes following her as she walked away from him. Her magical bracelet lit up puddles and weeds as she picked her way along the filthy streets lined with vacant warehouses. Kate had never seen such a disreputable place. All her instincts told her to run away as fast as she could. But the King's Wife Charm rode her shoulders like a stylish piece of jewelry, and her husband lay somewhere ahead, held prisoner by powerful magic. Kate sighed. Her childhood friends probably never had days like this.

Charm hissed and tugged her into the shadows. A few seconds later, a thickset figure plodded silently past them, not even looking their way. "That was Thaydar!" said Kate. She hurried up behind the burly goblin, but he didn't turn around. When she tried to tug on his coat, her hand passed right through him without encountering anything solid at all, but in another second, the dematerialized goblin reached a door in a crumbling brick building and jerked it open decisively. He might be air, but his grip was as strong as ever.

Kate caught the closing door as Thaydar went through it and stepped into a narrow, leaky hallway lined with brick walls. The ground was covered with wet paper and decaying trash. Beetles skittered softly along the walls and among the moldy papers, fat, sleek, and smoothly black. Her attention caught by the large bugs, Kate tugged her gown off the floor. Then she realized that she was alone. Thaydar had come through this door just seconds ago, but now he was nowhere to be seen.

Kate stepped gingerly down the nasty space, trying to avoid the puddles and insects. A large gray rat hurried along the wall beside her, intent on business of his own. Charm watched him closely, but he made no threatening moves. As Kate neared the end of the hallway, she saw a door to her left. She was reaching for its handle, feeling very concerned about what might be beyond it, when a small child burst out crying practically in her ear. Kate jumped and whirled around. Charm whisked out of sight, hugging her arm tightly, but its coils didn't collapse into a resting state. Kate approved of its judgment. This was no place to rest.

The child continued to wail pathetically. Kate looked up and down the hallway and held her bracelet toward the stained and spider-hung wooden rafters, but she saw no sign of it. In another minute, the door swung open beside her. Kate turned, almost falling as she slipped on a fat bug. A man stood in the doorway.

"Welcome, my dear!" he said in a gravelly voice. "Always a pleasure to have pretty callers. You're looking for the baby, aren't you? Why don't you hold your magical jewelry a little higher and look at the wall there?"

Feeling that her lighted bracelet was rather unfortunately conspicuous, Kate nevertheless did as he suggested. At first she recoiled, seeing what appeared to be a large spider on the wall. Another moment's examination and Kate felt distinctly sick. A shriveled, skeletal little hand was nailed into the brick beside her. Kate dropped her arm and turned back to the man, completely disgusted.

"Isn't it clever?" he rasped. "Isn't it an interesting bit of magic? It cries whenever a woman walks by because it's still looking for its mother. Rather impractical, I'm afraid, since it won't cry when a man comes in, but must we always be practical? Some things we do just for their own sake." The man beckoned Kate into the room, and she walked in, but in another second she gave a loud cry and jumped back into the hall, the baby's voice wailing once again beside her. "Oh, don't be alarmed," called out the man in his hoarse voice. "Come right in, and I'll tell you all about it."

Kate stepped slowly back into the small room, her hand over her mouth. In a large iron cage lit by two candelabra lay the decaying body of Hulk, his insides distended with gas. The tiny room was full of the most unbearable stench, and Kate could see that the large body was teaming with bugs and worms. She choked, sure she would vomit in the close space. The sorcerer came to stand beside her, gazing down at the dead feathered ape.

"Who says monsters don't exist, eh?" he inquired gruffly. "You never expected to see such a sight in your life, and you'll never guess where I found him. Not the Himalayas, no, not even the Andes, but right here in our own British Isles! He's a goblin, my dear. They do exist, you know. Isn't he a beauty?"

Trying to control her stomach, Kate concentrated all her energy on studying the sorcerer. The man was unremarkable in every way. He was of medium height and build, gray-haired and slovenly. His ordinary face might have belonged to any grandfather of Kate's experience. But when he turned toward her, she discovered that his pupils were ruby red. She had seen many an unusual eyeball in the last year and a half, but every single one still had black at the center.

"Come along," he said hoarsely, picking up one of the candelabra and leading her through a door at the other end of the small room. Kate found herself in a very large, low room, the original warehousing space of the building. The dancing lights of the candles and her own diamond bracelet could not illuminate its dim corners. The floor was littered with the remains of smashed boxes. She hooked her dress on a piece of packing crate and had to stoop to work it loose. When she turned around, the sorcerer was waving her courteously through a narrow doorway. She stepped through, trying to avoid a flattened bit of fur that looked as if it had once been alive. As she did so, the sorcerer pulled a door of iron bars out of the wall. He slammed it shut with a clang, and Kate was a prisoner.

"What are you doing?" she demanded in surprise, seizing the bars.

"I'm going to kill you," rasped the man. "You're obviously a powerful sorceress, and I'm not going to give you any more time to do your work."

"I certainly am not!" said Kate indignantly, wondering how she would get out. When Charm bit him, it would have to locate the key and release her. "My coachman tried to kill me, and I was trying to find help. I saw a man walking this way, and I followed him."

The sorcerer turned at the doorway, holding up the candelabrum. Those red pupils glowed eerily from that comfortable face.

"If you weren't powerful in magic, your coachman would have succeeded in killing you and saved me the trouble," he growled. Kate reflected unhappily that this was true. "Perhaps you can explain why you were snooping about my property with magical lights, but I doubt it. Not that it matters; I'd kill you, anyway. I can use your hair and your liver, and I think I have a spell that calls for your left ear, too." He turned and went out.

"Charm," called Kate quietly, "why didn't you bite him? Don't tell me he's not a danger to the King's Wife!"

Charm glided up from her sleeve and peered out through the bars at the gloomy space beyond. "You are in terrible danger, King's Wife," it hissed softly. "Only three King's Wives before you have been in more danger. I cannot bite this man. He is what Thaydar was, a manifestation of the spirit. He can kill you, but if I try to bite him, I will seem to be biting the air."

Kate glanced around her long, narrow prison in dismay. "But what can we do? How can I escape?"

"His body is elsewhere, like the King's," whispered Charm. "I must have a body to bite. You are the one hundred and sixty-eighth King's Wife I have guarded, and you may be the last."

"If his body is elsewhere," said Kate firmly, "then you have to go find it. Surely he wouldn't leave it too far away."

Charm hissed for a few seconds and then unwound itself, gliding down to the floor at her feet. Now that she was finally rid of the snake that she had detested for so long, Kate felt horribly unprotected.

"Look everywhere, Charm. You have to save the kingdom," she called. "Don't worry about what happens to me." The magic snake stopped and reared up to look back at her. It seemed like a long, thin bar of gold.

"I do worry, King's Wife," it hissed. "You are carrying the Heir. If you die, there will be no more Kings, and that means no more King's Wives."

"The Heir?" gasped Kate. "Charm! What are you talking about?"

"Your son, of course," buzzed the snake. "Yours and the King's. Stay alive until I return."

"Wait!" cried Kate, but it whisked under the door and was gone.

Kate paced up and down for some time in the cell, turning this news over in her mind. So she was going to have a baby. Wouldn't Marak be thrilled! She couldn't wait to rescue him so that they could talk about it. I wonder what the baby will look like, she mused. Maybe my hair and Marak's eyes. I'm not going to cry when I see him, she thought happily. And that sorcerer had better not try to hurt my baby!

A click at the far door told Kate that the sorcerer was returning. Bulk sidled through behind him, carrying a large, curved sword. Kate stared at him in astonishment. Although the goblins had a well-stocked weapons room, none of the King's Guard carried anything but a knife. They relied on magic to subdue enemies.

"You were so interested in the dead goblin," said the sorcerer, "that I thought you would enjoy being killed by his twin."

"But how can you be sure he's a goblin?" asked Kate. "He just looks like a funny monkey to me."

The sorcerer turned to look at the pale ape, who crouched with the sword in his huge hands. "Oh, he's a goblin. They all look different. I have sixty of the horrible monsters now, and they carry out any command. You would think, to look at them, that they were designed just for hell. They don't even have to kill on their errands. People run at the sight of them."

This speech made Kate absolutely furious. Bulk was not a horrible monster, and neither were any of the other goblins. They would have scorned stabbing a woman in the back, as the handsome Bingham had tried to do, and they certainly wouldn't kill a guest in order to use her left ear. Kate glared at the avuncular sorcerer. How happy she would be to live with horrible monsters if she could only get away from him!

"That's fascinating," she said coldly. "How did you even know they existed? Did you just meet one by accident?"

"We're wasting time." The sorcerer hesitated. "But it's such a good story, and a few minutes won't matter." Kate fervently hoped that he was wrong. "My brother is a doctor, and he wrote me a year ago, very excited about a new patient of his. This madman claimed he'd been enchanted by goblins, and you'll never guess what they did. They stuck him to the ceiling! I couldn't believe it when I saw him. I'd give anything to learn how to do it."

The sorcerer couldn't have wished for a better audience. Kate stared at him openmouthed. So he had learned about goblins from her very own guardian. Wouldn't Marak be furious with himself when he learned that his revenge had endangered the whole kingdom!

"That fat man skittered back and forth across the ceiling like a bug," continued the sorcerer, "telling me all about the goblins who stole his wards. Of course, no one but me believed him. Everyone was sure he had killed them himself. I wasn't about to let another magician profit from his excellent information, so I killed him before I left. And you'll never guess how I killed him!" Kate couldn't speak. Her guardian, dead?

"I hanged him, of course!" The sorcerer burst into a loud, raucous laugh. "There he hung, neck snapped, feet dangling, but they dangled toward the ceiling! That big body twisting to and fro on the rope, pointing straight up into the air. What an unbelievable sight!"

Kate stared at the man, horrified beyond words. Hugh Roberts had meant real harm to his wards, but she could never have wished such an end for him. She remembered how he had looked crawling around on the ceiling and closed her eyes with a shudder.

"Well, time to kill you," the man said abruptly. "I'll be able to try something new tonight with that ear. Do you command that bracelet to light, or does it light by itself?"

"I don't really know," Kate said, gazing at it. "I don't think I do anything." In answer, it flared a little brighter. The sorcerer looked annoyed.

"Go ahead," he told the feathered ape hoarsely, handing him a key. "Unlock the door and then kill her." Bulk shuffled forward, head down. He turned the key in the lock, and Kate stepped through the open door. Bulk looked up at her, his yellow eyes strangely darkened, and shuffled back a step. Kate walked out into the room, stepping over the flat fur thing, and he moved farther away, looking at the floor.

"Now what's happening?" growled the sorcerer. "Are you working a spell on him?" He crossed to the ape and stared at his face, slapping him a couple of times. Kate was surprised that his hand didn't go right through. Maybe spirits could hit each other.

"Go kill her!" he demanded, pointing at Kate. The ape shook his head pitifully. Bright flames engulfed the feathery body, and he howled silently, writhing in torment. "Go kill her now!" But Bulk crouched down and hid his face.

"I can't believe this!" The man eyed Kate uneasily. "I think he's afraid of you. They lose their memory, voice, and hearing, so their fears are almost the only thing they have left. But why you?" Kate considered the question herself. Bulk must be afraid of being bitten, she thought. Every goblin was raised to know what the King's Wife Charm could do.

"I'll fetch another one," the man muttered. This time he didn't lock her up in the cell; in fact, Kate noticed that he gave her a rather wide berth as he headed for the door. Bulk disappeared after a minute. Kate hurried to try the two doors out of the large room, but both of them were locked. What a shame, she reflected bitterly, that this powerful sorceress couldn't work a simple Unlock Spell.

The sorcerer came back with Sayada and Tinsel, a giant of a goblin with thick, corded silver-gray arms. Adele had named him for his hair, which fell like bright tin threads around his face. Neither goblin would approach Kate at all. The sorcerer bullied them and burned them, but they refused to lift their swords. The gray-haired man wiped the sweat from his face and studied the slight, pretty girl with real alarm.

"I can't imagine what they think you'll do," he complained. "It's times like this that I wish they could speak."

"Maybe they're just gentlemen," Kate suggested calmly. "They certainly look like gentlemen to me." The sorcerer stared at her in astonishment and turned to study the two phantoms. He had been sure she would scream at the sight of the one without a nose, but she gazed at the freakish creature as serenely as if she saw it every day. He hesitated, taken aback, trying to think what to do. Then he snapped his fingers in sudden inspiration.

"I know which one will kill you," he said gleefully, turning to leave. "He's the best one, the very best, and he's not afraid of anything."

Unlike you, thought Kate in disgust. You can take on helpless things without a qualm, but you're afraid of one mysterious girl. She glanced up scornfully as he returned, his plain, comfortable face wreathed in smiles. Then she gasped. Right behind him was Marak, eyes on the ground, curved sword in his six-fingered hand.

"Oh, so you're afraid of this one, eh?" The sorcerer turned to look at the silent goblin. "That's funny, I don't think he's so bad. A little grotesque, but nothing compared to those nose holes, I would have said."

Kate stepped forward quickly. "Marak," she called out in goblin, "look at me. I've come to help you escape. Can't you work any magic at all?" The goblin King didn't even move. His face was shielded by his impossible hair as he leaned on the curved sword.

"No working spells on him!" barked the sorcerer. "I don't want you damaging him! Now, kill her," he commanded the goblin. Marak swung the sword up and stepped toward Kate without hesitation. She reflected bitterly that the sorcerer had been right to pick him out. The goblin King had nothing to fear from the King's Wife Charm. He would never be bitten, no matter what he did. If only he would look at her!

"I wasn't enchanting him, I was talking to him!" Kate said indignantly, stepping away from her husband's advance. "I just said hello. Why didn't he answer?"

"What, you know him?" shouted the man in disbelief. "Wait a minute," he ordered, and Marak stopped at once, staring at the ground. "He only hears and knows what I hear and know. If I were out of the room, he'd hear nothing at all. What language was that? How do you know about goblins? Why are they afraid of you?"

"His name is Marak, and he is the King of the goblins," she said, ignoring the questions. "He is a great magician, much greater than you will ever be, and he protects his people with his magic. He doesn't need to carry around candles like you do. He lights the entire kingdom with his spells. And I asked him why he had a sword in his hands. He doesn't need a sword. He kills with magic."

The sorcerer looked excitedly at the motionless goblin King. "What a shame he can't speak or remember! Have you watched the spells? Do you know the words?" Kate's heart gave a leap. As the sorcerer talked, she saw Marak make a movement of his own. He was fingering the sword thoughtfully as if he were thinking about her last statement.

"The goblin King's magic wouldn't work for you," said Kate coldly. "No human could work it. No human can ever work magic. They talk the demons into working it for them."

The sorcerer flinched, and his pupils glowed bright red. "Kill her!" he roared angrily. Marak raised the sword again, but this time he didn't step forward.

"Marak," cried Kate desperately, "I know you won't hurt me. You never did, unless it was very important," and she held out her scarred hands. "I know you won't kill me because the lines say a long life. A long life for both of us."

"Stop! Where did those come from?" The sorcerer studied the magical lines with interest, and Marak put down the sword. This time Kate thought he was looking at her, but she couldn't be sure because his hair was still in his face.

"They're from the wedding ceremony," she explained. "From the magic worked to protect the King's Wife. Nothing matters to the King as much as his wife and his son. Remember, Marak? Your wife and son!"

The sorcerer stared at her, amazed. "You're his wife?" he demanded. "You're married to that monster? A pretty girl like you and a freak like that!" He bellowed out a laugh. Behind him, the goblin dropped his head once more.

"He's not a freak!" cried Kate in indignation. "Goblins are strong, not pretty, and he's worth a hundred of you! Marak, you have to come home," she begged. "You're asleep right now in your own palace, and you have to wake up!"

The sorcerer turned to look at his servant, and the goblin turned to look at his master. Marak hesitantly reached a hand up to push the striped hair out of his face.

"Stop that!" cried the sorcerer. "You know you can't move on your own! That's enough of your magic!" he snarled at Kate. "You came here to kill me, but you'll be killed instead by your own precious freak." He whirled back to the goblin. "Kill her right now, and be quick about it!"

At the command, Marak advanced decisively, sword up. When he looked at Kate, she saw the same distant expression he had worn when he cut her hands open. She didn't think he knew her at all.

"Fight for us, Marak!" she begged. He raised the sword in his right hand and brought it slashing down, but at the same moment he shoved her as hard as he could with his left hand. Kate sprawled onto her back in a filthy puddle as the blade flashed past.

"Stop trying not to kill her!" the sorcerer screamed. "Kill her, and this time really do it!"

Kate tried to scramble away, but the goblin stepped on her arm, pinning her to the ground. His impassive gaze showed only the faintest flicker of unease, the faintest hint of puzzled recognition. He swung the sword up to chop off her head, and she couldn't get away.

"Marak," Kate whispered in goblin, "I'm going to have a baby." Then she closed her eyes tightly as the sword came slashing down again. She felt a burning pain and reached up to touch her face. A shallow cut stretched across her cheekbone, but the weapon clattered to the ground.

"My wife and son!" Marak cried. "Kate, our baby! Do you mean it?" He looked around in surprise. "What are we doing here? Where are we?" And he reached down to help her up out of the puddle. The sorcerer glared at them both, beside himself with fear and horror. A dog started howling somewhere below them.

"The watchdogs!" the sorcerer spat at Kate. "This is all your fault. Sixty monster servants, and I have to kill you myself!" He snatched up the sword and raised it, but Marak wrapped his arms around the furious man. Kate stepped back from the struggling pair, unsure what to do. "Let me go!" howled the sorcerer, his eyes like red lamps. Marak was wreathed in flames now, his face twisted in agony, but he held the sorcerer in a tight grip. An unearthly keening came from below, joining the howling dog.

"The wizards! The wizards!" shouted the frenzied sorcerer. "Let me go!" As the stricken Kate watched, Marak glowed brightly all over like molten metal. He collapsed onto the floor, still glowing, and the sorcerer broke free, charging straight at Kate and swinging the sword wildly. One second she was staring at his livid face, mouth open, spit flying, weapon swung back to kill her. The next instant she was staring at the dim room beyond as the sword toppled onto the ground. She seized it and looked around frantically, but there was nothing to see. The room was completely empty.

Holding the sword, Kate moved to the center of the room, gazing around in bewilderment. She reached a hand up to her cut cheek and wiped away the blood, staring at the silent, dingy space and listening to the water drip from the rafters. She remembered the howling and the keening. Now there was no sound at all. A golden flash caught her dazed attention, and in another second Charm twined rapidly around her arm until its head reared up before her face. As she blinked at the snake, it bared fangs in an exultant grin.

"I have just bitten a man," hissed Charm triumphantly.

Chapter
Thirteen

Kate picked her way carefully down the rotted wooden stairs under-neath the warehouse building, still clutching the sword. She was beginning to regret having asked the golden snake to show her the sorcerer's body.

"Charm, did you know all along that I was going to have a baby?" she asked.

"Yes, I knew, King's Wife," hissed the snake.

"And you let the baby and me leave the kingdom?" demanded Kate in amazement.

"The kingdom was not safe. The sorcerer could reach inside it to bring harm to you and the Heir. I needed to come to the sorcerer to protect my Wives."

They reached the bottom of the stairwell. Two large gray wolves were chained there. One of them was long dead, rolled onto its back with its legs out stiff. The other one appeared to be sleeping. Its beautiful fur was matted with filth, and the gray coat wrapped a desperately thin body.

At the end of an unlit hallway, Kate came to a thick wooden door, splintered and twisted from its hinges. She stepped cautiously past it and caught her breath sharply. At her feet lay two hideously desiccated human corpses wrapped in dirty bands of cloth. Their dark brown skin was tough and leathery, stretched taut over the bones beneath. One was missing a hand, and the other had no lower jaw. The upper teeth stuck out into the air, yellow and uneven.

Sudoku 139

5			6				4	8
		9	4		7			
	6					3		
	5							7
			3	1	8			
1							2	
		4					7	
			1		6	8		
8	9				2			4

Sudoku 140

	6							
			2	1			8	
7			4	9		3	1	
		6		7		1		
	4						6	
		8		5		4		
	3	4		6	5			1
	7			3	9			
							7	

Sudoku 137

						7	5	
5			4	6				
			9			8	4	6
		6		8	4			
		9				4		
			5	2		3		
3	1	7			6			
				9	3			7
	2	8						

Sudoku 138

		1		4				
2	5			1		3		7
7				6	9			
								9
	3		2		5		8	
1								
		2	8					4
8		3		6			2	1
				5		8		

"When I was here before," hissed Charm quietly, "these two were awake. I did not bite them because they did not try to stop me. I am only a magical charm, and they are here to combat the living."

Kate stepped over the mummified forms as well as she could, keeping a worried eye on them. Then she looked up and stopped short.

Before her lay the sorcerer on a low stone table, his comfortable face calm and his body motionless. Kate gripped the curved sword tightly, reassured to be the one holding it now. She saw in horror that his red-lit eyes were fixed on her. They were the only thing about the body that could still move.

"I have just bitten a man," hissed Charm with deep satisfaction. "There he lies, awaiting the King's Judgment."

Kate stared at the grotesque red lights in the pleasant face, remembering her husband's glowing body lying on the ground. She didn't even know if Marak had survived. She thought of the bloated Hulk, who lay here so far from home, and the little child's hand still longing for its mother. A hard lump rose in her throat as she glared at those sickening eyes, and she lifted the sword and brought it down with all her strength. The sword rang hard against the stone table, sending a shock up her arms, and the sorcerer's head bounded off his body and rolled into the corner. Kate stared, startled, at the rush of dark blood inundating the sword blade. Perhaps she hadn't needed to use all her strength.

"There you are, Charm," she said shakily, wiping the bloody blade. "I don't think we need to bother the King about this one." As Charm buzzed like a hive of angry bees, Kate looked around the room in disappointment. "Where are the goblins? Are they already freed?"

"No," said the snake. "They are upstairs in jars. I found them in my journey looking for the body. I am sure the King would have planned an excellent revenge for it."

"Then he should have gotten to it first," replied Kate, stepping over the mummies again.

They went upstairs to the sorcerer's workroom. Kate, used to Marak's tidy ways, was disgusted at the mess. Scrolls, parchments, and open books littered the tables and the floor, and the room reeked from the many nasty mixtures that rode the sea of paper. Kate reflected that goblin magic and demon magic must be very different. Marak's magic relied on herbs, minerals, and other inanimate objects, whereas the flies buzzing about the stinking remains in this room told a very different tale.

Standing along one wall were rows and rows of ordinary glass jars, each with some hieroglyphs painted on its lid. Kate picked one up carefully. It was very light, but she could see something inside that looked like colored water. "What should we do?" she asked. "Should we open the jars or take them back to the kingdom? Maybe if we break the seal, the goblin inside dies."

"I do not know," admitted the snake. "I interest myself in no magic but my own. Here are some that are not goblins," it added, gliding over two old jars at the back. "Open them and see what happens."

Kate carefully pried up the lid of the first one, breaking the wax seal. A cloud of orange smoke streamed out like steam from the spout of a teakettle. It flowed swiftly past her and was out of the room before she could blink. The other jar was filled with yellow smoke that sped after the first.

"Well," she said doubtfully, "they certainly knew where they were going, but how do we know we did the right thing?" She went back to the other jars, looking for Marak. Charm found his jar, and Kate held it up to the light from her bracelet. It was only half full, she noticed with concern. The others were completely full.

A rasping noise behind her made her turn around. The two

desiccated corpses from downstairs shuffled slowly into the room, one propping himself upright on the other, who was crawling. Their noseless, leathery faces turned toward Kate, and she saw with a shudder that they looked at her without eyes. The one without a hand had orange sparks glowing in its empty sockets, and the one without a jaw looked at her with twin yellow sparks. The handless one spoke in a mumble, propping its inadequate form on a paper-strewn chair. Kate let out a terrified squeak as the jawless one crawled a pace nearer.

"They mean no danger to the King's Wife," hissed Charm. "It is just that they have been dead for a very long time—they were wizards long ago when I was young. They wish to thank you for freeing them from the sorcerer's control." Staring at the hideous corpses, Kate remembered the orange smoke and the yellow smoke that matched the flaming eyes.

The mummy spoke again, holding its hand below its shriveled jaw to help itself form the words. "They go now to the place where they belong," translated the snake. "They serve a greater power than this paltry man. They have had a tiresome few years putting up with his arrogance." It listened closely as the corpse spoke on in a mumbling whisper. The crawling figure knelt upright now, almost at Kate's feet.

"They ask a favor," Charm hissed. "They wish to take the body of the sorcerer with them. They say there is always danger from a dead body that held such powers, and also, there is the matter of their revenge."

Kate stared at the two ghastly forms before her. Their flames glowed very brightly at her as Charm spoke. The voiceless one kneeling at Kate's feet gave a vigorous nod to show his enthusiasm. He did this by reaching up with his bandaged hands and rocking his skull back and forth on its bony neck.

"Do you think I should let them?" Kate asked doubtfully.

"I think so," hissed the snake. "I can feel their hatred for the sorcerer. Their desire for revenge is real."

"All right, then," said Kate. "In return, ask them what we should do with this place. We need to make sure that this magic can't be used again and that the spells worked here are undone."

Charm spoke quietly to the wizard, and he mumbled out an answer. "They say that when fire consumes the spells and enchantments, they will all be broken." Kate considered the difficulty of this task rather unhappily. The standing mummy spoke, and the crawling corpse nodded his skull. Then they turned and shuffled slowly from the room. "They thanked you again," hissed the golden snake after they left. "They said it was a great pleasure to meet such a powerful young sorceress, especially such a pretty one."

"Charm!" said Kate indignantly. "Why didn't you tell them the truth?"

"Eighteen of the King's Wives have been powerful sorceresses," hissed the snake. "Five of them were powerful when young. But only one other King's Wife besides you was powerful, young, and pretty all at once." Kate sighed and gave it up.

Confident now of obtaining the goblins' freedom, she pried open jar after jar, releasing smoke of every color. Some almost exploded. Others streamed out more calmly. They all headed resolutely for the door and vanished, one after another, down the hallway.

Kate saved Marak's jar for last. When she had counted the others to make sure no one was missing, she pried up the lid of the half-empty jar. Nothing came out. She tilted the jar, and the dark green smoke poured out like water, collecting in a swirling puddle upon the floor. As she watched, almost in tears, it rolled slowly toward the door. She could have walked beside it and kept up.

"Oh, no! Charm, what have I done? How is he supposed to get

home like that?" wailed Kate. The golden snake twined around her waist, bending low to study the rolling cloud.

"The King isn't looking well," it hissed quietly. They watched in silence as the cloud vanished into the dark hall.

"And now I have to burn this place!" cried Kate, still distraught about her husband. "Oh, dear, the wolf! I can't burn it down around her ears."

The wolf danced and yelped frantically at the end of her chain. The golden snake bared its fangs in anticipation, but she only pawed Kate, whimpering pitifully. Kate unfastened the buckle on her tight collar, and the gray form barreled past her and whisked up the stair-case, running toward the back of the building.

Kate followed the wolf down another bug-filled hallway. She emerged at one end of a long, unlit room filled with rattles, squeaks, and roars, clapping her hand over her nose and retching at the hideous smell. Beside her in the short end of the room was a large, wide door. Unlatching it and pushing it open as far as she could, she stepped into the alley beyond. She stood outside for a minute in the drizzling rain of the late night, breathing in the sweet, smoky air.

The wolf jumped into a low pen across from the door and laid herself down among small puppies, but only one emaciated pup crept to his mother. The other three lay stiff, insects crawling over them. Holding up her bracelet, Kate discovered that the room was filled with cages of all sizes. Animals growled, hissed, and banged the bars, and the floor was covered in waste and filth. She didn't think she could stand it.

"I can't destroy this place now, Charm," she said, aghast. "I can't burn these animals alive."

"I have seen them," whispered the snake. "Many of them you can simply release. Some of them would be a danger to the King's Wife. I can bite them, and you can leave them to the fire. But if you do not want to burn them alive, you will have to kill them yourself. My bite does not kill."

This, Kate decided sadly, was the only thing she could do. She retrieved the sword from the jumbled workroom and forced herself to look into one cage after another. Many animals in the cages were long since dead, and living animals crawled over their rotting comrades, quarreling with each other for the bones. Kate released a tide of mangy rats, stepping back quickly as they poured toward the open alleyway. She let out three young foxes and a number of kinds of birds. The bear, one eye gone, roared desperately at her, and she had to force herself to stab the poor brute. Charm whizzed busily about the cage of poisonous snakes, biting its living copies faster than they could react. Then Kate cut down the middle of the cage, dividing the motionless bodies.

She came to the cage of a small monkey and opened the door gingerly, hoping as much for its sake as hers that it wouldn't try to bite her. She expected it to run to the alley, and she felt unhappy about it, knowing that such an exotic creature could never survive in the cold and damp. But the monkey hopped to a nearby cage and opened the door, reaching in. A white mouse crawled onto the monkey's paw and let itself be carried out to freedom. The monkey squatted down by the cage, cuddling the little mouse, who snuggled against the brown fur and curled its tiny tail around its body. Kate noticed with a sick feeling that the little white mouse had only one front paw. The other had been severed neatly at the elbow, doubtless for some special spell.

As they approached the last cage, Charm whispered, "This one is no danger to the King's Wife." Kate peered into the cage and almost fainted. A baby girl pulled herself up by the bars and looked out at Kate, giggling in delight. She was round and rosy, her black hair and bright eyes shining in the light from the bracelet. She stretched up toward the sparkling light, waving one hand through the bars. Kate bent down, and the child caught one of her fingers and held it firmly in her fat little fist.

"How can we possibly find her mother?" breathed Kate, kneel, ing by the cage. She saw, revolted, that the cage already contained other sets of small bones and rags.

"Are you sure she still has a mother, King's Wife?" hissed the snake. "The child's dress is stiff with blood."

Kate stared for a long moment at the baby in its simple, thread, bare dress. She imagined a mother, young like herself, struggling with the sorcerer as he fought her for her child, falling, fatally stabbed, but still clutching the baby close as her eyes glazed in death. Or perhaps—Kate's heart stopped at the thought—perhaps a gob, lin servant had pulled away the baby. Perhaps her own husband had wielded that deadly knife.

She headed purposefully toward the workroom, the baby in her arms. As she left the room, the mother wolf rose and picked up her puppy in her mouth. The little monkey glanced up and scampered after them. When Kate reached the door of the workroom, she looked back in surprise. The monkey rode on the wolf's neck now, clinging to its long fur, and the tiny white mouse rode on the mon, key's shoulder.

Kate went to fetch the candelabrum burning by the cage of the dead Hulk. But now the huge body glowed with a multicolored light, covered with bright patches of smoke, the freed goblins who had stayed to protect their dead comrade from the insects. The sight blurred before Kate's eyes, and a lump rose in her throat. Marak had said that goblins stayed together. That was their strength.

"Burn the body," Charm whispered, "and the goblins will leave it. They will know there is nothing more to be done."

Kate brought paper and books to the cage and spilled candles over them. Then she tossed the shriveled little hand onto the pile, the child's voice wailing in her ears. Once lit, the paper went up quickly, and the candles melted in the heat. One by one, the colored smokes streamed away.

She hurried down the hall and dropped a candle in the work, room, igniting that sea of papers. Then she started a fire in the room of cages. Smoke was already pouring out the wide door as she stepped into the alley, and she could hear behind her the crackling and roaring of flames. Holding the baby, she walked off into the damp night. The wolf trotted behind her, the monkey clinging to its neck.

⌒

The next morning, Kate was riding back home in a carriage with the baby on her lap, the wolf and pup at her feet, and the monkey stroking its little mouse on the cushioned seat across from her. "Charm," she called, and the snake awoke with a zing. The baby screamed in excitement and clutched the golden coils with both hands. "You did a great thing last night, Charm," said Kate. "You saved the kingdom, the King, the King's Wife, and the Heir."

The snake considered this as well as it could while being tugged about. "I have always saved the King's Wife," it pointed out softly. "The rest was important only insofar as it saved my Wives."

Kate pried the baby's hands loose. "I've decided to name her after you," she announced, "because you saved her life."

"You wish to call her Charm?" whispered the snake. "I will never know which of us you are talking to."

"Oh," said Kate, taken aback. "I didn't think of that." The snake examined the child curiously as she bounced up and down on Kate's lap.

"I am sensible to the honor you do me," hissed Charm. "Perhaps you would let me name her. I would like to call her Matilda, after one of my favorite King's Wives."

"Matilda," said Kate experimentally. "That's nice, Charm. We'll call her Matilda. But," she added wickedly, "I didn't know you had any favorite Wives."

"I have guarded one hundred and sixty-eight King's Wives, and fourteen were favorites," hissed the snake. "Their names are Ada, Merneith, Dara, Hesione, Olwen, Clodia, Unna, Kala, Matilda, Eleanor, Kiba, Madge, Adele, and Kate." Kate smiled at the last two names. Matilda worked her hands free and grabbed for the snake again.

⌒

The next evening, Kate stood before the iron door that led into the goblin kingdom. This trip underground was quite different from the one she had made before. Then, Marak had brought the unwilling Kate inside by force as she gazed longingly back at the stars. This time, Kate barely noticed the night sky as she hurried inside to see her husband. All that the guards could tell her about the King was that he was gravely ill. She shifted the baby nervously from one arm to the other as she looked up at the massive iron door.

"Hello, door!" she called out. "Let me back into the kingdom!" It rattled in consternation.

"King's Wife!" it boomed. "What are you doing outside? I didn't let you out."

"No, you didn't," said Kate. "Quick, let me back in. I need to see the King."

There was a pause. Perhaps it wasn't a long one, but to the anxious Kate, it certainly seemed to be.

"I can't open for the King's Wife," explained the door.

Kate started to reply, but a metallic zing made her pause. "Listen to me, little door!" buzzed Charm ominously. "You are endangering my King's Wife with your stupidity. If you do not open immediately and without further discussion, I will twine myself through your lock and your hinges and throw you down twisted and broken, and the goblins will put in a new door that understands its obligations."

The door creaked open, rattling sulkily as Kate swept in with the baby, the golden snake twining majestically about her shoulders and the wolf with its pup and riders marching behind.

"I never knew that snake could talk," muttered the door.

Kate hurried to the banquet hall. She peeked in anxiously, and her heart stopped. Of all the pallets she had left here a few days ago, only one remained, and she knew whose silent figure lay upon it. She ran pell-mell across the hall, the wolf galloping behind her.

"Marak, Marak!" she cried, dropping down onto the pallet and staring, heartsick, at his still face. "Please wake up! You have to wake up now!"

"All right," he agreed in an amiable whisper, and he opened his unmatched eyes to smile up at her. Looking into those eyes, Kate realized that she had lied to that loud woman after all. Of course she had lost her heart to him right away. For two days she had been thinking of things to tell him, but now she couldn't think of one. She just stared at him, her heart full.

Marak freed one arm from the blankets and reached up to touch the cut on her cheek.

"I remember that," he said softly. A metallic zing sounded, and the golden snake was with them once more.

"Oh, King," hissed the snake ceremonially, "I have bitten a man. He lies in the city of Liverpool, awaiting the King's Judgment. I bit another man, too," Charm continued with an unhappy buzz, "but he no longer requires your attention."

Chapter
Fourteen

Marak was ill for months, exhausted from fighting the sorcerer. Unable to go to court, he took care of important matters from his bed, and he continued to rely on Seylin's help for some time to carry out the Kingdom Spells. He sent Thaydar out to deliver the King's Judgment on Bingham, but Thaydar returned with the news that the paralyzed coachman had already been killed. Marak was disappointed. The goblin revenge that he had chosen for the young man would have been considerably worse than death.

It was in part Marak's desire to work the Kingdom Spells that kept him bedridden for so long. Given only so much strength, he preferred to spend it on useful magic rather than on walking. Always practical, he embarked on a review of the King's Wife Chronicles as a way to use his convalescence. Kate spent hours every day reading to him in her stumbling goblin while the wolf and pup slept by the bed and little Matilda played on the floor beside them. The dwarves were already making her elaborate baby toys, but Til enjoyed playing with the wolves more than anything else. She pulled their fur and disturbed the King's rest with her laughter until the servants came and took her away.

As soon as he had the strength, Marak erased the Door Spell, judging that he had no right to withhold freedom from someone who had braved such dangers to free him. He asked only that Kate wait until their son's birth before using her newfound liberty and that she confine her outside visits to the goblin lands. Before, Kate would have been wild at the long wait, but now she was resigned. She had seen enough horror outside to feel content in the goblin kingdom for some time. But she did go often to visit the front door. "I am the King's Wife," she would call. "Open up." And the poor door would have to open. It didn't try to argue with her anymore.

"Thank you," Kate would say, "but maybe another time." And she would walk back to the palace again, leaving the door rattling back and forth in frustration.

Emily was disappointed that Kate had forgotten her almond brittle, but the gift of the little monkey made up for everything. "I never had a pet who had a pet before," she said wonderingly, watch^ ing her monkey cuddle the one^armed mouse. Emily had rather ordinary human looks, but when she went about in bright silks and satins, with her hair done up in ribbons, her hands, arms, and neck covered in jewelry and the monkey and mouse riding on her shoul^ ders, she went as far as an average human could toward attaining a bizarre goblin presence. Certainly, Kate had misgivings when she saw her little sister thus and wondered what their father would say if he could see her.

The wolf mother refused to be given away to anyone. She never left Kate's side if she could help it, trotting behind as Kate went from place to place and lying down on her feet the minute she stopped. This achieved two important canine goals. First, Kate always knew that someone loved her devotedly, and second, every bright gown received a generous sprinkling of coarse gray hairs. The thin pup grew into a handsome beast in time. Having spent his early months at the side of the convalescing Marak's bed, he formed a strong attachment to the goblin King and followed him everywhere. Kate, dipping into her educated past, tried to name the pair Helena and Constantine, but Marak persisted in calling his companion Dog, or, when they were both in the room together, Your Dog and My Dog.

Kate decided rather disgustedly that this was to be expected from a husband who shared his own name with one hundred and sixty-seven of his predecessors.

The goblin King was well by the time the Heir was born. As he had long ago predicted, the birth was a very hard one, and it took all his attentive magic to get Kate through it. "And very lucky you are, little elf, to be married to a goblin," he told her firmly, "or you'd have gone the way of your mother, her grandmother, and the grand-mother's own mother, I expect." Kate, pale and sweaty, didn't open her eyes to acknowledge this smug remark. After the last twenty-four hours, she didn't feel lucky to be married at all.

"A new Marak!" announced Agatha, bringing over the goblin baby. Kate heard the old Marak give a cry of delight. She reminded herself decisively that she was ready for this moment. Nothing about the son she had had with her beloved husband could possibly upset her. Opening her eyes, the exhausted Kate took one look at her baby and promptly burst into tears.

She didn't cry because the baby, larger and longer than a human baby, was staring at her steadily with one green eye and one blue eye. His skin was more silvery than Marak's, and his lips were consider-ably closer to a rosy color. She didn't cry about the hair, lying in silky locks around his high forehead, although that was a bit of a disap-pointment. As the King had predicted, the baby had his mother's golden hair, but marbled among the golden curls were soft locks of Marak's own beige. No, it was the right hand, or rather, the lack of it that had the weary and somewhat hysterical Kate bawling into her pillow. From the shoulder to the elbow, the right arm was a chubby baby arm, but from the elbow down it was the forearm and paw of a tiny lion cub.

Marak couldn't have been more thrilled as he held his newborn son and watched him wave the fuzzy, speckled paw in the air. "What a King he'll be!" he declared happily to his sobbing wife. He stroked the soft baby locks, stirring their golden and pale curls with a finger. "Kate," he added with a puzzled frown, "I thought you hated my hair."

"I do hate your hair," sniffed Kate indignantly. But then she remembered all the times she had seen him looking at her through those pale wisps or jerking out the ribbon and running his hands through the wild mane as he thought. "Oh, well," she said with a tired giggle. "I suppose it made an impression."

"Just look at him," insisted her husband joyfully, setting their son down on the bed beside her. "What a stunning boy he is, every inch a goblin King! What could you possibly be crying about?"

"But, Marak," Kate protested, "he has a paw!" She looked at it dubiously. She was somewhat calmer now that the shock was wearing off, but she still wasn't happy about it.

"And do you remember the last goblin King who had that paw?" demanded Marak. "Lionclaw, the greatest of all the Kings. Marak Lionclaw led the goblins to this kingdom and ended the migration. He was the greatest magician the goblins have ever had. The records say that he was the one who enchanted Hollow Lake to hold up the water. Just imagine," he exclaimed, "what magic he'll work with that right hand!" And as his tired wife wiped her eyes on her blanket, Marak played with the little paw, pressing it gently to make the sharp claws extend.

"Look, Kate!" he hooted. "It's just like a cat's paw!" And Catspaw was the son's name from that moment until the day he became Marak in his father's place.